'James Bradley is a writer of ideas and this prescient, thrillingly imaginative novel shows us what's to become of humanity. Bradley's most intimate book to date, *Ghost Species* asks hard, heartbreaking questions about the price of our separation from the natural world. Do we have the right to alter nature? What do we destroy when we seek to enhance it? And is it really possible to love another species as we do ourselves? An urgent, frighteningly timely novel about ethics, technology and love, *Ghost Species* made me think again and again of the poet Rilke's command: *You must change your life.*'
Charlotte Wood

'*Ghost Species* is a remarkable novel from one of Australia's most engaging writers. This is great storytelling, gripping the reader from the first pages to the final sentence. *Ghost Species* is the story of our shared experience within families, communities and the nation. It is not a story of the future, but a vital narrative of the times we live in. In a time of uncertainty and potential catastrophe, James Bradley has delivered a story vital to any understanding of how we choose to live with each other and the precious planet that provides us with life.'
Tony Birch

'At once haunted and haunting, this deeply moving book has the heft and power of myth or prophecy. It is a lament from the edge of a darkening world, giving voice to the grief and loss of this time and to the universal need for hope and love. Look, it says, look, and don't look away. This is what we're choosing.'
Lucy Treloar

PRAISE for *Clade* by James Bradley

'Epic ... Riveting.'
Missy Higgins

'This is the unstinting dreaming and devoted craft-work of a deeply serious, marvelously accomplished artist taking on the absolutely essential.'
Thomas Farber

'*Clade* opens up to become that rarest of novels: one that stares down its harrowing beginning to find a sense of peace and even of wonder, while being true to itself. All the way through, the prose is achingly beautiful.'
THE SATURDAY PAPER

'*Clade* triumphs ... It is impossible not to be swept along by the sheer pace of the narrative.'
THE AUSTRALIAN

'The book works. It stays with the reader. In the end, *Clade* does what apocalypse stories do, from the epic of *Gilgamesh* to *The Walking Dead*. It tells us that life will go on, even after the end of the world.'
THE MONTHLY

'At once intimate and epic ... The apocalypse is happening, even as our messed-up lives distract us.'
THE GUARDIAN (UK)

'A beautifully written meditation on climate collapse, concentrating on three generations of an Australian family ... Bradley's short, intense novel is as much a hymn to hope as it is a warning.'
NEW SCIENTIST

'Complex and beautifully paced, *Clade* is the first great novel of climate change. So well does it predict our possible future, it is unlikely to be the last.'
KILL YOUR DARLINGS

'A compelling story of the triumph of hope over devastation ... *Clade* is a visionary book.'
THE WEST AUSTRALIAN

'A melodic, intense rendering ... sharp, inventive and ultimately hopeful.'
THE HERALD SUN

GHOST
SPECIES

James Bradley is an author and critic. His books include the novels *Wrack*, *The Deep Field*, *The Resurrectionist* and *Clade*, a book of poetry, *Paper Nautilus* and *The Penguin Book of the Ocean*.

GHOST

JAMES BRADLEY

SPECIES

HODDER*studio*

First published in Great Britain in 2020 by Hodder Studio
An Hachette UK company

This paperback edition published in 2021

1

A CIP catalogue record for this title is available from the British Library

Paperback ISBN 9781529358100
eBook ISBN 9781529358094

Printed and bound in Great Britain by Clays Ltd, Elcograf S.p.A.

Hodder & Stoughton policy is to use papers that are natural, renewable
and recyclable products and made from wood grown in sustainable
forests. The logging and manufacturing processes are expected to
conform to the environmental regulations of the country of origin.

Hodder Studio
Hodder & Stoughton Ltd
Carmelite House
50 Victoria Embankment
London EC4Y 0DZ

www.hodder.co.uk

For Mardi,
and for Annabelle and Lila.

'The animals on the walls are the animals in our minds, and neither have yet faded from view. Stand and look at them long enough and we may begin to grasp what they meant and why they matter. Refuse to look and they will stay asleep, like Arthur's knights under the hill. But unlike Arthur's knights in those old legends, they won't rise up to save us in our hour of need. Nothing will rise but the roots and the tendrils, growing over the remnants of our projects and our wishful thoughts, as they have done so many times before. And the bison and the ibex will still be there, deep in the rock, waiting to be found again.'

Paul Kingsnorth, 'In the Black Chamber'

Some nights, when the wind is up and the power flickers and fails, she tells the child stories, as if this thread of words might be enough to bind them together, to bear them through all that is to come, like a boat, or a leviathan.

She knows she is not alone in despairing for what the future holds, in wanting to find ways to hold it back for as long as possible. But no matter how hard she tries she cannot keep it at bay forever. For a time is coming – soon, sooner than she wants it to be, sooner than either of them will be ready – when the child will have to venture forth into the world we have made and find a way to survive. The onrush of that time, the feeling that their years together are already falling away, shadows her life, a drumbeat of loss behind the moments of joy, a reminder every instant is precious. But when they are here, isolated by the power or the wind, it is not time's flight that frightens her; instead it is the knowledge that the child is alone, and that one day soon she will understand that. And so she does what mothers have done since the beginning of time, since before we were human: she draws filaments from the darkness and weaves them together to create meaning, purpose, shape, arranging the elements to reveal the world, or perhaps to make a new one.

Before the child, if you had suggested this might be something she could do she would have laughed, told you she was not a storyteller. But in the years since the child arrived in her life she has found the habits of breath and suspense that make a story live were already there, waiting within her, just as the eagerness for it is in the child, her capacity for rapt attention.

How far back does this strand of connection go, she sometimes wonders. Did we require language to discover story, or did language evolve to sustain story? Are we the only animals that tell stories? Do the birds? The fish? The elephants? The whales and dolphins? And if they do, what shape do those stories take? For surely story is as much a way of being in the world as a way of describing it? A means of comprehending the way all that surrounds us hums through us as we live?

It is not a thought she lingers on, for to consider it is to invite a different kind of grief, an awareness of what is being lost, extinguished as the animals disappear, one by one, the irreplaceable wonder of their knowledge of the world wiped away with them.

And so instead, she sits in the dark and rocks the child and tells her stories. Tales about forests, and snow, half-remembered myths about wolves and bears, fables about talking birds and singing stones, each containing some glimpse of a world they have forgotten how to see. In the daylight she sometimes wonders how much of the power of these stories grows out of her desire for something solid, something to connect their unanchored world to the past. But at night, as she tells them, she can feel their power moving through her, and knows it is more than that, that they come from some deep place, somewhere before memory, before time.

Sometimes, though, when the child is on the edge of sleep, she tells her one particular story, a story unlike the others, a story about a people long ago, a people who were not quite us. For as long as they could remember this people had lived on the plains in Africa, moving in bands through its vast spaces, hunting and singing. Their world was a place where animals ruled, its grasslands and forests thronged by elephants and rhinoceroses so huge the earth told of their approach long before they arrived, its wetlands and rivers stalked by crocodiles, its skies filled by flocks of birds so immense they blotted out the sun. The people dreamed of the animals, dreamed themselves, weaving stories to teach those who came after them how to honour the animals, how to honour the land.

Millennia passed, and the people were happy, until one day, some of them grew restless and decided to head north, through the mountains and across the desert, into the green lands beyond.

These were new places, peopled by new creatures – bears as tall as trees, fish as long as men that lay dreaming in the rivers, vast herds of wild horses and deer – but in time the people learned their songs and as the generations slipped by they began to dream of them.

And then one day the snow began to creep south, carpeting the land, and bringing the ice with it. This new world was harder than the old, but the people learned to survive, secreting themselves in the caves and dark places to wait out winters that lasted nine months, learning to hunt the animals that came south with the snow, the mammoths and the elk and the deer, crafting clothes from their furs and treasures from their bones. And through it all they stayed true to the land, its voices, its presence.

But though they could not see it, the cold was changing them, and as the millennia slipped by they became heavier, stronger, adapting to their world just as the animals had. And when they sang the land, they knew they were part of it, that it sang them as well. And when they dreamed the world, they knew that it dreamed them as well. Until at last they were no longer the same people, but a people who lived by firelight, a people of snow and ice.

It is a story she tells only on the edge of sleep because she does not want the child to ask her how it ends. For if she did she would have to speak of the others, the people they had left behind in Africa, of the way they grew more numerous, more intelligent, their fingers shaping the world, crafting tools and weapons, until one day they too began to move north, through the deserts and across the mountains. In the countless millennia since the people left, the newcomers had forgotten they ever existed, so when they finally reached those distant lands they were startled to find others already there, a people like them but also different; larger, stronger, wilder, their skin pale, their hair orange and brown.

What did these newcomers make of their ancient relatives when they first encountered them, she wonders. Did they see them as brothers and sisters? Or did they see in them the face of something different, something lesser, monstrous even? It is said that when the Europeans first arrived on Australian shores the Aborigines thought them ghosts; did these newcomers think the same, glimpse in their pale skin the shiver of death, an intimation of the fate that awaited them? Or did they seem misshapen and bestial? All those stories of ogres and giants and trolls, their origins buried in the deep past – do they come from them? Whichever it was, the newcomers drove them back, until finally the people who had come first were almost gone, forced back to the sea on the furthermost peninsula. And though it might have seemed that this was their end, it was not, or not quite, because they were not gone. Because there is her.

IMPOSSIBLE THINGS

Later, Kate will wonder whether any of it would have happened if they had been somewhere less isolated, whether normality might have put a brake on their actions if they had been closer to other people. For though in those years that very notion – normality – had already begun to bend, giving way as the planet itself began to buckle and shift, there is no doubt that up there, cut off from the rest of the world, it sometimes seemed that anything was possible and nothing was forbidden. When she comes to look back she will realise that this was not an accident, that even though Davis's other schemes had come to naught, this at least he had understood, planned for even, and the realisation that he had manipulated them will make her feel ill.

Today, though, she thinks none of this. Instead, as the helicopter shoots over the forest, its sleek shape slicing through the coiling breath of the mist that rises from the treetops, she is absorbed by the landscape beneath, its silent presence. For years now there has been drought here, but as the canopy moves past below there is little sign of it. Instead the forest that carpets the hills and the enfolded flanks of the mountains with their outcrops of grey, volcanic stone looks impenetrable, primeval.

Only the scurf of smoke on the horizon betrays the truth, the degree to which this landscape is already convulsing.

In the seat beside her Jay sits, unspeaking, his dark eyes focused on the view below. His silence is perhaps a sign he is anxious about what lies ahead. When the invitation arrived Kate had recoiled from its gnomic wording, the assumption they would drop everything to head south to meet with an unidentified benefactor who was interested in discussing a mysterious project they thought the two of them would find 'intriguing'. 'American,' she had snorted contemptuously when she first saw the email. 'Or Chinese.'

But Jay had grinned. 'We should go. After all, what's the worst that could happen? We get a few days to ourselves in Hobart? I could do with the time away; we both could.'

Aware he was making an effort, she had forced herself to smile and agree. And so, a week later, they are here, in a helicopter somewhere over the Tasmanian bush, heading for a rendezvous at an unknown location with a potential employer whose name they did not know.

Jay twists in his seat, his attention caught by something below. She follows his gaze. At first her eyes cannot makes sense of what she is seeing: the cubic buildings scattered on the hillside are rendered almost invisible by the way their smoke-grey glass exteriors reflect the surrounding landscape, dissolving the perfection of their geometry into a mirrored infinity of grass, stone and sky.

In front of her in the cockpit the assistant – Madison, she reminds herself – swivels in her seat and looks back, her face hidden behind her oversized sunglasses, the inscrutable armour of her pale makeup and carefully painted lips. In the two hours since she met them at the airport she has offered no hint of where they are going or, indeed, any personal information at all.

'We have to walk the last bit,' she says, lifting her voice over the roar of the rotors and engine. 'Helicopters aren't permitted to approach the facility.'

Jay leans forward. 'Facility? What is this place? Are those buildings labs?'

Madison smiles and stares over their shoulders. Kate realises she is looking at some kind of display in her sunglasses.

'You'll be given a full briefing once we're on-site.'

The helicopter swings around, passing over a low hill towards an open space on its far side. Jay leans back into his seat. 'Who the hell are we meeting?' he says, his voice pitched low enough to ensure only Kate can hear him over the engine. Kate just shakes her head and looks out the window again.

The grass flows outward in waves beneath them as they descend, exposing the bleached textures of its roots, the darker hues of earth and stone. At the last moment the helicopter seems to hesitate, the pitch of the engine rising, then there is a jolt as the rear wheels make contact with the ground, followed by the gentler bump of the front. A moment later the engine spins down, the space left by the absence of its sound immense.

With a practised motion the pilot opens the door and climbs out. Reaching up she takes their bags, one by one, then helps each of them down. As Kate climbs out she catches a glimpse of herself reflected in the plexiglass canopy. At Jay's insistence she dressed well, taking more care than she has in months, the black shirt and dark jeans she has chosen emphasising her lean figure. Yet when she looks at her face, its thinness beneath her pulled-back blonde hair emphasised by her scrubbed skin and hollow cheekbones, all she sees are her eyes, lost, numb, emptied out.

Picking up her bag she stares up the hillside while she waits for Jay to arrange himself, dully grateful she packed lightly and is not required to drag a suitcase over the ground.

Once Jay has his bags Madison heads off up the slope, moving remarkably sure-footedly given she is wearing heels, Jay beside her. Kate watches them ascend for a second or two and then follows, a few metres behind.

The hill is high enough to block the view of the facility – or, Kate realises, to block the facility's view of the landing area – so it is only as she reaches the top that she has a chance to observe it properly. Seen from ground level it is, if anything, even more beautiful than it was from the air: its interconnected cubes seem to float above the hillside opposite, as weightless and inscrutable as some kind of alien artefact.

Jay stops to let Kate catch up with him. 'Who do you think designed this place?' he asks. Kate glances at him – he is easily seduced by wealth – but before she can answer, a strange cry echoes across the hillside, a strangled howl like nothing she has heard before. She stares around.

'What was that?' she asks.

Jay shrugs. 'A bird? Some kind of possum?'

Kate stares at him. Jay is a creature of the city, his interactions with wild animals and the bush confined to the occasional documentary, yet even so she cannot believe he is not at least slightly unsettled by the sound. Ahead of them Madison is already halfway down the hill. Adjusting her bag on her shoulder Kate stares across the open space towards the building one more time, the cloud-filled surfaces of its mirrored walls depthless, unbounded. Then she adjusts her bag on her shoulder and heads down after Madison, Jay beside her.

Madison stops by the base of the nearest cube. Where its cantilevered shape meets the hillside a door is cut into its side, the outline almost invisible; beside it a small panel is set into the surface at chest height. Madison waves a hand in front of the panel, and the door slides open. Stepping aside, she motions to Kate and Jay to enter. Inside is an entrance area, its double-height space subtly illuminated to emphasise its simplicity, the way its stark lines are rendered calming, even comfortable, by the perfection of its dimensions. One of Kate's colleagues once joked that you always know you're in the presence of real money – corporate money – when there is no sign of advertising, an observation that comes back to Kate as they are led through the space and up a staircase into an open area above.

Unlike the quiet atmosphere of the entrance area, this second space has the hushed power of a stone circle or temple. Unfurnished save for a long table in its centre and a pair of chairs to one side, its angles direct the eye to narrow floor-to-ceiling windows set into the walls, each of which frames a different slice of the landscape. Kate comes to a halt.

Off to one side, somebody moves. Kate turns to see a male figure standing by one of the windows. As if Kate's attention were some kind of signal he steps into the light, his pale eyes focused on her and Jay.

Kate hesitates, aware he is familiar but unable to place him. He is young – no more than thirty, or perhaps thirty-five – with tousled blond hair and the narrow frame and large-eyed, slightly ungainly features of a 1960s pop star, although under the rumpled Nirvana T-shirt he wears his body looks well maintained. He stops in front of them, and as he does Kate realises who he is. Davis Hucken. Tech billionaire. Founder of Gather, the social network whose user base now surpasses those of Instagram and Twitter combined.

Next to her, Jay has fallen still.

'You came,' Davis says, opening and closing his hands as he speaks. 'I was worried you might change your minds.'

His voice is oddly pitched, almost adolescent, its carefully neutral Californian tones not quite disguising the edge of something harder beneath. Still startled, Kate realises she remembers reading about him buying large areas of land here in Tasmania, supposedly because of its relative isolation and potential resilience in an unstable world.

'This place belongs to you?' she asks.

Davis blinks. 'Technically it belongs to the Hucken Foundation, but yes, I suppose so.'

Kate keeps her face blank. 'What is it? Some kind of retreat?'

Davis smiles again, his expression unreadable. There is, she sees now, something odd about his affect, an awkwardness, as if his reactions are not natural but somehow acquired.

'What do you know about the Foundation?'

Kate and Jay exchange a glance.

Jay steps forward. 'A little. It's an offshoot of Gather, a kind of charitable or benevolent arm of the main organisation. You've been funding the creation of seed banks and genetic repositories, and giving money to a whole range of environmental programs, a lot of them in developing countries. I'm pretty sure I read about something to do with river dolphins in the Amazon just recently? And the coral restoration program in East Africa? Also I know you were involved in the work Narayan and her team have done tweaking plankton DNA up in Alaska.'

'That's correct. The Narayan project in particular has been a huge success. And we have twelve of the repositories now, all fully self-sufficient and capable of surviving ten thousand years without maintenance. We're also working on repositories for cultural materials: artefacts, literature, music, technology. Again, all designed to last a hundred centuries.'

Kate doesn't speak. This kind of talk has always made her

uncomfortable; the very qualities people like Davis find so intoxicating seeming arrogant and preening to her.

'But there's another strand to our work. One that's less public.' Davis glances at Madison. 'Have they signed the non-disclosure agreements?'

Madison checks her screen and tells him they have. Davis nods. Turning away from them, he moves back towards the window and stares out. Looking at his slim figure silhouetted in the light Kate is struck by the disconcerting sense that they are watching a rehearsed performance, as if he is acting out a private TED video. Or is it just that he has so internalised this mode of performance it has become second nature?

'When we set up the Foundation we thought we were in the business of saving things, of doing what we could to stop what we have disappearing. That's why we built the repositories. The seeds and biological material stored in them mean we have a safeguard that will allow the planet – and us – to survive an extinction-level event.'

'Like an asteroid?' Jay asks.

Davis turns back to them. His eyes are a colourless blue; combined with his sandy hair and pale lashes they make him seem almost transparent.

'Did you see the news this morning?'

Jay and Kate look at one another.

'The last white rhino. Gone.'

Kate nods. 'I saw. But what does that have to do with this facility?'

'Let me tell you a story. A hundred thousand years ago there was megafauna all over the world. Woolly rhinoceroses and mammoth and elk in Europe and Asia, giant sloths and sabre-toothed tigers and monster armadillos in the Americas, huge marsupials and massive reptiles here in Australia. But then, about eighty or ninety thousand years ago, they began to disappear. If you plot those disappearances on a map it looks like a wave, washing across the world, following the migration of our ancestors across the planet's surface. Some places lasted longer: in America the megafauna survived until twelve thousand years ago, in New Zealand the moas and the giant eagles lasted until about six hundred years ago. In the southern oceans the whales and the seals survived until the beginning of the nineteenth century. But wherever you look, these collapses coincided with the arrival of *Homo sapiens*.'

He stops and stares at them both for a second or two. 'And the megafauna was just the beginning. In the past fifty years we've killed two-thirds of the wildlife on Earth. The handful of megafauna species that survived our arrival – the elephants, the giraffes, the rhinos – are almost gone, bird numbers are in freefall, insect populations and ocean ecosystems are collapsing. And that's only going to get worse. We're on track for – what? Four degrees? Five? Six? I was in the Arctic last week, at an archaeological dig near Alakanuk in the Yukon. A decade ago the permafrost was only a few centimetres below the surface. Now it's a metre down. The ground is collapsing. There are fires on the tundra – fires! This last winter it barely snowed. The sea ice is almost gone. We're not at a tipping point, we're past the tipping point. The world we knew, it's over. Our civilization is already dead. The question now isn't how to save what we had, it's how we make something new.

'Obviously part of that process is technological. We need to develop better energy systems, more effective farming techniques, better ways of managing water. But if we're concentrating on that we're missing the big picture. This isn't just about technology or economics or politics. It's goes deeper than all of them. We have to accept that the old binaries, nature and technology, the human and the environmental, no longer make sense, that it's up to us to re-engineer the world.'

'You're talking about, what?' Jay asks. 'Genetic engineering? Synthetic biology? Biotech?'

'Partly. We're working on engineered species: plants that will sequester carbon dioxide, plankton that absorb acids to help slow down ocean acidification, corals and mangrove species that grow faster and are more tolerant of temperature variation. But that won't be enough.'

Jay and Kate must look confused, because Davis smiles.

'Come with me. I want to show you something.'

He crosses to a window and waves his hand in front of the wall. With a soft whirr the glass slides away to reveal a narrow balcony. Davis steps out and gestures to the two of them to follow him.

The balcony looks out along the valley, offering a view of the hillside, the dark line of the trees above, the grassy space beyond the last of the cubes. On the ground just beneath it, a stand of eucalypts has taken root in the lee of a broken hump of stone, their pale limbs twisted, warped and wizened by the wind. Kate folds her arms against the chill, but Jay is so focused on Davis he seems not to notice.

Davis looks up the slope. 'It won't be long.'

A moment later the cry Kate heard earlier echoes out again, only this time it fades away to become a series of strangled yelps. Stepping closer to the edge of the balcony, she closes her hand around the timber railing, suddenly alert. For several seconds nothing happens. Then, a lean shape appears from the trees above. It pauses briefly, then lopes down towards them. A second or two later another appears, and then another, the three flowing down the hill together, like a pack, until they reach the stand of eucalypts. At first Kate thinks they must be dogs, but then she registers their curious gait and the black stripes on their backs and gasps.

'How?' she manages to say. 'When?'

'Three years ago.'

Kate nods, only half-hearing him. Davis whistles, and the three creatures look up as one and then dart around the base of the eucalypts towards them. Davis picks up a bucket that stands against the wall of the building and extracts a piece of meat. Holding it up so they can see it he waits for a moment and tosses it down to them. They shoot forward, growling and snapping, but the largest is too quick. Clutching the meat in its jaws it backs away, dragging the other two after itself, until they finally relinquish. With a shake of its head the victor jogs away and drops its prize on the ground.

Davis slings another hunk of meat after the first, and the remaining pair fall on it, snapping and snarling. Kate cannot take her eyes off them. Although they are right in front of her her mind rebels at the sight of them, their presence weird, unnatural, like glimpsing dinosaurs or aliens. Yet unlike the jerky film of the last specimen pacing around its cage in the 1930s, they are pulsing, alive, and – perhaps most unsettlingly – fitted to the landscape.

Davis throws down a third piece of meat, watching impassively as they leap on it. And then from somewhere up the hill there are voices. Beneath them the creatures freeze, listening. Somebody laughs, and, as one, the three of them turn and lope away, disappearing back into the trees like ghosts.

Kate and Jay stare at one another. Kate is not sure whether she is horrified or elated, but Jay's eyes are wide with delight.

'It's incredible,' he says. 'People have been talking about de-extincting thylacines for years, but you've actually done it.' He hesitates, and Kate can see him turning the possibilities over in his mind. 'Obviously they're a good choice – relatively intact genetic material, living analogues, but still, they look healthy, self-sustaining.' He pauses. 'What did you use to gestate them? Devils?'

'Dunnarts. Although because they're born relatively undeveloped and raised in the pouch, we also created an artificial pouch based on the design of humidicribs.'

'Are they fertile?' Kate asks.

Davis inclines his head. 'That's been more complicated, but yes, we believe so.'

She glances back up the slope to where the creatures disappeared. She can feel Davis watching her. She knows she should be excited, exultant even, but she is afraid to give way to the feeling, afraid of where it will lead.

'And they're living wild?'

'We raised them with as little human contact as possible.'

'Is this why you want us?' Kate asks. 'So we can help you re-create ... what, dodos? Auks?'

Davis shakes his head. 'I said before that the time had come for us to realise we are no longer separate from nature, that the binary between nature and technology no longer makes sense. What surrounds us is a new nature, one in which humans play an active part.'

'By resurrecting extinct species?'

Davis smiles. 'When I first thought of this program I imagined it would be a way of saving species that were in danger of extinction. Even if the technology wasn't there for resurrection yet, it would be soon, and at the very least we could preserve the genetic information, provide the infrastructure for when it eventually did become feasible. We now know we can do more than just pull species back from the brink. We can actually reverse extinction, resurrect species that were lost decades – even centuries – ago.'

'But?' Kate prompts him.

'The problem is that until now our horizons have been too limited. The damage we've done to the planet doesn't go back fifty years, or a hundred, or even five hundred, it goes back millennia. That means it isn't enough to bring species back. Animals don't make sense in isolation, they only make sense as part of a living whole. That means that if we're going to do this we need to do more than resurrect individual animals, individual species, we need to reconstruct entire ecosystems.'

'I don't understand. What are you proposing? Geoengineering?'

'In the first instance. As you perhaps know, we have several facilities in Russia and Canada. As the Arctic warms, the forest is spreading north, covering what used to be tundra. The trees are darker than grasses, so that increases the albedo and makes the land absorb more heat—'

'Which is causing the permafrost to melt faster,' Jay says.

Davis looks at him and blinks. 'That's correct. And as the permafrost melts, the methane that is locked up in it is being released, hastening the warming that's already taking place. If we can't slow that down, it's game over for the climate.'

'But how do the thylacines fit into that?' Kate asks.

Davis smiles. 'A few years ago, there was a project to reintroduce wolves to Yellowstone. At first they thought the wolves would help control the number of deer and other herbivores in the park. But as the population of herbivores fell so did their impact on the banks of the streams, meaning the rivers began to change course and grow more winding. Before long beavers moved back in as well, creating ponds and waterfalls and new habitat for fish and other species. Within a few years the entire landscape was transformed. What that study demonstrated was that reintroducing even one species can have profound effects on the landscape.

'In the case of the tundra, it's mostly grassland, which is a relic of the last Ice Age. But the grasses only exist because large herbivores prevent the forest from taking root. Those large herbivores are now almost gone, meaning the forest is free to spread. But as the example of the wolves demonstrates, if we can reintroduce large herbivores we can re-create the conditions of the last Ice Age and keep the forest at bay.'

'Thereby slowing or even preventing the release of the greenhouse gases in the permafrost,' Jay says.

Davis nods. 'Precisely.'

'When you say large herbivores, what do you have in mind? Reindeer? Elk? Moose?'

'Musk oxen. Aurochs. Mammoths. And the Arctic is just the beginning. We need to reconstruct ecosystems all over the planet. Rebuild what's been lost. What we've destroyed.'

There is a moment of silence. Jay glances at Kate. He is smiling, his excitement palpable.

'You think what you're describing is possible?' he asks.

Davis pauses, then takes a step forward. 'We know it's possible. Ecosystems are really just cycles of energy. We have the computational power to model them, to understand the way energy flows through them. But I want you for something else.'

Kate shifts uncomfortably, but Davis has not finished.

'The further we've come with this project the clearer it's become that resurrecting lost species and re-creating ecosystems is just the beginning. We're talking about entirely re-engineering our relationship with nature. But to do that we need to reimagine ourselves, the way we think, the sorts of attitudes that have got us where we are. We're so used to the dichotomies between human and nature, the individual and the whole, we can barely imagine the world without them. But we have to. And if we're going to do that we need to let go of the idea we're distinct, separate, unique.'

Kate and Jay glance at one other. 'I don't understand,' Kate says.

'Yes you do,' Davis says, staring at her.

Kate hesitates. 'You're talking about creating other human species?'

Davis nods. 'Not creating. Re-creating.'

'You mean, what? Neanderthals? Denisovans?'

Davis smiles. 'To begin with.'

'Why?'

As he smiles again, Kate feels the uneasy prickle of something. Charm, or perhaps the power to change the world that often passes for it.

'Because we can. Because it gives us the chance to undo the wrong that was done when they were wiped out. But also because we need them; the world needs them. Look at the Earth, at what our carelessness has done to it. We can't let that happen again. We need to be tested by other minds, other perspectives. We need to learn how other eyes see the world. Think what we could learn from them, from their minds! Imagine speaking to another species!'

Kate shakes her head in disbelief. 'Without an evolutionary context, a community, they wouldn't be another species, they'd be an exhibit, an experiment. All we'd see when we looked into their eyes would be a reflection of our own hubris.'

Davis gives her an oddly blank look. 'Perhaps at first. But you know as well as I do that the nature of life is to adapt, to change.'

'Even if you could reassemble the genetic material, you would require human surrogates,' says Jay. 'As well as human eggs. And I can't begin to imagine how you'd get ethical clearance. Human cloning is banned in almost every country in the world.'

Kate looks at him in dismay, aware from his tone of voice that he is thinking the idea through, weighing its possibilities. But he does not notice.

'We've already had some very productive conversations with both state and federal governments, so we're confident that suitable exemptions can be arranged.'

'But what about the scientific community?' Kate asks. 'They're likely to have significant objections as well.'

Davis smiles. 'That won't be an issue. The arrangements we've made with the relevant authorities are confidential.'

'And they agreed to that?'

'These are exceptional times. They call for exceptional measures.'

Kate hesitates at this non-answer. In recent years Gather has come under attack for its business practices, with widespread allegations its executives have manipulated government policy through lobbying and donations. Jay gives her a warning glance.

'You'd also need significant resources,' she says.

'That shouldn't be a problem.'

'I still don't see where we fit in,' she counters.

Davis blinks. 'Don't you? You two know as much about human genetics as anybody alive. Your work as a genetic programmer is without parallel, and Jay's recombinant techniques have shown remarkable results.'

'Why not use the team behind your thylacines?'

'They're working on the Arctic project.'

'Making mammoths?'

Davis nods. 'Among other things.'

Jay steps forward. 'You must know that what you're talking about is orders-of-magnitude more complicated than thylacines or mammoths. And the level of failure that can be tolerated is much lower.'

'Yes,' Davis agrees. 'That's why I want the two of you.' As he speaks he turns to Kate. For several seconds there is silence.

'And you know I have problems at present,' she says in a flat voice.

'Everybody has setbacks,' Davis says. 'I've had them as well. They're how we learn.'

'Like evolution,' Jay says. Kate glares at him, her stomach lurching in disbelief, but Jay only smiles.

Davis smiles. 'Exactly. Now perhaps I could show you the rest of the facility?'

That night they eat alone, seated in the room in which Davis was waiting when they arrived, the meal is delivered by black-uniformed staff. And when they are done they retire to a suite in one of the residential cubes, a pair of austerely beautiful rooms whose lofty ceilings and subdued lighting would not be out of place in a luxury hotel.

'Do you think he means what he says?' Kate asks, once they are alone. 'That the world can be re-engineered?'

Jay unbuttons his shirt and hangs it on the back of a chair. 'When you have his kind of money almost anything is possible.'

Kate gestures at the walls, the delicate play of light upon them. Their concrete surfaces bear the imprints of the timber palings used to mould them, the effect subtly softening the geometric simplicity of the structure, making what might otherwise be cold and stark warm and organic.

'With what this will cost he could do other things, though. Improve conditions in Africa or India, invest in education. Help reduce poverty.'

'It's too late for that,' Jay counters. 'We don't need change in a generation, we need it now. Hell, we needed it twenty years ago. What

Davis is talking about is a way of leapfrogging past all that, of creating the beginnings of a new world, one where we can do all the things you're talking about.'

'But he's talking about making people, about playing God.'

'Look at the world, what we're doing to it. We've been playing God for a long time. Perhaps what Davis is doing is offering us a chance to do that consciously.'

'And what will happen to these children if we make them? Who will raise them? Who's going to teach them? Where will they belong? We both know people who won't have kids because they don't want to bring children into this world. How is this different?'

'Because this has the potential to change everything. I mean, imagine the possibility of encountering another species. One that sees the world differently from us. Imagine what that might mean, how it might change the way we see the planet. Imagine connecting us to our deep past like that.'

'Are you sure we want to be connected to that past?' Kate asks.

'What do you mean?'

'We exterminated them.'

Jay laughs. 'Exactly! Which is all the more reason to do this. This is our chance to undo that mistake, to give them another chance. And anyway, Davis is right: imagine what we could learn from them.'

'If it can even be done.'

'It can be done,' Jay says. 'You know it can be done.'

'You don't think you're underestimating the technical problems? Where do we get the genetic material? How do we implant it? How do we bring the child to term?'

'We can work it out. With the resources Davis has at his disposal we can work anything out.'

'But it isn't just about the technical problems, is it? This is a life we're talking about. A child.'

'Davis will do it anyway,' Jay says. 'If we do it for him perhaps we can learn something. Perhaps we can control it.'

She shakes her head. 'That's your gambit? If we don't do it somebody else will? Really?'

Jay stares at her for a long moment. 'Are you sure we're talking about the same thing here?'

She returns his stare. 'What?' she asks, incredulous.

'I know this isn't a great time for you, that this can't be easy.'

Kate stares at him coldly.

Aware he has overplayed his hand, Jay hesitates. 'I'm sorry,' he says. 'But you know what I mean.'

'Get fucked, Jay,' she says, her voice low and hard.

'I just want to be sure.'

She glares at him.

'All right,' she says at last. 'I'll think about it.'

Standing up she walks into the bathroom and, closing the door, sits down on the edge of the bath to steady herself. She is shaking, and when she closes her eyes she can taste bile in her throat. It is only when the trembling finally subsides that she stands, and, approaching the sink, brushes her teeth and washes her face, moving through these rituals wordlessly, mechanically, as if it might be possible to erase herself in their repetition. Once she is done she returns to the room and undresses in silence, aware of Jay watching her. But when she climbs into the vast expanse of bed she does not turn to face him or reach out to touch him, unwilling to let the distance between them be bridged.

*

It has not always been like this between them. When they first met, seven years ago, Kate had just returned from California for an interview. She was in two minds about the job: when she left Sydney a decade earlier she had done so without regret, and the thought of returning to a place where her old life was so close at hand made her uneasy. Yet the prospect of a five-year research appointment was too attractive to pass up.

Their first encounter was at the lecture she was required to give as part of the selection process. She was nervous, keenly aware her years away and lack of contacts had made her an outside candidate, but after deciding to emphasise her research profile by approaching the lecture relatively formally she was dismayed to realise the audience seemed to have found her cold, mechanical. Following a couple of desultory questions from the head of department and a member of the selection committee silence fell, until finally Jay spoke up with a series of queries that she quickly realised were designed to open up the discussion in a way that allowed her to seem warmer, more expansive.

After the lecture he approached her. 'I'm Jay,' he said. 'Jay Gunasekera.' He was slim, handsome, his thick black hair stylishly cut.

She shook his hand. 'Thank you for that.'

'Don't worry. It's not about you,' he said, smiling. 'There's talk of funding cuts. They're all in a panic.'

To her surprise she found herself smiling as well. 'Well I suppose that's good news.'

Somewhat to her surprise she got the position. But although she half-hoped to run into him again, she had been back in Sydney for almost a month before she bumped into him amidst the evening tide of people heading up Abercrombie Street towards Redfern station. He greeted her warmly, delightedly, and before long they were deep in conversation.

When they disembarked at the same stop he suggested they have a drink some time, his offer so casual that it was not until later

Kate realised he had been asking her out. Over the next few days she wondered about the wisdom of her decision to accept: although she had had occasional partners she was usually careful to avoid possible entanglements at work. In the end, though, she went.

As they got to know each other better, she came to realise how different they are. The youngest son in a family in which academic success and the ability to handle oneself socially is celebrated, Jay has always approached life with the confidence of one who believes the world is full of possibility. In the early weeks and months of their relationship, Kate found this optimism and certainty liberating to be around, even as she worried she was failing him by being unable to share in it. In time she came to realise it was at least partly a deliberate strategy, a way of navigating a world in which he has always been, to some extent, an outsider. But as the years have passed she has also come to suspect it is also a kind of greed, an assumption others will give themselves over to him and bend to his will.

She does not like this withholding side of herself, although she understands its source. She was thirteen when she finally understood her mother was an alcoholic. By then Kate had already taken refuge in her own abilities. Instead of friends, she had books, computers, study for tests; instead of love she found comfort in the clarity of numbers, the certainty of facts. Her mother not only didn't understand it, she was made uneasy by her daughter's certainty and apparent self-containment. As she grew older Kate came to understand that the times her mother appeared in her room and lay on the bed alongside her or drew a chair up beside her while she was working were not because she loved Kate – they were because she wanted Kate to love her, or at least to nourish her need to be loved. And with this understanding came contempt for all her mother's desire for approval, the wheedling narcissism at its core.

It was only when she left home that she finally began to feel free. Even then, of course, it wasn't possible to entirely escape her history, or the way the gravity well of her mother's free-associating phone calls and desperate, needy presence constantly threatened to draw Kate back in. By the time Kate was in her third year of university her mother was living alone and unemployed in a flat in La Perouse, and on what would prove her last visit Kate was shocked by the sight of her, the way her skin had grown bruised and fragile, the overdyed hair, the puffiness of her once-striking features. Unable to bear the way her mother's neediness opened her, made her vulnerable, Kate had finally excused herself and walked out the front door, never to return. Somehow that made it easier to stop answering her calls, to simply absent herself from her mother's life, a decision she reached without ever quite trying. During her Honours year she changed her mobile number, and practised an almost monastic isolation. She abstained from social media, unwilling to submit to its shallow, greedy chatter, thereby denying her mother any of the usual avenues for finding her. Part of her understood the violence of this act, yet she could not find it in herself to regret it.

Jay knows some of this but not all. And while she understands he often wishes she could give him more, he does not press her, or not usually. But sometimes she wonders whether she has any more to give, whether the ache inside her is a need or simply a kind of absence.

The next morning Kate wakes to soft light. Sitting up she sees low cloud has blown in while she slept, the trees on the hillside opposite spectral in the mist. The room warm, quiet, the only sound a faint hum somewhere on the edge of hearing.

Jay is standing by the window. Seeing she is awake he smiles as if the night before had not happened.

'Davis has arranged for us to go walking with him,' he says. 'Then he wants us to review some of the other team's research.'

She nods slowly, wondering when he has received this information.

'I haven't got any walking shoes,' she says.

He picks up her robe and hands it to her. 'Davis says they have boots we can borrow.'

Once Kate is dressed they return to the room they ate in the night before. Once again, a meal is delivered to their table by a black-clad server. As he disappears back through the door at the back of the room Kate wonders whether they will continue to be cared for in this way if they agree to work on the project. The day before, as Davis had walked them through the buildings, gesturing to the labs and meeting rooms it had been like nothing she had ever seen before.

'Once we're fully staffed we should have two hundred people based here, although there will be many more working remotely. Finding housing for that many people was always going to be challenging, but we've got accommodation for forty on-site and we've commissioned housing in various places nearby to try to take some of the strain off the local economy,' Davis said at one point, before showing them one of the water recycling plants.

'We're also completely self-sufficient,' he said. 'So, in the event of some kind of breakdown, the records and data stored here can be kept safe.'

'Will the staff also be kept safe if there's a breakdown?' Kate had asked, but Davis had been unfazed.

'It's a good question. It depends on whether they're critical to the facility's operations or not.'

Davis appears as they finish eating. He is in jeans again,

although this time his T-shirt is emblazoned with the cover of a Velvet Underground album, its faded fabric suggesting it is original, or close to it, and his Converse have been replaced with what look like lightweight hiking boots. Not for the first time she finds herself curious about his decision to spend time here, with them, the notion of the head of a global corporation worth billions of dollars devoting so much personal energy to a project that will generate little or no revenue.

'There's some weather coming in from the south,' he says. 'We should be back before it arrives but we'll need to keep an eye on it.'

Kate doesn't reply. Instead she watches Jay, suddenly aware of how totally he seems to have given himself over to Davis's charm, the eagerness with which he responds to the younger man's promptings. She can already sense the pull of this thing, the way the possibility is feeding upon itself, expanding into the world like a genie leaving its bottle. Or a contagion.

The cloud that lay across the valley an hour earlier is already gone by the time they emerge, and the sun is warm on her face as they head up the hill. Davis walks fast, moving with a quick, practised stride; amidst the grass and low trees and broken stone, he looks even more boyish than he did the day before.

Halfway up Jay quickens his pace and falls into step with Davis, Kate allows herself to drop behind, enjoying the opportunity to be alone. To the south the sky is blue, its edges curiously faded, a reminder that this is, in some real sense, the end of the world, only empty ocean separating it from the distant ice of Antarctica. To the west the sky is darker, though, heavy cloud gathering. Remembering Davis's warning about approaching weather, and stories about careless groups of walkers trapped in the mountains by unexpected squalls, she quickens her pace.

On the far side of the hill a series of ledges descend into a gully in which ferns grow amidst stones and tree trunks, their lushness a surprise after the alpine grasses and low scrub on the far side. The air cool, fragrant with the smell of damp and rot. Near the bottom Davis stops beside a tree.

'Here,' he says, touching the trunk. 'What do you see?'

Jay steps closer. 'Some kind of lichen?'

'That's right. It's based on a species endemic to this area, but it's been engineered to increase its capacity to absorb CO_2.'

'You aren't worried about releasing it into the environment like this?' Kate asks.

Davis glances at her. 'I think we're past the point where that's what we should be concerned about,' he says.

Kate is about to reply when Jay interrupts. 'How quickly does it grow?' he asks, extending a hand and holding it above the trunk.

Davis nods approval and Jay touches the plant. 'We've altered its genetic clock to make it faster-growing than conventional lichens. We're working on refining that process, but thus far we've sped up its spread by almost fifty percent.'

'Doesn't that mean it will out-compete the un-engineered lichens?' Kate asks.

'Probably. Although we're looking at a project to engineer multiple species, so we can preserve as much diversity as possible.'

Davis steps back. 'There's something else I want to show you.'

He leads them along a path that winds up the opposite side of the gully. At the top of the hill a line of scrub blocks the path, but Davis pushes a branch aside and ushers them through. On the far side scrub gives way to rows of seedlings, each encircled within a cylinder of cloth and attached to some kind of sensor.

'What are they?' Jay asks.

Davis crouches down next to the nearest of the trees. 'A modified form of eucalypt. Super-fast-growing, with an enzyme in the structure of the wood so the cellulose sequesters twice as much CO_2 as normal timber.'

Jay kneels beside him. 'Amazing.'

Davis nods.

'We've got trial plantations at about a hundred sites worldwide, and we're working with governments to fast-track approvals. As soon as that's done we'll begin planting at scale.'

'Will that make a difference?' Jay asks.

'It's part of a larger strategy, but yes,' Davis says.

Kate stares at the rows of seedlings marching away down the slope. It is astonishing how much Davis has already achieved, and in such secrecy. Resurrected thylacines, mammoths, genetically engineered plants, a plan to re-create the conditions of the Pleistocene in Russia and Canada. How much more is there they aren't being told? Where else has some version of this conversation taken place? Aware of a shift in temperature, a flickering of the light, she glances upward. The clouds she glimpsed earlier loom overhead, occluding the sky. A cold wind licks through the grass.

'Perhaps we should get back,' she says.

Davis stands and glances at his watch. 'I've been monitoring the front,' he says. 'We should have time. But yes.'

As they retrace their steps Kate finds herself staring at the trees and plants around them, wondering how many of them have been altered, what other processes are taking place around her. Just below the crest of the hill she stops by a low gumtree. It has grown at an angle, its trunk leaning out into the open space of the valley. She reaches out and touches it, the smooth surface warm beneath her hand. How long has it stood here? Ten years? Twenty? A hundred? Each year spreading its seeds, reproducing itself. She has read about the networks of trees, the slow linkages of genetic memory and shared information that pass between them, connecting them into a shifting whole, the life of which spans centuries. What will it mean if Davis's trees overtake this one, overtake all of them? Will the engineered trees do the same? And what if they do not? What will be lost? Not just these trees but an entire way of being. Grief grips her, sudden, vertiginous. From the south there is a rumble of thunder, and a drop of rain strikes her, heavy, then another, and another, until all at once it is pouring, the rain sheeting down in an icy wall.

She turns and runs, bounding down the path. Ahead of her Jay has stopped, and is standing, staring back; as she reaches him he grabs her arm, and the two of them race on together. By the time they stumble into the entry area to find Davis waiting they are both laughing, the tension of a few minutes before wiped away by the sudden ferocity of the weather. Their faces alight, breath steaming in the sudden cold, they shake their hands and wring their hair, sending water flying.

'You see how much we've achieved already,' Davis says as they lean against the wall to remove their muddy boots. In the cold his skin has grown paler, his freckles standing out against it, his sandy hair plastered limply against his skull.

'It's remarkable,' Jay says. He doesn't look at Kate.

'It's only the beginning.'

'I can see that.'

'And you, Kate?'

She nods. 'It's extremely impressive.'

Davis smiles. 'Once you're dry, perhaps we could talk about who you might want on your team?'

*

They reconvene in a meeting room they have not seen before, its space bounded on two sides by floor-to-ceiling windows. Outside, the rain is still sheeting down and a grey pall of cloud fills the valley.

Davis is waiting by one of the windows when they arrive. He has changed as well, in his case substituting one hoodie for another, although his hair looks unbrushed, its back springing up in tight curls.

He indicates they should take a seat but does not do so himself. Once they are settled, he turns.

'The first thing I want you to understand is that if you agree to our offer you'll be part of the Foundation, and have full access to the Foundation's resources. That means that although the specifics of your project won't be public, even within the organisation, you'll be able to call on the expertise of any of your colleagues.'

'I assume that works both ways,' Kate says. 'That they'll be able to ask us for advice as well?'

'Of course.'

'And our research. What happens to it?'

'You mean commercially? Commercially it belongs to the Foundation.'

'And in terms of publication?'

Davis blinks. 'Insofar as you don't breach the broader requirements of non-disclosure you're free to publish.'

'In practice though, most of it would remain secret?'

Davis nods. 'Obviously.'

'And what about staff?' asks Jay. 'You talked about us choosing our team?'

Davis steps forward and touches the table. Its surface lights up in front of each of them, displaying the faces of possible candidates. 'That's right. We've already put together a shortlist of individuals we think will meet your requirements, but if there are specific people you want to bring, or candidates you think we've missed, just let us know.'

Afterwards, as they stand to leave, Davis speaks her name, asks if she might stay for a moment. She glances at Jay, who shrugs and then walks out, closing the door behind him.

Davis turns and looks out the window. This time she knows what he is about to say has been rehearsed.

'You know we chose you two because we think you're the best, don't you?' he asks at last.

There is a pause Kate knows he expects her to fill. Finally she complies. 'But?'

Davis glances around. 'I don't want you to think I don't understand why this might be difficult for you.'

Kate stares back at him. All the air seems to have drained out of the room.

'I know you don't trust me, but I want you to know I'll understand if you say no.'

She places a hand on the table to steady herself. She isn't sure whether she is angrier that Davis had been investigating her life or that he is suggesting she might make her decision for psychological reasons.

'My objections to the project are ethical, not personal.'

'I undertand that. And I respect it.'

'Do you?'

Davis smiles. 'Of course.'

As she walks back to the room her legs are shaking so much she is afraid she might fall. Jay is seated by the window, flicking through his phone. Seeing her expression, he gets to his feet, moves towards her.

'What is it?' he asks, reaching for her. 'What's wrong?'

Kate pushes past him and sits heavily on the bed. Lifting a hand, she stares at it. It is trembling.

Jay sits next to her. 'Kate? What happened? What did Davis say?'

She shakes her head. 'It's nothing.'

'You know we don't have to do this, don't you?'

She nods. 'The child. Will they have rights? We need some kind of guarantee they will be protected by the law, that they'll have the same rights of self-determination as a normal child.'

'We can make sure we have that.'

'And when the time comes what will we tell them about themselves?'

'The truth. Or whatever version of it the people responsible for their psychological welfare think best.'

'That's not enough. They deserve to know the truth. We owe them that much.'

'Of course.'

'And how will they be brought up? Who will care for them?'

'Davis is talking about some kind of team. Psychologists, paediatricians, nurses.'

Kate glances at him. 'So, not us, then?'

Jay shakes his head in surprise. 'No. Not us.'

Kate closes her hands, steadying them.

'Okay then,' she says. 'I'll do it.'

They were at dinner the first time Jay suggested having a baby. Kate laughed.

'I don't think we're ready for that,' she said.

Jay fell silent, staring at her across the table.

She hesitated, realising she had missed something in his tone. 'You're serious?'

'Of course,' he said.

They had discussed children when it first became clear their relationship was going to endure. Kate had said she wasn't sure, that after her own childhood it didn't seem right. Jay waited for her to reply.

'Please, Kate,' he said when she didn't. 'If you don't talk to me, I can't help.'

But she only shook her head, refusing to look up.

Finally he reached across to her, touched her cheek. 'I know how you feel about this. But it wouldn't be like it was for you. We'd be us.'

Still off-balance, she turned his hand over. His palm, smooth, soft, so different from her scrubbed skin.

'Is this the right time?'

'Is there ever a right time?'

She didn't reply, and a moment later their meal arrived, interrupting them. But afterwards, as they walked home, she had wondered about her resistance to the idea. Was it just about her past? Her mother's failures? Or was it something deeper? She was almost thirty-five, the women around them were having children, yet she couldn't imagine herself as a mother.

Jay didn't return to the subject that night, or the next, though she knew he had not let the idea go. Despite his irritation with his parents' frequent observations about he and Kate's continued childlessness, she had seen the delight he took in the company of his nieces and nephews, and knew how much that expansion of the world mattered to him. Occasionally when she was with his siblings and their families she understood it as well, but more often she felt awkward, as if she were an intruder.

And then there was the sense things were unravelling all around them.

A week later, she turned to him in the bathroom as they were getting ready to sleep. 'Look at the world,' she whispered. 'How could we bring a child into this?'

'We can't be afraid like that. By making a child we say we believe in the future, that things can get better.'

'And if they don't?'

'They will. They have to.'

She shook her head. He pulled her towards him. 'And anyway, I don't care about the world, only you, us.'

In that moment his tenderness seemed incomprehensible to her. She was so angry, so unreachable.

'Why do you love me?' she asked.

'You know why,' he said, stroking her hair from her face.

'No,' she said, 'I don't,' and turned her face into his neck.

Perhaps that is where it would have ended. Yet over the weeks that followed Kate found herself returning to the question. She had never thought of herself as somebody who was good with children – in fact, they usually made her feel uncomfortable – but now she found herself watching them on trains and in parks and at social events. Gradually she realised it wasn't the children themselves that frightened her, it was something deeper, less easy to articulate. Not just the loss of autonomy over her body, her life, but of being vulnerable in that way. Because were it to happen, she would have to let Jay closer, show him things she did not know how to express.

The night she told him she would do it they were in bed together. It was dark, and he went still beside her. Finally he touched her hand.

'Are you sure?'

She hesitated. 'I'm sure.'

*

The Foundation arranges their relocation with remarkable smooth-ness. Offered their choice of accommodation, they select a house in an area of bushland just under half an hour's drive from the facility. It is set back from the road with views over a valley, the only sign there are other houses nearby the ribbons of smoke that rise from their chimneys on winter afternoons or the occasional roar of an engine in the distance.

'I feel like the Unabomber,' Jay jokes on their first evening there.

Kate laughs, aware it is the first time in his life he has lived more than a few minutes from a supermarket. 'Don't worry. I don't think we'll be here all that much.'

Nor are they. For the past few weeks they have been assembling a wish list for their team. Because of the nature of the Foundation's work, much of the support they need can be sourced internally, especially when it comes to the more specialised computing. But Jay has ideas for several staff from outside. Some of them are people Kate knows, or at least knows of – Torill from the University of Copenhagen, Dulani from Cambridge; but there are others she only knows by reputation, most prominent among them, Mylin, whom Jay knows from his post-doc days and who has had remarkable success creating stem cells from DNA recovered from frozen cells.

Although all are required to sign non-disclosure agreements, not everybody is made aware of the true focus of the project. How much each does understand depends less on their level of seniority than on their need to know. The scope of the project makes this easier than one might expect: at Davis's direction they are to work on several different animals at once, allowing the more sensitive parts of the project to be kept secret.

Still, only one of the people they speak to refuses to be involved. Of the others it is Mylin who is the least fazed. 'We all know the science is there,' she says. 'What we need to do is let go of the outdated thinking that's holding us back.'

'The technical challenges are immense,' Jay says to Davis on the day they begin. 'We might have a sequenced genome but, as you no doubt understand from your work on the thylacines, that's very different to having the building blocks of a human being. We need to re-create an individual genome, invent a person. And that is only the first step. Once we've got that we need to create a fertile egg and an embryo, successfully implant it and bring it to term.'

As Jay speaks Kate finds herself shifting uncomfortably in her seat. It still astonishes her, that it is possible to exhume the history of life from the deep past, that with a sequence of chemicals it is possible to create a living creature – a living *person* – in a lab. Yet when she steps back from the scientific questions her larger unease remains. Should they be doing this? Should *she*? Folding her arms she forces herself to concentrate on Jay's words, the structure of the task ahead of them.

They begin with the genomes sequenced in the early years of the century, augmenting them with samples drawn from various sites around the world. As they proceed Kate is surprised over and over again by the Foundation's reach and the technical wizardry of the people it employs, their ability to extract usable material from samples that are, in most cases, forty or fifty thousand years old. In the end a significant amount of material is extracted from a tooth recovered from a cave exposed by a retreating glacier in the French Alps. The remains are skeletal, yet the unusually cold conditions mean enough DNA has been preserved to reconstruct many sections of the genome that had eluded them, and once passed through a battery of scans provides them with vital information about the subject's physiology. Although no one refers to her that way, all of them know that this woman, this member of a separate species dead for five hundred centuries, is as close to being the mother of the child they are making as anyone could be.

The work is consuming, and because of the facility's relative isolation they take to spending most of their waking hours in the lab, often not returning home until late in the evening. Occasionally on the weekends she and Jay do the ninety-minute drive into the capital, but as the months race by they make the trip less and less often, and instead spend their weekends alone or at the facility.

At first Kate finds pleasure in the work, and, rather to her surprise, in working so closely with Jay. Although there are still days when she feels the darkness rising around her like a tide, more often she feels focused, clear, like her old self. She knows that if she looks she will find the cracks, that she cannot go back, but for the most part she moves ahead of it.

Perhaps Jay notices as well; certainly he is less wary of leaving her alone. Yet as the months pass the workload begins to take its toll. By the time they arrive home most nights it is dark, the house cold and silent, and while Kate reads or watches TV on her laptop Jay works, often not coming to bed until after she is asleep. At first it seems not to matter, but it slowly becomes clear to Kate that they are drifting apart, and, though she does not like to admit it even to herself, that she is no longer upset about that.

Through it all, the work continues. With the material gathered it falls to Kate to oversee the final reconstruction of the genes, a task she approaches using the procedures for synthesising DNA she has developed over the past decade in combination with the processing power offered by the Foundation and Gather. And once they have a complete set of chromosomes, they begin to create eggs and, eventually, embryos.

The final stage in the process is to use a surrogate. The woman selected for that role arrives towards the end of the second year. Kate encounters her as she steps out onto the pathway leading to the labs, startled to find a young woman she doesn't know standing, looking out over the valley.

'Can I help you?' Kate asks, approaching her. The young woman – girl, Kate thinks, correcting herself – turns to face her. She wears her long blonde hair straight, a blunt fringe above her eyes like one of the Manson girls, a wide-boned face with the unassailable beauty of the privileged, yet there is something myopic about the way she stares at Kate, as if she hardly sees her.

'What are you doing here? Did somebody let you in?' she asks.

The woman gazes back coolly. 'I'm Marija. I'm the surrogate.'

Kate stares at her. 'Really. And you're here to see who?'

'Jay. He told me to get some air.'

Jay is in his office. He swivels his chair towards her as she closes the door.

'What the fuck?' she demands.

He looks puzzled. 'What?'

'I've just met our surrogate.'

He hesitates, composing himself. 'Marija? Yes. She arrived this morning.'

'And when were you planning to tell me about her?'

'I assumed you knew. Davis found her.'

Kate stands, staring at him. When they first joined the Foundation they agreed Jay would act as project leader, both because his networks were better and because he was more practised at negotiating organisations. They both knew this was unlikely to be without its costs, but she has managed to ignore the way his increasing involvement in the Foundation's internal politics has altered him. But until now it had not occurred to her that he might be deliberately withholding information from her. Cold fury boils up as she remembers his friendliness over breakfast a few hours earlier, though she is unsure whether she is angrier about the breach of trust or the realisation he thinks she needs to be managed in this way.

She is unsurprised it is the issue of surrogate selection that has brought them here, because they have argued about the question before. Right from the outset she has been uncomfortable about Davis's demand they allow the Foundation to facilitate the choice of surrogate, all too aware of the ethical slipperiness of it all.

'How much does she know?'

Jay glances out the window, as if unwilling to meet her eye. 'Not much. Davis wants the focus of the research to remain private.'

'She doesn't know the baby she'll be carrying isn't human?'

Jay looks uneasy. 'It won't make any difference to her.'

'That we know of.'

'She's signed the agreements.'

'The agreements?'

'Jesus, Kate, what is it you want from me?'

Kate stares at him without speaking. Then she shakes her head and stalks out the door.

Meanwhile Davis appears and disappears, seemingly at random. Some mornings they arrive to find him already there, seated in the lab, their findings open on his tablet. Often when that happens he will be eager to talk, to review their progress, his grasp of the fine detail alarmingly precise.

'The insertions look encouraging, but have you considered shifting the parameters of the search?'

The first time it happens Jay is furious, incensed at the invasion of his privacy.

'He can't just sweep in here, open up private files,' he rages.

'They're the Foundation's systems,' Kate reminds him. 'He probably has back doors into everything anyway.'

Jay considers this. 'That makes it worse. How are we to know who else he's sharing our data with? Who else has access to it?' Kate knows Jay has become convinced they are not the only team Davis has working on this, that there are others, elsewhere. She knows it angers him, although whether that is because he is being kept out of the loop or because he is worried about others using their results without their knowledge she isn't sure.

Whenever Davis visits Kate is careful to keep her distance. Davis seems a different kind of being, untethered by ordinary human concerns. Despite his occasional charm, his careful observance of the mores of contemporary sensitivity, there is something oddly absent about him. Yet simultaneously she is in no doubt about his ruthlessness, his preparedness to do whatever he needs to in order to achieve his goals. Is this something about his psychological makeup, or simply a function of his wealth, the way it insulates him from normal human concerns? In the weeks after they joined the project she made a point of reading up on him, working her way through the biography published two years earlier, the profiles in *Wired* and *The New York Times* and Bloomberg, the more critical pieces ferreted away in less frequented parts of the web. Yet despite the glimpses of his early life – his parents are both psychiatrists, perhaps explaining Davis's studied blankness – the facts were oddly unrevealing, the man emerging as little more than the sum of his mantras about transformative change and the need to let go of the past. One detail had stuck with her, though, an observation made by the journalist Davis had commissioned to write the story of his life and then fired, resulting in the most famous piece about him, a defiantly unhagiographical treatise running to twenty thousand words published in the *London Review of Books* that told the story of the three months its author spent following Davis around. The version of Davis that emerged in it was not so much as the evil genius many make him out to be but something rather stranger; a man whose understanding of the world was circumscribed by the limitations of his experience, his assumptions about his own intelligence, his experience of success. Repeating Davis's mantra about refusing the constraints of conventional thinking – 'the best solutions are often the most frightening' – the author asked whether it was really just the distillation of the adolescent fantasy the entire world is simply a computational problem, capable of being solved by an algorithm or an app, a way of avoiding the unfortunate fact the world is nothing of the sort, that its problems are often messy, intractable, or in the parlance of Davis and his cohorts, uncalculatable.

At other times Davis just appears, turning up in one of the kitchens or dining areas. On these occasions he gives the impression he has been there all along, that his sudden appearance is entirely unremarkable, sometimes going so far as to offer to make them coffee, or push some meal he has been preparing in front of them.

One night, when they are reasonably confident he is elsewhere – just as she is never entirely convinced Madison and the others aren't robots, Kate is never quite certain Davis doesn't have a secret living space hidden somewhere in the complex or devices monitoring their private conversations – Jay mentions their benefactor has raised the question of connections between autism and Neanderthal genes.

'When was that?' she asks, deliberately casual.

'He messaged me the other day.'

'I didn't know you two messaged each other.'

Jay's expression remains studiedly neutral. 'We don't, or not often.'

'Why do you think he wants to know?'

Jay laughs, and for a moment Kate remembers her affection for him. 'You don't think Davis might have a personal interest in autism?' he asks.

'Davis isn't on the spectrum,' she says, taking a sip of her wine. 'He's a sociopath.'

Jay smiles, amused.

'I'm serious,' she says.

He laughs again, more dismissively this time. 'Jesus, Kate. Give the guy a break.'

'Who? Our billionaire puppet-master boss? Doctor fucking Evil in a hoodie? Listen to yourself, Jay.'

He purses his lips. Kate is reminded of how much he hates conflict, and more particularly her anger. For the most part she can control it, but tonight she finds she doesn't care.

'Is this about him or you?'

'Fuck you, Jay. It's about *us*, this project, all of it. We're making a human being, not because they're wanted but because some rich white guy likes the idea of playing God. Doesn't that bother you?'

Jay stands up. 'Forgive me if I'm misremembering, but as I recall it was *your* idea we stay.'

'And if I'd said no? Would you have walked away with me?'

'You'd need to have told me what you thought or felt for that to happen.'

Kate stares at him.

'I'm going to bed,' he says. 'You do what you want. You always do anyway.'

The lights are off when she follows him into the bedroom, but she knows Jay is not sleeping. She undresses, lies down next to him. For a long time neither of them speak, the presence of the other in the darkness palpable. Finally Kate extends a hand, touches his back, and Jay turns towards her. She presses her face to his, kisses him; he responds, and for a time their bodies move together, wordless, urgent, each of them straining towards a closeness they have lost.

Afterwards Jay rolls onto his back, his breath slowing as he slides into sleep almost immediately. Kate lies staring at his profile in the darkness. Not for the first time she finds herself struck by how little she really knows about him, how little he really knows about her. Are all relationships founded on this unacknowledged incomprehension? Is it even possible to understand another human being? So much of the time we do not even understand ourselves. And what happens if we do come to understand those we love? Can we still love them? Or is something lost, some possibility?

Finally, unable to sleep, she gets up and, dressing, goes out into the darkness and drives towards the facility.

It is past midnight by the time she gets there, and the offices and corridors are empty. When she was younger she loved to visit the university labs at night. Something about the institutional nature of them, the silence and liminality of them appealed to her. When her friends left to drink or watch Netflix she had often stayed behind, simply to be there.

These labs are different: newer, better equipped, infinitely cleaner, yet as she opens her screen in the half-lit space she feels the same sense of calm the labs she had worked in as a student had given her.

After a few minutes she becomes aware of a presence behind her, and turning, finds Davis standing there.

'Hello, Kate,' he says, smiling.

Kate regards him warily, unsure how long he has been there.

'Davis.'

He walks towards her and seats himself on the bench opposite her.

'Am I interrupting?'

She shakes her head. 'I didn't realise you were here.'

'I arrived earlier this evening.'

'Are you staying on-site?'

He shrugs. 'I don't sleep much.' There is a moment's silence, in which he looks at her, as if expecting her to ask him something else. 'I hear you're working on the woolly rhinoceros as well as the main project.'

Kate closes her screen and places it face-down on the bench. Although the woolly rhinoceros de-extinction program is taking the less challenging path of re-engineering the DNA of modern rhinoceroses, the project has been a source of ongoing problems for months. 'There were a few kinks that needed ironing out. Jay and I agreed that would happen quicker if I got involved.'

'Excellent.' Davis pauses for a moment. 'And the main project?'

She hesitates. 'You know where we're at.'

He waits for her to elaborate. When she does not he leans back against the bench. 'You're still not comfortable with what we're doing here, are you?'

'No.'

'But Jay is?'

'I don't think it's that simple.'

Davis looks at her, and for a moment she has the unpleasant feeling he has rehearsed what he says next.

'When I was still at school, some friends and I found a back door into the broadcast systems of Fox News. It wasn't a big thing, just a piece of code they hadn't closed off properly. At first we were content just to know it was there, to know that we could slip inside their systems, move around at will. But one day I had an idea: *What if we used it?* We were really just kids, chatting on an encrypted server, but I remember the way that suggestion set us alight, the way it brought us to life. And eventually we decided we would use it to make a statement.

We made a sort of set in my friend Ravi's basement, and set it up so there was nothing that would identify the space. And then, one evening, we slipped in that back door and jammed their signal.'

Kate looks at him. 'You're talking about the broadcast with the guys in masks? The ones explaining what would happen if global warming wasn't slowed? That was you?'

Davis nods. 'All twenty minutes of it.'

'I thought they caught somebody for that.'

Davis shakes his head. 'They questioned some kids who had nothing to do with it. And a lot of activists. But they never got near us.'

'Why are you telling me this?'

Davis smiles. 'I wanted you to see the way knowledge can disrupt the system. The way even the smallest door can open onto something larger.'

Kate stares at him for a moment, aware something is being asked of her but unsure what it is, except that she does not wish to give it.

'This is where I'm supposed to say, "Or we should leave the door unopened?" I suppose?'

Davis's smile does not falter. 'Except I know you're too smart for that.'

They called it a miscarriage but it wasn't that, or not quite. There was no unexpected bleeding at two months. She had been almost six months' pregnant when she was hit with cramps one afternoon at work.

She does not talk about it often, if at all, but when she does, there is one detail she cannot bring herself to speak about. Because when she felt the cramps she was at the lab, in the middle of a cycle, and instead of calling Jay she kept working.

It hadn't been a long time, just long enough to finish the cycle, but when she stood up at the end she knew immediately something was seriously wrong.

On the way out of the building she called Jay. He was in a meeting on the other side of town, but he called back almost at once. His voice trembled as he pressed her for details, and she knew at once she couldn't tell him.

In the taxi she felt something wet between her legs, and looking down had seen blood. In the mirror the driver's eyes were on the spreading stain, his face half-sympathetic, half-frightened. As their eyes met she wondered if he was working illegally, what it might mean for him if something happened to her while she was in his cab.

'I'll pay for it,' she said, willing her voice not to shake. 'Just get me to the hospital.'

In the hospital they called her obstetrician and left her on a gurney to wait. Every few seconds she would reach down, touch her belly. In the first weeks of her pregnancy the idea she was carrying a baby had seemed if not quite abstract – after all, how abstract could it be if she was carrying it around inside her? – then removed from her, as if she were a passenger on a journey she had not quite committed to. But over the months since then she had felt herself changing, the baby, its presence within her so wondrous that the idea she might lose it, that its matter might be sundered from hers was unbearable, unimaginable.

Jay was still on his way when the nurses came for her, meaning she was alone as they took her into the delivery room and guided the baby from her.

She knew it would be tiny, not yet ready to be born, but in fact it was its perfection that shocked her. A girl, not much larger than a kitten, yet fully formed and so beautiful it was difficult to believe she wasn't alive.

They wanted to keep Kate in hospital for two days, but she refused. Instead she demanded Jay call a taxi, and, refusing his help, walked out into the street to wait for it. Back at home she crawled onto the bed, turned her face to the wall, and wept.

She knew her decision to wait didn't really matter, that the outcome would not have been any different if she had gone to the hospital immediately, but still, the uncertainty gnawed at her. What if she had left sooner? Might the baby have lived?

At Jay's urging she asked for a week of leave, but once the week was up she could not go back. Instead she remained at home in their apartment. At first she just slept, weighed down by an exhaustion that seemed to have no beginning, no end. But as the weeks passed she took to reading, chasing through the internet in search of articles about the ruination of the world. She realised that while she had been sequestered away in her discipline, she had somehow let the scale of the situation elude her, but now, as she read and read, she felt the enormity of the tragedy that surrounded them begin to swallow her. Every day there was a new study, a new catastrophe, new evidence of systemic collapse. Every day she felt less able to control her sense of impending disaster.

Part of her understood she was not in her right mind, that this was depression, but knowing didn't help: it was as if she were outside herself, observing something over which she no longer had any power.

Jay did his best. But it was not until he agreed to give a keynote in Boston, a commitment that would require him to be away for more than a fortnight, that it became clear how bad things had become.

'I'm frightened to leave you,' he confessed a week before he left.

'What do you mean?'

He gestured at her laptop on the table. 'All this. I know you're hurting, but you have to try.'

She stared at him. 'I'm fine,' she said.

'You're not. And you haven't been for a while. We can't go on like this.'

Kate caught herself before she suggested they didn't need to. 'Okay,' she said.

Jay drove her to the doctor, where they sat in the waiting room in silence. In one corner stood a model house, large enough for a child to enter, its interior piled with plastic blocks and toys. After they had been there a few minutes a woman entered with a girl of three or so; obviously familiar with the waiting room, the girl let go of her mother's hand and, hurrying over to the house, entered it and began to remove the blocks and pile them on the chair beside it.

Kate and Jay watched, unspeaking. The girl was small and fair, her blonde curls pinched back from her face by a coloured band in a way that emphasised the bones in her forehead. At one point the mother glanced up from her phone, and catching Kate's eye, smiled at her; Kate looked away, tears filling her eyes.

In the surgery Jay sat in silence as Kate explained she was feeling unwell, that she was worried she was depressed. Only a few months earlier she had sat here smiling as this same doctor offered advice about stretch marks and dispensed folk wisdom about using the shape of the bump to predict whether the baby was male or female. But even as she spoke Kate had to struggle to keep talking, her words, language itself, blunt and ill-made. The truth was she felt exposed, raw, as if everything that protected her from the world had been scoured away, leaving nothing but the past she had tried so hard to leave behind.

The doctor prescribed a course of anti-depressants, and gave her the number of a psychologist. As Jay ushered her out the door Kate caught the look that passed between him and the doctor, grateful on his part, solicitous on hers. Back in the car she was so tired she could hardly speak.

She saw the psychologist once but did not go back. Instead she let herself fall into the anti-depressants. After a time she realised she was no longer depressed, but she was not better, or not better in the way she knew Jay wanted her to be. He suggested more and more often she think about transitioning back to work, but she did not, could not: the thought of it seemed trivial, absurd. Finally she told him she wasn't going back.

'Then what will you do?' he asked.

She shrugged. 'I don't know.'

Davis isn't there on the morning they attempt the nuclear transfer; instead, he is at a press conference at the Foundation's facility in Siberia. Neither Kate nor Jay nor any of their team have heard anything about the event, or even the project, so they are surprised when they emerge from the lab to find an alert on their phones asking them to join the feed.

When they connect, Davis is surrounded by a collection of people whose faces Kate recognises, though it takes a moment or two to realise they are famous: two actors, a pop star she remembers from a scandal a few years before, a reality TV star who was briefly involved with Sea Shepherd.

After a brief introduction Davis steps to the microphone, blinking in the light. He looks uncomfortable, like an animal caught in the spotlight, but then he gathers himself, and Kate sees the weirdly oblivious self-belief she knows so well reassert itself.

'Many of you will know that two years ago I negotiated an agreement with the Russian government for the control of almost two million hectares of state land in areas characterised by continuous and semi-continuous permafrost and forest. This arrangement was completed on the understanding the Hucken Foundation would study the effects of warming on Arctic and Subarctic ecosystems, and explore projects that might slow the changes that have already begun to transform these areas.'

On a huge screen behind Davis images dance by, a dizzying montage of accelerated footage of melting ice and calving glaciers, of a lake of blue water where ice should be, of rivers tumbling down through tussocked grass, of land subsiding, collapsing into thermokarst valleys, of animals and plants emerging from the frozen ground.

'I'm pleased to announce today that we've met a series of milestones in that process, and also that the Foundation has plans to extend our brief by setting up a program to restore a number of extinct species to the park, beginning with the auroch.'

There is a murmur from the assembled crowd, scattered applause. Davis waits awkwardly for it to finish. Kate glances at Jay, who is watching with his arms folded.

'The Nazis wanted to breed aurochs,' Jay says. 'They spent years working on a program to re-create them through elective bloodlines.'

'You didn't know, then?'

Jay shakes his head. On the screen Davis is talking again.

'This is just the first part of a larger scheme to rebuild the ecology of this area. We have plans in place to de-extinct other species—'

'Mute it,' Jay says, and the screen falls silent. Kate watches him, surprised again by how transparent he can be. He is annoyed that Davis has let his attention drift, that other teams are more important to him.

'What now?' she asks.

He shrugs. 'We wait to see whether the embryos take,' he says.

With each failure the mood in the project team becomes increasingly tense. Jay grows distant, irritable.

And then, just when it looks as if it will never work, a healthy embryo is produced. Kate suggests the team celebrate but Jay refuses, afraid they will jinx it. She laughs at him, and is surprised when he glares at her.

That night she expects him to be distant, but in the darkness he reaches for her, and they fuck wordlessly, his body no more than a shape in the gloom. Closing her eyes she imagines the embryos in the lab freezer, the surrogate's body, and for a moment it is not Jay above her but Marija, or somebody else she does not know.

A fortnight later they implant, Kate watching the operation on a screen. For a week they wait, and when the news comes that the embryo has taken they all cheer, until Jay motions to them to calm down, assuring them there is much more that needs to be done.

As summer bleeds into autumn they monitor Marija's pregnancy closely. There are hiccups, but for the most part it proceeds normally. One day, at the gym, Kate encounters Marija. She is swimming, her stroke clean and strong, her angular body barely altered from the back. As she wheels up the lane Kate watches her, wondering at what they have done here, at the notion the child in her womb is not human. How much does Marija guess, Kate wonders. Some? All? None?

In her bag her phone buzzes, and pulling it out she reads an email from Jay and fires back a quick answer. As she puts her phone away again she is startled to realise Marija has climbed out of the pool while she was distracted and now stands a short distance away.

Out of the water the younger woman's body is long and lean, the only sign she is seven months' pregnant the gravid weight of her belly, which protrudes at an improbable angle from her body, her heavy breasts. She does not acknowledge Kate's presence. Eventually Kate turns towards her, speaks.

'You swim beautifully.'

Marija doesn't look at her. Instead she looks at the pool.

'I did squad when I was younger.' She has the slightly blurred accent of the young, that indeterminacy that makes it sound like it is straining eastward, across the Pacific.

'It shows,' Kate says.

Marija continues to dry herself, as if the conversation is over.

Not for the first time Kate is struck by the way Marija repels all attempts to engage with her. It is difficult to tell whether it is lack of interest or a peculiarly obstinate stupidity. Were there always so many people who were so unengaged by those around them? Or is it a new thing? An evolutionary response to technology or social conditions? She has heard Marija on the phone to people who must be her friends, her words flowing out of her, as if she were describing a video that just happens to be her life in which anybody not in her field of vision is irrelevant.

'I saw some of the results. You seem to be doing well.'

Marija glances at her, her flat incuriosity deflected for a moment by the fact they are talking about her.

'They said.'

'And you feel well?'

She nods, grappling the wet mass of her hair into a thick rope as she wraps it in a towel. Kate watches her thoughtfully.

'I'm curious,' she says. 'What made you sign up for this project?'

Marija looks at her. 'I wanted to help.'

Kate hesitates. She feels as if she is on the edge of something. 'Help with what?'

'Help Davis.'

'Why would you want to do that?'

'Because I believe in what he's doing. Because he's trying to make the world a better place.'

'But this is a baby you're making,' Kate persists.

Marija smiles. 'It's my body,' she says. 'If I can make somebody else happy that's a good thing, isn't it?'

In the last weeks of the pregnancy, there are a series of meetings to review the question of whether a vaginal delivery or a caesarean would be safer. Although the decision is ultimately one for the medical team, Jay and Kate and several other of their senior colleagues are included in the discussions. Although the baby seems to be developing as anticipated, her weight is lower than expected. It is unclear if this is normal or due to some unexpected developmental delay, but in the end the medical team decides to operate, thereby eliminating one vector of risk. The decision is communicated to Marija by Jay and the head doctor in a conversation that is livestreamed to Davis, Kate and other members of the team. The camera is on the ceiling of the conference room, its angle queasily reminiscent of footage from some kind of exposé.

Although Kate had assumed Marija would be upset, or at least concerned about the possibility of post-operative damage, she seems entirely unmoved by the news, receiving it impassively.

More troubling to Kate is the decision Marija will not be allowed to see the child. To achieve this it has been decided she will be sedated during the procedure and then removed to a recovery suite immediately after the incision has been closed.

'She deserves to hold her, to see her,' Kate says, but Davis refuses.

'We're worried the shock might lead to her breaching her confidentiality agreement,' he says, his voice oddly hollow through the speakers.

On the day appointed Marija is prepped and moved to the delivery suite. Although they are not part of the medical team Kate and Jay have been given permission to attend the procedure; together with Davis and a videographer they stand to the side of the room as Marija is wheeled in, her body swathed in a surgical gown, her long blonde hair falling on either side of her face.

The operation is quick, unproblematic, but as the scalpel pierces Marija's skin and the flesh parts to reveal the blue-grey form of the child, Kate begins to shake, the memory of her own time in surgery coming back to her. Reaching down, she grips the chair and wraps an arm around her middle. Nothing is ever truly over. She turns to Jay, but above his mask his attention is fixed on the obstetrician, so she closes her eyes and focuses on breathing.

And then, sooner than seems possible, there is a gasp. Kate opens her eyes to find the obstetrician holding a blood and vernix-smeared form in his white-gloved hands. She is so still, her tiny shape so immobile that Kate's breath catches. But as the nurse lays the tiny form out on the resus trolley, it coughs, then with a rasping wheeze begins to cry, and all at once the moment rushes in, filling her, filling all of them. Above his mask Jay's eyes are creased with delight; on the far side of the suite the obstetrician leans back in relief. Pushing closer, Kate stares down at the child, her tiny face contorted as she cries out in shock and fear at being torn from the world within and thrust into the light, a sound not heard for forty thousand years spilling out into the air, filling the space around them, Kate's only thought that she is so small, so beautiful. So human.

The hours after the child is born pass in a daze, the world around them only half-real. Jay and the other team members are elated, suspended in a mixture of relief the procedure has been a success and wonder at the less easily parsed miracle of her being. Still clad in a gown, Jay is interviewed by the videographer, his words coming in a rush as he attempts to describe his feelings, glancing around every sentence or two to look at the child – Eve, as Davis has demanded they call her – nestled in the arms of the nurse. When he is done the videographer approaches Kate, but she lifts a hand and backs away, uncomfortable committing her emotions to words at this moment.

There is much to be done, of course – not just medical tests but records of size and weight, heartbeat and blood chemistry, reflex responses and more, as well as photographs and video. But even before they begin it is apparent to all present that she is healthy and strong, no different, in many ways, from a normal baby.

But even a superficial glance is enough to reveal she is not normal. Beneath the thick red-brown hair plastered against her scalp her head is larger, the face more simian, the rounded cheeks and jaw reminiscent of those of a chimpanzee, her subtly shorter forehead emphasising the unusual largeness of her eyes.

Yet it is not these differences that strike Kate most forcefully, but her fragility, the wonder of her. She is them but not them, human but not human, extinct yet somehow here, in the world. But most of all she seems to embody a kind of possibility, something both dizzying and terrifying to contemplate, her presence in the world changing everything. And nothing.

The scientist in Kate is dispassionate enough to want to probe these responses. Are they simply relief and excitement? A natural reaction to a newborn child, or perhaps some kind of delayed response to her own trauma? Or is there something deeper going on, some hardwired response to the sight of a different species? We are, after all, programmed to recognise our own kind, and, conversely, to know when somebody or something is not one of us.

They have produced a formula with which to feed her, engineered to provide minerals and proteins they anticipate she will need. It is a decision Kate resisted, arguing they should allow her to breastfeed, an argument that was overruled by Davis and Jay. Technically it is the responsibility of the nurse to whose care Eve has been entrusted to feed her, but when Kate asks her if she can hold the child, the nurse smiles and places her in Kate's arms. And as Eve takes the bottle Kate realises it does not matter, that in the end the world narrows down to this one thing. The way that bond connects both, one to the past, one to the future, or in this case, folds back in on itself, disturbing time, abstracting meaning.

It is only when she looks up that she sees Davis standing to one side, watching her. During the procedure he had stood on the other side of Jay, barely speaking, his eyes above his surgical mask focused on Marija and the doctors. Once or twice Jay had said something to him, but Davis had seemed to hardly notice, not even glancing around as he replied. In the moments after the birth he had been interviewed by the videographer; clad in his scrubs he had spoken of the Foundation's goals, the fact their achievements had propelled them into the future. 'We are at a moment of historical decoupling,' he said, his manner shifting from something almost messianic to a performance of humility so disingenuous Kate was surprised he couldn't hear it himself. In recent weeks there have been a string of negative stories about Gather sharing information with the Russian and Chinese intelligence services; watching Davis's performance Kate found herself wondering whether his oddly unsettled demeanour is connected to them.

Still lost in the wonder of the child, she smiles.

'Would you like to hold her?' she asks.

Davis doesn't move. 'She looks happy where she is.'

Kate smiles again. 'Are you pleased? Is this what you expected?'

Once again she sees the sheen of mania she glimpsed when he spoke to the videographer in the fixity of his gaze. 'The whole point was to move us past expectation. Into somewhere new.'

Kate hesitates, unsure how to respond. But before she can recover herself Madison appears at Davis's elbow and whispers something to him.

'I'm sorry,' he says. 'I have to go.'

It is only after he has left it occurs to Kate that at no point did Davis hold or touch the child.

Kate does not see Marija again, although later she is told she was discharged and returned to the mainland the day after the birth. Davis disappears as well, supposedly back to Oakland to discuss the buyout of another company, although that same day Kate sees photos of him at a music festival in Costa Rica and a meeting with Saudi sheikhs. With them gone it is as if some crucial link with the wider world has been severed. Isolated not just from the other staff at the facility, but even those in their own team who are not privy to the true nature of the project, Kate finds herself struck by the sense the rest of the world has fallen away, leaving only her and Jay and the others involved in Eve's care.

At least at the outset this proves easier than anybody had anticipated. Eve is strong, alert, surprisingly untroubled. Although there is no way of knowing for certain what constitutes normal development in a non-sapient child, she seems healthy and happy.

In principle Eve's day-to-day care is the responsibility of a team of nurses. Although all have been carefully vetted Kate sometimes wonders what they think of the project, and of those involved in it: more than once one in particular asks pointed questions about when they plan to move Eve into a more normal environment, and on several occasions Kate interrupts conversations none of the nursing staff seem in a hurry to resume. Yet still, as the weeks pass, she finds herself in the suite more and more. Sometimes she has an excuse – data to review or samples to collect – but more often she is there simply to be close to Eve, her hours passed watching the child sleep or cradling her tiny body, undone by her presence. One evening, when Eve will not settle, Kate offers to take over from the nurse, holding the bottle as Eve's restlessness gives way to calm. As Eve slips into sleep Kate becomes aware of somebody behind her, and looks up to find Jay standing there. He smiles solicitously, and she smiles back, suddenly aware of the way they recapitulate the iconography of the family: infant, loving mother, attentive father.

Jay places a hand on her shoulder. 'You mustn't bond with her,' he says gently. 'She isn't ours.'

She starts, struck by his use of the word 'ours'.

'But that's the point, isn't it? She should be somebody's. All children should be.'

'And she will be. You've seen the plans. Davis has arranged for carers and educators.'

Kate's stomach twists. 'You know that's not the same. She deserves parents.'

Jay nods. 'You're right. But we understood when we signed up that it would be like this. That she would be part of an experiment.'

'Are you sure that was the right choice? We could find another way, surely?'

'Please, Kate,' Jay says. 'Don't do this.'

That night, back in their room, they argue.

'So, what?' Jay demands. 'You think they should hand her over to us? Let us play happy families? You know that's a fantasy. It's never going to happen.'

Kate stares at him. 'I don't think you understand what it's like to grow up without people who care about you,' she says, willing her voice not to waver.

'If I don't, it's because you've never talked to me about it,' he replies. For a brief moment Kate wonders if he will say more, but he does not. Finally he relents. 'I'll talk to Davis. Perhaps there are ways the plan can be finessed.'

But two days later Kate is startled when Jay stands up in a team meeting and says he thinks the time has come to begin developing new candidates.

'If we can make one child we can make more,' he says, his voice clear, confident.

There is a murmur of voices. Kate grips the arms of her chair. She wants to stand up, walk out the door, but she cannot move. Opposite her, Mylin catches her eye. Several times in recent months she has sought Kate out and sat with her in the cafe, seemingly eager to establish a bond between the two of them. Mylin holds her gaze for a few seconds, then Kate looks away.

Twenty-four hours earlier Davis had been in the facility, staring at Eve in her crib, his expression unreadable. Only when the nurse prompted him by asking if he wanted to hold her did he seem to remember he was not alone and look up, regarding her and Kate with his pale eyes.

'Kate,' he said. 'I didn't see you there. I hear you've been spending a lot of time with her.' His voice was pleasant, conversational, but not for the first time she was reminded he was not like her, not like any of them, that he inhabits a world in which his whims have the force of reality.

Afterwards, before he met with Jay, she had caught Jay in his office and reminded him of his promise. He smiled and told her he hadn't forgotten.

That evening Kate watches him sitting in their living room, working on something on his notebook, and realises she no longer knows him. Looking down she sees her hand is shaking.

The next day she wakes before dawn. Outside, the first murmuring of light. Slipping out of bed, she pulls on a jumper and steps out into the morning air. She hears birds in the distance, their cries echoing across the valley. The grass is wet as she crosses towards the forest and sets off up the hill. On the slope the trees are speckled with grey where the lichen is taking hold. Looking out over the landscape, she understands with the force of a blow something she should have understood long before. This project is wrong, not because it is an exercise in vanity, because it places humans at the centre of things or pretends to godhood, or for any of the other arguments they have rehearsed at various stages in the process. Instead it is wrong because it fails to see their solution is part of the problem, a misplaced belief that this is another problem they can manage, engineer, control.

Eve is not an experiment, she is a conscious being, she deserves the right to find her own path, to be her own person. She deserves love, not just people hired to care for her. But more than that, she deserves to grow up on her own terms, unburdened by other people's expectations to discover what she is for herself.

The day rushes by. Ordinarily she could rely on her work to anchor her, on her ability to push everything else aside and lose herself in it, but today she cannot. She feels she has passed beyond some kind of boundary, that there is no going back, nor, without knowing what to do next, any going forward. It is only when she returns home late in the evening that she suddenly understands what it is she must do. For a moment she just stands, drinking in the simplicity, the almost mathematical purity of it, then she turns, and heads back towards the house.

Inside Jay is seated on the couch, headphones on, absorbed in something on his screen. They have barely spoken all evening. For a long moment she stands, staring at him. What will this do to him, she wonders, and her chest contracts. Her heart beating fast she hurries into the bedroom, and taking out a bag, stuffs clothes into it, money, documents, anything she can lay her hands on. Although she is working fast she does not feel panicky or afraid, instead she feels curiously calm, the edges of the world around her delineated with a strange and unfamiliar clarity. Once she is done she opens the drawer beside the bed and drops her phone in, and heads out to the car.

The facility is quiet, its halls empty when she arrives. Glancing up at the red lights of the cameras she knows she is being recorded, that they will have a video of her arrival. In the room beside Eve's the night nurse sits with her back to the glass, the screen in front of her glowing in the dark. She does not look around as Kate slips past.

As she enters the nursery she knows she cannot stop, that if she lets herself falter she will lose the certainty she needs to do this thing. She picks up a bag, begins to pile in wipes, nappies, bottles, formula and all the other paraphernalia. Then, shouldering the bag, she turns to the crib.

Eve is asleep, swaddled in her blankets, her mouth half-open. Reaching down, Kate strokes her hair, aware that if she does this, there is no turning back. Somewhere nearby a door closes, and Eve murmurs, shifting in her sleep. Without looking around Kate reaches down and lifts her up, cradling her sleeping form to her chest.

Although it is late she is braced to encounter one of the guards or assistants in the hall, but as the lift doors open on the lobby she sees the entry hall is empty. For a moment she wonders whether she had been hoping somebody would be here to stop her, to divert her from her path, but instead she walks out, into the waiting darkness, and on, towards the car.

FOUNDLING

In the mornings Kate wakes early, surfacing into unwelcome consciousness. The first glimmers of light leaking around the blanket she has suspended against the window to keep the sun out, Eve still snoring softly beside her. In the pre-dawn light her memory of Eve's four a.m. feed suspended somewhere in the netherspace of dream.

At first she could not understand what it is that rouses her at this hour: save for the occasional car passing on the road below and the first cries of the birds outside the room is quiet, peaceful. But in the three months since they left the facility she has realised it is not the sound from without that wakes her but an almost indiscernible change in the pattern of Eve's breathing, some subtle shift in its register as she transitions towards consciousness.

For those first few minutes Kate always lies unmoving, listening to the soft rise and fall of Eve's breath and wishing this moment might stretch on, that she might sink back into sleep. But even though her tiredness is immense, geological, she knows she will not.

It is remarkable to Kate that she should have become so attuned to Eve's presence, that the rhythms of their bodies should have meshed so completely, so unthinkingly. When Eve stirs in the night Kate wakes; when Eve laughs Kate feels the dopamine rush of love. She is even immediately alert to the timbre of Eve's wordless utterances, cries of anger or frustration setting her on edge, wails of distress cutting through her like a knife, murmurs of hunger making her body ache with the need to sate Eve's appetite.

Often this pre-dawn sense of dislocation remains through the day and into the evening, heightened by the way the light lingers long after she feels it should have faded and passed. Even after four summers on this island she still finds the length of these southern summer days dislocating, a reminder she is near the edge of the world. Some nights, after Eve is finally asleep, she goes outside and stands in the small space of grass that passes for a lawn in front of the house. Alone in the near-dark she drinks in the smell of the leaves and the grass and the dust and gazes out at the hills to the west, still blue beneath the fading sky. This summer the heat arrived weeks early, and has worn on longer than ever, a blanket of hot air that will not shift; sometimes she smells smoke, glimpses the plumes of fires in the distance. On the hottest days Kate has taken to bathing Eve in cool water to keep her comfortable.

Mostly, though, what she feels is alone. Since they arrived here her contact with the people in the town nearby has been minimal, confined to brief exchanges with the older man who works in the petrol station or the two teenage girls in the small supermarket on the main street, whose harried lack of interest in her and Eve she has come to value.

The reasons for this isolation are simple and immutable. Although it is incredibly unlikely anybody not associated with the project would guess the truth about Eve, Kate knows she cannot risk drawing attention to the two of them. There are questions she cannot answer, and, more frighteningly, people searching for them. Already the world, this new world she and Eve inhabit, delivers blows: although she keeps Eve hidden behind a shawl in her pram when they are outside the house, on those occasions strangers do glimpse her they tend to glance around, ready to smile, then freeze or look away, suddenly reluctant to make eye contact with Kate. Yet even despite this there are moments when Kate has to fight her urge to show Eve off or extol her achievements, the impulse surprising her every time it happens. Only a week ago, in the supermarket, a woman who noticed Kate adjusting the shawl stopped and asked how old Eve was. 'Six months,' Kate said before she could catch herself. The woman glanced up in surprise, then took a step back, as she murmured Eve was big for her age.

And so Kate's delight in Eve is something she has come to think of as essentially private, contained within their circle of two. Perhaps all children are wondrous, their development astonishing, but for Kate, Eve is doubly so. In the first weeks at the facility there had been some concern that she was reluctant to interact and slow to smile – so slow, in fact, that were it not for her physical strength and capacity to hold her head up they might have thought her delayed – but over the past three months she has hit her other milestones as soon or sooner than a sapient infant would have.

Kate has found this reassuring but is becoming less comfortable with the desire to compare. Even the terminology makes her uneasy. To speak of *Homo sapiens* and *Homo neanderthalensis* is clumsy, yet still preferable to depending on the term 'human', and its implication that Eve is not. Better again is the distinction she has taken to drawing between sapient and Neanderthal, though even this makes her uncomfortable.

Yet no matter what words she uses there is no question, the differences are considerable. Although at birth Eve was no larger than a sapient infant, her musculature was already surprisingly defined, especially around the neck and shoulders, and as she has grown she has developed faster than a sapient child, learning to sit by four months and crawling by five. Despite Eve's obvious intelligence, it is difficult for Kate to escape the feeling that she is also different in other ways from a sapient child: not withdrawn exactly, but warier, less attuned to social contact. Kate was in the lab the first time Eve smiled; she remembers the delight that filled her body. But as the weeks have passed she has also come to recognise how inward it is, that like the soft, wheezing sound of Eve's laughter that she so loves, it does not come easily, readily, but from somewhere deeper in.

This sense of divergence between Eve's physical and social development should not be a surprise: studies of Neanderthal teeth show they breastfed for less time than *Homo sapiens*, a fact some argue suggests their children grew faster, and were less closely bonded than sapient children. She does not want to believe this: there is no question she and Eve are bonded. But sometimes, when she watches Eve staring at the play of light upon a wall, she wonders whether she is different in some deep way.

Or perhaps she is imagining it? Could it be this is all a form of confirmation bias? That she is simply seeing what she is looking for? That Eve is more normal than Kate allows her to be, and Kate's fear of others observing Eve is actually a terror that she will be caught, exposed as a kidnapper.

It is this last thought that preys on her mind as she wakes in the pre-dawn each day. For though she still believes she did the right thing, that Eve is better off here with her, she is stalked by the thought that they might be found, that Eve might be taken from her. Night after night she lies awake, conjuring scenarios in which she is arrested, and Eve returned to the facility or, worse, put into some kind of care or remanded for study, the possibilities spiralling away from her.

She is reassured by the isolation of the house, which is set back from the road a kilometre out of town. But she has also been careful to avoid situations where she might be drawn into conversation, only visiting the few stores when absolutely necessary. During the day she and Eve rarely venture beyond the backyard.

Yet as this strange, protracted summer has worn on, she has taken to walking with Eve at dusk, partly to escape the heat in the house, partly because she feels the need to be out, in motion. The first few times she went she followed the road, enjoying the quiet, the heat radiating from the asphalt, but more recently she has taken to heading back towards town, and the small recreation area on its outskirts.

Concealed behind a line of trees, the space is divided in two, one half given over to a play area featuring a swing set and a desultory slippery dip set in the middle of a rough circle of bark, the other to a picnic table and benches. Kate has only seen other people there twice: once while walking to town for supplies she glimpsed a pair of women and three small children; the other time two middle-aged women stood watching while a fox terrier raced here and there, their backs to the road, faces hidden behind dark glasses, arms folded.

Though the area is clearly barely used, Kate is careful to only frequent it at dusk, when the chance of encountering other parents is minimised. All the same, she has come to love the window in her day when she can walk the kilometre down the road and sit beneath the trees. Most evenings she brings a blanket and lays it on the grass so Eve can watch the branches move against the sky, or the ribbons of cloud moving slowly overhead.

This is what she is doing one evening in February when she notices a woman walking up the short path that leads from the road. Startled, she places a hand on Eve's chest, tensed to grab her.

The woman wears a loose blouse and narrow pants that emphasise her lean, angular frame but look oddly out of place out here in the country. Although she has obviously seen Kate and Eve she does not approach them immediately. Instead she crosses to the far side of the grass and then, turning back, walks towards Kate. Aware leaving now would seem strange, Kate forces herself to remain where she is. The woman pauses just in front of her.

'I hope I'm not intruding,' she says with a smile. Her diction is very clear and slightly formal, as if English is not her first language.

Kate forces herself to smile. 'No, of course not.'

The woman kneels. Kate tenses, alert for any hint of recoil.

'She's yours?'

Kate hesitates, then nods.

'How old?'

'Six months.'

'She's lovely. What's her name?'

'Eve.'

The woman gestures to the patch of ground next to Kate.

'Do you mind?'

Kate shakes her head, trying to keep her expression calm and welcoming, and the woman sits down beside her. She looks to be in her late-thirties – Kate's age, or perhaps a year or two older – her black hair streaked here and there with grey. She appears blessed with the sort of self-possession Kate has always envied.

'I've not seen you around here before,' the woman says. 'Are you staying somewhere nearby?'

'Yes,' Kate says as casually as she can. 'Just up the road.'

'Just the two of you?'

'Yes,' Kate says.

The woman does not reply, and Kate does not elaborate.

'And you?' she asks.

The woman looks up. 'I live that way,' she says. 'The blue house. You're Australian? American?'

Kate looks at the woman in surprise. 'I'm Australian, but I spent almost a decade in the US.'

'Ah. Hence the accent.' The woman smiles. 'I still have trouble telling.' Reaching down, she slips her hands around Eve. They are worn and battered, perhaps by sun, but strong. 'Is it okay?'

Kate stifles the urge to snatch Eve back. Is it possible the woman is some kind of spy? A private detective? She forces herself to shake her head. The woman lifts Eve and lays her on her shoulder.

Until now Eve has paid the woman only passing attention, but now she turns to her and, to Kate's surprise, smiles, her wide face opening up into a look of delight. The woman smiles back.

'She's got beautiful eyes,' she says. 'They're so big.'

Kate nods, the woman's recognition of the beauty she sees in Eve almost painful.

A lock of the woman's hair has come loose, and hangs beside her face. Eve reaches up to grab it. As her hand closes around it the woman laughs and, dropping her head, lets Eve draw her face closer. Even from where she sits Kate can see the shift in Eve's manner, the way she recedes into herself.

'You're good with her,' Kate says in an awkward voice. The woman nods.

'I have a son only a little older.'

'Is he with his father?'

The woman's expression changes. 'No. A neighbour. I needed a few minutes to myself.' She passes Eve back to Kate.

'I'm sorry. I must go. Perhaps I will see you again. My name is Yassamin.'

'Kate.'

'I am very pleased to meet you, Kate.' Yassamin smiles. 'Perhaps your Eve might like to meet my Sami.'

'Yes,' Kate says.

Kate does not move as the woman walks away, instead she sits and watches her receding back, a fixed smile on her face. But as soon as Yassamin is out of sight she sweeps Eve up and hurries back along the road, glancing behind herself over and over and fighting the urge to break into a run.

That night she cannot sleep. The rational part of her knows Yassamin's friendliness was almost certainly no more than it seemed, but another, darker voice tells her she cannot discount the possibility that her presence in the park was not a coincidence, its urging converting every sound from outside into an approaching car or footsteps.

This anxiety is not new: it has shadowed her since the moment she fled the facility. She had no clear plan that night, only a determination to get away, find somewhere safe for her and Eve. In the car park behind the buildings she placed Eve in the footwell of the car, bundling her in so she was safe, then, climbing in, accelerated away into the night. Although her mind was racing she knew she could not let herself think too hard about what she had done; instead she gripped the steering wheel and stared ahead, into the darkness. But a few kilometres from the facility she glanced down at Eve in the footwell and felt the irreversibility of what she had done begin to dawn on her. Taking a deep breath she forced herself to focus on what to do next.

She knew it would not take them long to discover Eve was gone, what she did not know was how soon they would realise it was her that had taken her. Presumably one of their first acts would be to call Jay, who would realise she was missing, and, probably sooner rather than later, make the connection.

Would he try to find her himself? Or report her absence to security? She had left her phone back at the house, but as long as she was in her own car she knew she was vulnerable. As darkened farmland and bush gave way to sleeping houses she pulled the car to the side of the road and, gathering her bags and Eve, set off along the road on foot. Mercifully the night was mild, and traffic on the road sparse, yet still she was relieved when she glimpsed a petrol station up ahead. Wary of being caught on camera, she did not enter the illuminated space of the station, instead lingering by the road a little way back. Over the next half-hour cars passed in ones and two, until finally a taxi pulled into the station. She waited while the driver filled his tank, then as he drove back out towards the road she stepped out into the light, one hand raised.

She climbed in, ignoring the driver's curious glances in the mirror. She had already decided to head for a motel she knew on the road out to the airport, but wary of travelling straight there she directed the driver to drop her at a row of shops a little further up the road. Along the way Eve fussed and stirred, but Kate calmed her, rocking her gently as she watched the sleeping city pass outside.

It was well after midnight by the time she climbed out of the taxi. She waited for the driver to pull out and disappear into the night before she headed back along the road towards the motel. The office was locked, but she knocked anyway, rapping on the glass until a middle-aged man appeared from a back room. He sized her up through the window then turned the lock and opened the door.

She could see him regarding her carefully, no doubt aware of the reasons women turn up in motels with babies in tow after midnight.

When he asked her for her driver's licence and credit card she told him she needed to pay cash; to her relief he didn't argue, just told her she would have to pay in advance.

The room was worn, bland, a loveless box with a television and a wardrobe along one wall, and a bed and two bedside tables on the other. The curtains were a murky mess of purple and red across the window facing the car park. For a moment Kate remembered a similar room with her mother, many years before, a week spent in a motel after one of her relationships dissolved. Lowering the sleeping Eve to the bed, she sat down beside her, and all at once began to sob.

That was the last time she would cry, and even then she did not let it continue long. Instead she wiped her face, trying to think through what came next. The impossibility of untangling this thing she had done slowly revealing itself. Whatever happened now, her old life was gone.

Step by step she began to think through what she needed to do next. First, and perhaps most importantly, she needed cash, as much of it as she could lay her hands on. Then she had to find somewhere to stay, somewhere she and Eve would be safe. The rest of it – transport, communication, clothing – could come later.

With the outline of a plan forming in her mind, she lay down beside Eve. She would be awake soon, demanding food, but though Kate was so tired her body hummed with exhaustion, she knew she would be unable to sleep. And so instead she lay there, staring blankly at the ceiling.

She realises now it was always in her, this talent for extremity, the preparedness to embrace solutions without concern for their implications. Yet that night she was afraid, not just of what she had done, but of whatever she had unleashed in herself. When morning came she took Eve and walked to the nearest bank, where she emptied her and Jay's accounts. Then she walked until she found a thrift store, where she bought an old stroller, blankets, clothes for Eve, ignoring the questioning stare of the woman behind the counter as she paid in cash.

She knew she would be safer if she could get off the island, but she could not risk a plane, and she assumed they would be watching the ferry. In a bigger city it might have been possible to disappear by losing herself in the suburbs, but that was not going to work here. So sticking to back streets she wound her way towards the interchange, where she bought a ticket on the first bus out of the city.

A few hours later she stepped out in the main street of a small town. Again she rented a motel room, then set about looking for a place to live. As she stood staring at her reflection in the window of the real-estate agent she realised there was no way they would rent her a house without ID or references, neither of which she could risk using. So, she pushed Eve in her pram a few doors up to survey the noticeboard mounted outside the supermarket. There, among the cards advertising lawn-mowing and guitar lessons, she found what she needed.

She called the number on the card from the phone box out by the road; a man answered, and an hour later she stood waiting for him in the driveway of a house on the outskirts of town. He was retired, a former overseer from one of the timber mills; the house had been his late sister's until her death a few years before. It was small, largely unfurnished, its bare rooms and empty kitchen stark. But it was isolated from the town and hidden from the road by a stand of trees. The bond and the first month's rent made an alarming dent in her cash, but once he was gone she knew she had done the right thing, that they would be safe here.

Over the weeks that followed she acquired things they needed, picking up a mattress from a cheap store in town, blankets from the charity shop in the same complex, a television left beside the road; none have been enough to make the house feel homely, or even lived in, but in the time they have been here she has remembered how little she cares about comfort.

She has been surprised how little she misses the constant connection of her former life. No phone without ID, no internet either, no credit cards or bank accounts or electricity or gas. Yet she has also begun to realise that it is possible to live without any of it, to make do. Her electricity is covered by her landlord, she has no need for a phone, and though print newspapers are now almost non-existent, she does not feel isolated by the lack of access to the outside world; quite the opposite, in fact.

More importantly, though, she sees now just how surveilled our lives are. It is not a new awareness – she has never really been comfortable with the constant intrusion of technology, the ways in which the self is performed and curated online – yet simultaneously it has only been these past weeks that it has become clear how entirely these systems entrap us, ensuring we are monitored, assessed, used. Suddenly outside them, she does not feel reduced or lonely, but somehow freer, more alive, more aware, her attention not constantly flicking between screen and world. Sometimes she wonders whether she is also relieved to be away from the constant cataloguing of crisis as well, the drumbeat of disaster and atrocity that has suffused her existence for so long. And while in part of herself she knows she cannot outrun reality forever, there are times when it seems possible to forget about it, quiet moments when she can feel herself expand, her awareness spreading out into the fading sky, the cries of the birds, the shifting wind.

Still, it is a fragile freedom, encircled by fear and doubt. About money, about the constant risk of discovery. About the knowledge of what her choices have cost Eve already, what they may yet cost her in the future.

In the days that follow she alters her routines, avoiding the park, walking a different path. Once she thinks she glimpses a woman watching them in the supermarket. Lifting an arm to draw Eve close, she abandons her shopping and makes for the street, head down, not looking back as she hurries back towards the house.

That afternoon, she decides they have no choice: they must move. Yet how, and where? Her money is almost gone, and she has no way to replenish it. And though the bus continues on, up the road, there is no guarantee she could find them another place to live.

Finally she decides to at least look, and gathering their things, she pushes the pram the kilometre to the bus stop to wait for the morning bus. The day is hot, still, and as the bus winds through the hills she holds Eve up so she can stare out at the passing countryside. All summer there have been fires to the north and west, some sparked by the lightning that rumbles across the landscape, others by humans, the smoke hanging in the air, turning the sunsets blood red, lining her throat. Some mornings she has woken to the yard carpeted in ash, the almost weightless remains of trees that took decades or even centuries to grow, an entire ecosystem reduced to floating flakes.

Only a fortnight ago the fires burned through these valleys not far from the town, running fast up the slopes: for two days smoke hung heavily and fire trucks rattled through the town. Eventually the wind shifted, and the fires marched away again, but looking out at the blackened stumps and ruined earth Kate realises how close the flames came.

Eve falls asleep just before they pull into their destination; as Kate clambers out she wakes and begins to fret. Outside, a wind has come up, blowing fitfully through the trees, and Kate smells ashes. The town is tiny, even smaller than the one she has come to think of as her own. The bus stop is beside a park; on its far side behind a pair of trees a church stands, its sandstone structure stained but still handsome; on the opposite side of the street a general store occupies another sandstone building, beyond which a pair of older buildings house a pub and a takeaway.

She knows at once it is no good. The town is too small, too exposed, the countryside around it too bare. She could not survive here. Against her chest Eve is struggling, growling and complaining fitfully.

The bus back runs twice a day, which means she has four hours to kill with a hot, disgruntled baby. She has food in her bag, but after heading up the main street, there is nothing more to see. She winds their way back towards the church and the park. Eve is finally asleep, so when she reaches the church she crosses to it and steps inside. The interior is grander than she had expected, a timbered roof soaring over pale sandstone walls. Taking a seat, she gazes around, observing the stained-glass windows, the altar, the organ nestled on one side. Cheap red carpet has been laid on the floor, but its artificial hue cannot detract from the elegance of the space as a whole.

She passes the afternoon in the church and seated in the graveyard by its side, watching while Eve stares up at the leaves of the tree. When the bus returns they board, and on the ride back Eve is distracted and cranky. For a time Kate worries that Eve has picked up on her agitation, her concern that they are in danger, and that night Eve will not settle, struggling and fighting in Kate's arms, pushing the bottle away. When Kate puts her down Eve stretches out, rigid, refusing her touch. More rattled than she would like to admit, Kate lies next to her, allows herself to slip into sleep.

Just after midnight she is woken by the sound of Eve wheezing. She reaches out to touch her cheek. Eve flinches away. Her skin is hot, and she begins to cry, the sound fitful, raspy. Switching the light on, Kate attempts to calm her. Although her face is contorted and she is crying, Eve is not awake; instead she writhes and shivers, her eyes closed, as if dreaming whatever afflicts her.

Something cold twists in Kate's gut. Throughout the process of Eve's creation they worried about her being exposed to viruses and other infections her body was not evolved to resist. Some had been possible to anticipate and so are coded into her DNA, and she is shielded from others by the transfer of Marija's microbiome during pregnancy and the battery of vaccinations she was given in her first weeks. But it is impossible to know whether there might be other potentially deadly diseases they have overlooked. So, while this may be simply a childhood infection, it might well be more than that, something her body is unequipped to fight.

Kate rattles through the basket of baby paraphernalia, finally closing her hand around the box containing the thermometer. She fumbles with the packaging, shaking it loose as she stares at the device, trying to understand how it works. Finally she finds the switch, and lifting Eve's arm holds it underneath: 39.2 degrees. She sits for several seconds, staring at the readout. Eve's normal temperature is 36.5, slightly lower than that of a sapient child, which means this is even higher than it would be were she a sapient. Yet what does that mean? Touching Eve's cheek again, Kate feels the heat radiating from her tiny body.

Gingerly she picks Eve up and rocks her from side to side, singing softly in an effort to comfort her. Outside it is windy, the house creaking. Earlier there were clouds on the horizon, a suggestion of rain, but it has not arrived.

Still cradling Eve in one arm she mixes a bottle of formula, presses the teat to Eve's lips, but she twists away, one hand raised to swat at the bottle.

In the cupboard she has drugs – ibuprofen and paracetamol – both of which she believes Eve should be able to take without ill-effect. But as she takes down the bottle of ibuprofen she realises she is frightened to use it. What if Eve's system is so compromised it harms her?

She stares at the bottle clutched in her hand. Then, before she can change her mind, she kneels beside Eve and, stroking her forehead, drips the liquid into her mouth.

Eve wrenches away from her, and coughs and splutters, then lets out a piercing wail. Kate closes her eyes, trying to block it out. Eve's cries go on and on, but finally she seems to succumb to exhaustion, her wails giving way to raspy snuffles and twitches. Careful not to disturb her, Kate climbs onto the mattress and arranges herself beside her, her hand on Eve's belly as Eve pants and whimpers.

The night passes, an ocean of time. By four it is clear that Eve is not getting better. Her fever has not subsided, and she seems to be drifting in and out of awareness of her surroundings.

It is unbearable, the waiting, made worse by Kate's own exhaustion. Finally, just after seven, she decides she can wait no longer, and after checking to make sure Eve is dozing, she pulls on her shoes and hurries to the door.

It is fifteen minutes' walk to the house Yassamin pointed out, but Kate makes it in five, running hard. At the gate she pauses, worried she may be making a mistake, but the thought of Eve alone back in the house pushes her on, and she hurries up the small path, barely taking in the plastic toys discarded by the entrance.

She knocks, first once, then again and again, until finally a light comes on and a shape appears behind the glass.

'Who is it?' Kate recognises the voice.

'My name is Kate. We met in the park the other day,' she says. 'I'm sorry to turn up like this, but I need your help.'

There is a moment's silence. Then the door opens to reveal Yassamin, a blue gown wrapped around her body, her dark hair pulled back.

'I'm sorry,' Kate says, aware she is repeating herself. 'But Eve, she's sick, and I'm on my own.'

Again there is silence.

'I wondered, could you come over? Just for a few minutes. I don't know what to do.'

Still Yassamin does not answer. A child gives a wordless cry in the background. 'Is it something infectious?'

'I don't know,' says Kate. 'I don't think so.'

'Sami is awake. I will have to bring him.'

'Of course,' Kate says.

Yassamin nods. 'Wait here.'

'Thank you,' Kate says. 'Thank you.'

A few minutes later Yassamin reappears, a dark-haired child in her arms. 'The heat,' Yassamin says. 'He cannot sleep.'

Kate nods. The boy stares at Kate. He is taller and older than Eve, his dark hair and eyes lending him an almost feminine beauty.

They hurry down the road to Kate's house. When they enter, Eve is silent. Yassamin looks around as Kate leads her through the house, and Kate sees her take in the bare walls and spartan furniture, the scattering of baby books and the play mat on the floor.

Eve is on her back dozing when they enter, her face and head twitching intermittently. Yassamin passes Sami to Kate, then touches Eve's forehead.

'She's so hot. Have you taken her temperature?'

Kate nods. 'It's 39.3.'

'Is it going up or down?'

'Up.'

'You should take her to the doctor.'

Kate looks uneasy. 'I can't.'

'Why not?'

Kate shakes her head. 'I just can't.'

Yassamin stares at her, then at Eve. Finally something shifts in her expression.

'Then we must give her medicine here. Something to bring the fever down.'

Kate shakes her head again. 'I tried.'

'Then you must try again.'

Kate nods, angry at herself for needing Yassamin's permission. Eve shakes and spits out the new round of medicine, but Kate scoops her up, cradles her in her arms.

'Now we wait,' Yassamin says.

Over the next hour Eve worries and cries, but she seems more alert, more herself. Finally she closes her eyes and falls asleep, her breathing rough but even, almost normal. Back in the kitchen Eve finds Yassamin watching as Sami totters about.

'She is sleeping?' Yassamin asks, and Kate nods.

'Yes. Thank you.'

'Why did you not want to take her to a doctor?'

Kate draws a chair back and sits down. 'It's a long story.'

'And there is nobody else who could help?'

Kate shakes her head.

Yassamin regards her carefully, her black eyes thoughtful. 'Is somebody looking for her?'

Kate nods. 'Yes.'

'And you are afraid of them?'

'I'm afraid I'll lose her.'

Yassamin looks at Kate for a long time. Finally she nods. 'Sami is hungry. I need to take him home. You should sleep.'

'Yes,' Kate says. 'And thank you.'

Yassamin nods, watching her. 'You should not be alone, Kate,' she says, but Kate doesn't reply.

When Yassamin has left Kate returns to the bedroom and lies next to Eve. Once again she strokes her hair, wondering at the force of life that moves in her tiny form, the force of love within herself.

She is woken in the early afternoon by Eve's laughter. She sits up. Eve smiles at her. Kate smiles back and reaching out, touches her forehead. It is cool, her fever gone. Eve grabs for Kate's hand and pulls on her fingers, her tiny hands closing over them one by one. Delighted, Kate resists and then succumbs, while Eve gurgles with bashful delight.

Kate is astonished by the rapidity of her recovery, the way the illness seems to have washed through her and away, leaving no trace. Yet while Eve seems unscathed by her fever Kate is not, the terror of the night just passed underlining the enormity of the risk she has taken with Eve's safety. She feels chastened – no, not chastened, ashamed – of her precipitousness, the negligence of placing Eve at risk in this way.

Nor does the feeling pass. Later in the afternoon as they sit on the grass at the back of the house, Eve rolls over and grasps Kate's finger, her eyes meeting Kate's for a long moment, her trusting face full of the shy affection Kate loves in her and, without warning, Kate's eyes fill with tears.

The next morning she walks to town and examines the noticeboard. There are ads from people looking for labouring and cleaning work, as well as notices advertising services such as tree-lopping and roofing. But nobody offering employment. Eve gurgles in her arms as Kate stares at the board, her mind casting back through memory, to days when she waited while her mother searched a similar board, the way she muttered to herself, then berated Kate for people not caring, not being prepared to understand how difficult things were for her. Closing her eyes, Kate leans forward and braces herself against the board.

Eve coos, and Kate shifts to rest her face gently on Eve's head, the scent of the thick, coarse hair warm and sweet. Finally she steps back and scans the board again. This time she notices an A4 sheet advertising an old computer for sale. She stares at it for a few seconds, then tears a number from the fringe of them at the bottom of the page, then walks through the arcade towards the payphone at its end.

The owner lives outside town, but within a few minutes she has bargained him down to $200 and arranged to meet him in the car park an hour later. As she hands over the money she feels a shiver, aware how little this leaves her. Outside the cafe she boots it up, logs onto their wireless. She knows she must take care, so she finds a free VPN service and sets up an email account under a false name. That done, she begins to sift through various websites, searching for something she can do.

She bypasses the usual scams – work from home and make $700 a week, $1000 a week, $5000 a week – one by one, searching for something real. Eventually she finds somebody looking for help proofing their thesis. The money is pitiful, but it is work she can do without leaving the house, or – she hopes – identifying herself. She creates a profile under her new name and submits a bid for the job, making sure her credentials are worded in a way that prevents them being easily identified, and before she has time to stop herself, hits send.

When she returns to the cafe the next morning she has a reply: the student is interested, but anxious to clarify a few points about why she is looking for the work. She tells them she has had a baby, is looking for some supplementary income. A few minutes later Kate has the job.

The work, when it comes, is more difficult than she had imagined: the student's prose is terrible, resistant to anything other than wholesale rewriting in many places, but over the next few days she does what she can, working in small bursts in the evenings and while Eve sleeps, and sends it back, appending a series of comments and suggestions. A few hours later the fee is released into the electronic wallet she has set up. She assumes that is the end of it, but two days later she receives a message from the student thanking her for her work.

She is not surprised the work is good: there is a rigour to her mind, a desire for perfection that demands she exceed expectation on everything she does, and although her months with Eve have altered its focus they have not blunted it. But still, she is surprised when, a few days later, she receives an email asking her to perform the same service for another student, and then a few days after that, another.

Within a few weeks they are coming regularly, and from all over the world, and while the money they bring is not vast, it is something. Yet each new request provokes a flicker of unease, a fear she is making herself too obvious, that somebody will question her credentials, or discover the name she has assumed is fictitious. Davis and the Foundation have too much money, too much intellectual capital invested in Eve to let her out of their sight forever. They must be looking for her, and with each transaction the risk of discovery moves closer.

There are good days and bad days, and on the bad she has to struggle to control the panic that rises in her, the certainty they are coming and that when they do, Eve will be taken from her. She has contingencies in place: a small amount of cash, a bug-out bag, a memorised escape route, and when she feels the terror creeping in she forces herself to think through her plan, its clarity something solid she can hold onto. Rarely a night goes by when she does not wake to a sound outside, her body immediately tense; while during the day even when she knows she should be calm, or fully present with Eve, her mind is elsewhere, circling the inescapable reality of what she has done.

For the week after Eve's illness she stops going to the park in the afternoons, preferring to remain indoors, or in the small yard, secluded. She tells herself it is for Eve's sake, a way of ensuring the child is not unnecessarily exposed to new infections when she is already weak, but the truth is, she is wary of encountering Yassamin again.

By Friday, though, she has no choice. They are almost out of food and she needs to use the cafe's wi-fi, so she straps Eve to her chest and ventures out to the supermarket. Overnight the heat has broken, and it is a cool, windy morning, clouds blowing raggedly overhead. As the seasons have wheeled across she has found herself more and more aware of the island's geography, the way the wind blows cold from the south, a constant, restless reminder of the breadth of ocean beneath. Once, in her first weeks at the facility, she and Jay travelled to the coast, walked along a beach by one of the bays. It was a day like today, the wind scudding across grey water, breaking its surface into whitecaps, the beach bleached white, dry as bone, the black volcanic stone tumbled at its end. Just offshore a whale surfaced, expelling the air from its blowhole with an explosive sound, its dark bulk briefly visible before it slid back into the water, and in that moment Kate had felt something of the immensity of the ocean, its wind-scoured emptiness. Where is Jay now, she wonders, does he miss her?

She emerges to find Yassamin outside the shop next door, her stroller in front of her. She stops dead, about to dart back inside, but it is too late: Yassamin has seen her.

'Yassamin! Hello,' Kate says, aware of the false brightness in her tone.

Yassamin returns her greeting with a smile, seemingly unfazed by Kate's brittleness.

'I've been meaning to come over to say thank you,' Kate says. 'But I haven't had a chance.'

Yassamin nods. 'I understand.' She steps forward to look at Eve. 'She is better?'

Kate nods. 'Yes.' She laughs in a way that sounds fake even to her. 'It's like it never happened.'

'They become so sick so fast. It can be very frightening,' Yassamin says, and for a moment Kate is aware of the keen intelligence and dignity in the other woman's eyes, the sense she is registering Kate's prevarications and silences yet simultaneously withholding judgement, and she relaxes.

'It was.' She looks at Sami, who is staring at her from his stroller.

'And Sami? Is he well?'

'He is,' Yassamin says. She looks past Kate and across the car park to the road. 'You are walking back?'

Kate hesitates and then, surprising herself, nods.

As they make their way back up the road they talk, carefully, circuitously. Kate tells Yassamin she is a scientist but she has taken time off. Yassamin glances at her, her assessing gaze lingering just long enough for Kate to be aware she is having trouble matching Kate's version of herself with her circumstances.

'And you?' Kate asks.

Yassamin hesitates. 'I was a lawyer.'

'And you stopped when Sami was born?'

Yassamin looks at her, considering her reply. 'I stopped before we left Iran. Five years ago now.'

Kate waits for Yassamin to elaborate, but she does not. 'And his father?'

'His father has problems he needs to work out.'

As Yassamin speaks they reach the turn-off to her house. She stops, fixing Kate with a careful look.

'Do not be afraid to ask me again if you need help.'

Kate smiles. 'Thank you.'

As the summer fades into autumn Kate finds herself spending more and more time with Yassamin. Eventually she discovers that Yassamin and her husband separated not long after Sami was born. She has been careful to avoid him, but he does not seem to have sought her out.

'We married young,' Yassamin says. 'Over time I realised he was no longer the man I had thought I was marrying, or perhaps never was. If it hadn't been for the war I don't think we would have stayed together as long as we did. Coming here was hard for both of us, but particularly for him. He was frightened, I think, of not having control.'

Kate suspects there is more that Yassamin is not telling her, just as she suspects Yassamin knows there is much Kate is holding back. Yet still, she is grateful for Yassamin's company. Her dignity and calm manner are reassuring, and to Kate's surprise Eve sheds some of her customary shyness in the cheerful presence of Sami.

Despite herself she keeps an eye on stories about Davis and his enterprises. As the questions about Gather's business practices and connections to oligarchs and authoritarian governments have proliferated Davis himself has come under increasing scrutiny, as have the activities of the Foundation. Yet in the week Eve first stands upright, the first de-extinct animals are released in Siberia, and as she gazes at the images of the auroch and mastodons his teams have created Kate is filled with a dizzying sense of the degree to which the world has spun off its axis.

Putting her computer aside she turns to Eve, who is standing with her hands wrapped around a leg of the table, flexing her legs as she bobs up and down, the strength in her limbs already obvious. What is she, Kate wonders for the umpteenth time. Human? Not human? And what does that even mean? Realising Kate is watching Eve beams, her delight in her own achievement so palpable Kate cannot help but laugh; at the sound of her laughter Eve drops her eyes bashfully and returns to her bobbing.

It is difficult not to compare Eve's progress with Sami's. He is a few months older but although Eve is bigger, stronger, her grip firmer, she is also shyer and less confident in company. In situations in which Sami will be cooing and playful Eve often seems elusive, preferring to engage in activities that allow her to ignore those around her, avoiding eye contact. This binds Kate to her even more powerfully: there are moments when Eve catches her eye, and smiles or reaches for her, when the child's trust undoes her.

But although Eve is difficult to coax into playfulness, there are still moments when she gurgles and laughs – that most human trait – delightedly. Kate does not need to hear it – Eve's humanness is beyond doubt to her – yet still, it is a thing of wonder, to be reminded of the affinity between their two species, an affinity that spans not just genetics but time.

And then Eve speaks. For weeks she has been cooing, the sound a little like an asthmatic dove, but one morning as Kate is buttoning her into her onesie Eve looks at her and says, haltingly, 'Mumma'. Her voice is surprisingly deep, throaty.

Kate stops and stares at her.

'What was that?' she says, happiness welling up inside, but Eve looks away, her eyes focusing on the window.

'Mumma,' she says again, more quietly this time, less certainly.

'That's right,' Kate says, touching her hand and feeling Eve's fingers close around hers. 'Mumma. Mumma.' Leaning down, she presses her face to Eve's belly and blows, and after a moment's hesitation Eve laughs her raspy laugh, her face still turned away, so Kate blows again, all of a sudden feeling like the world is speeding away from her.

Over the next few weeks Eve gradually acquires new words. Each one brings Kate joy, and the scientist in her, the perfectionist, ensures records are kept, and a diary of her more impressionistic responses and questions maintained alongside it. Through this she is calm and, she realises, content.

It cannot last, though. Just after Christmas that year Yassamin tells her she has found a job in the city, that she will be moving back. Kate does her best to look happy for her friend, but her sense of loss must show, because Yassamin touches her hand and tells her she will not be so far away, that Kate can always visit.

'Of course,' Kate says, but as she walks back to her house that night she knows she will not, that she cannot risk it.

In the weeks after Yassamin leaves they message each other, but it does not help the way the isolation comes rushing back, and with it, the fear of being caught. She continues to work hard to cover her tracks but she still wakes in the dark consumed by the ticking fear she has made a mistake, or that she has been caught. That winter is unnaturally brief, but as the spring gives way to summer she and Eve find a rhythm to their days, and to her surprise the anxiety gradually recedes, replaced by anxiety about fire and heat. But as their third winter in the house draws down it grows worse again, leaving her sleepless night after night, her tiredness making her jump. One day, out on the highway, a black SUV passes her three times, and she becomes convinced she is being followed. Lighting off up the track towards Yassamin's old place she walks back across one of the top fields, watching the pale ribbon of road on the hill below as she makes her way back to the house. Yet the car does not reappear, and she becomes convinced she has merely frightened herself, that it is all in her mind.

The next day she works, correcting a thesis while she watches Eve play. When it comes time for her nap Eve will not settle, and eventually Kate gives in, and they head out to walk to the park.

It is bitterly cold, the wind making her head feel tight and her ears ache, but Eve seems not to care. Indeed, as she rambles in the long grass, her red-brown hair blowing thick about her, she looks almost comfortable, her wide eyes alight, filled with the pieces of the landscape. Kate knows one thing without needing to keep record: Eve is no less intelligent than a sapient child. Despite the otherness of her, she is alert, focused, her mind quick and nimble as a fish.

It is growing dark by the time she gathers Eve up and they begin the slow trek home. Nearly the solstice, the days already short. As they walk, Kate is filled with something very like happiness, which is perhaps why she does not see him until she rounds the corner to the front door and stops dead, staring at him.

'Hello, Kate,' he says.

Eve tightens her grip on Kate's hand.

'Who's he?' she whispers.

Jay looks down and smiles. 'It's okay,' he says. 'I'm a friend of your mummy's.'

CHILDHOOD

At first Kate cannot move. She has lived in fear of this day for so long that now it is here she doesn't quite believe it.

Jay crouches in front of Eve, who is hiding behind Kate, staring at the ground.

'Don't be afraid,' he says, extending a hand.

Eve clutches Kate's leg tighter.

Jay smiles. 'Last time I saw you, you were just a tiny baby. You're so big now.'

Still Eve doesn't respond. Finally Kate undoes Eve's hand from her leg and ushers her towards the back of the house. 'You go and play,' she says. 'I'll talk to him.'

Eve looks up. Her eyes are wary, and for an instant Kate sees the animal in her. Kate smiles reassuringly. 'It's all right,' she says.

As soon as Eve disappears around the corner Jay turns to Kate again.

'It's good to see you.'

Kate wants to run but knows it is too late. 'Are you alone?' she asks.

For a brief moment Jay looks wounded. Kate is reminded of his dislike of conflict and tendency to assume things will turn out as he wishes. He nods. A kind of hopelessness washes through her.

'Come inside,' she says.

As they step through the door Jay looks around, and Kate sees the place as he must see it: poor, threadbare, broken-down, the cheap second-hand blanket that covers the couch a desperate attempt to disguise its meanness. How has she ended up living in a repeat of her childhood after all these years?

Jay follows her through to the kitchen. He stops by the small window and stares out into the backyard. Eve is crouched near the back fence, half-turned away, already intent on some game. She wears a blue corduroy dress, the 1960s look of which Kate liked when she found it in the shop, but its shape emphasises the blockiness of her build. Atop her head sits a pair of pink and white rabbit ears, her red-brown hair dark in the fading light.

'She's beautiful,' Jay says.

Kate doesn't answer. She does not quite believe he is here, but simultaneously cannot believe he was not here sooner. He seems entirely familiar yet different in ways she cannot place.

'She is.'

He crosses to a group of drawings stuck to the wall; scribbles of colour, a scattering of clumsy potato-shaped figures, a tree, a black cloud with what looks like teeth that has always made Kate vaguely uncomfortable.

'These are hers?'

Kate nods. Jay touches one.

'Does she draw a lot?'

'She does.'

'No problems with grip or manipulating the pen?'

Kate shakes her head. 'No. Pinch is strong as well.'

Jay looks like he is about to ask another question, but then he catches himself. Stepping away from the wall, he stares at her for a long moment. Neither of them speaks.

'What did you think you were doing?' Jay asks finally, his handsome face a mask of concern.

'What we were up to was wrong.'

'You chose to be a part of it.'

She nods. 'I did. But that didn't mean I needed to stay a part of it.'

'But what about Eve? Without medical back-up she could have grown ill, had developmental problems, anything. Did you consider any of that?'

Kate doesn't reply. Jay turns his head and stares sideways in a look she knows means he is thinking about what to say next.

'Were you depressed? Was there some kind of incident I don't know about?'

Kate knows she should claim there was, but she finds she cannot do it. She shakes her head slowly.

'Then help me understand why you did it.'

'What are you going to do? Take her back?'

Jay leans. 'I don't know. I don't think it's been decided. But you know you can't keep living like . . .' he tilts his chin to indicate the room, the house, 'this.'

'We're okay,' Kate says, her tone hotter than she meant it to be.

Jay hesitates. 'I'm sorry.' He glances back through the window. 'She seems . . . happy.'

Kate looks at Eve outside. 'She is,' she says, then shrugs. 'Or I think she is. She's very self-contained.'

'Abnormally so?'

Kate glances up. She knows that tone, Jay's desire for evidence.

'I don't know. I don't have a lot to compare it with. But my impression is she's more self-contained than a sapient child.'

Jay nods. 'And have you kept track of other developmental markers? Speech? Sitting? Walking?'

Kate hesitates. One of the things that had attracted her and Jay to each other had been the intellectual excitement of dissecting a problem or exploring an argument, and though she suspects Jay is deliberately using this to bring them closer now, she still feels something of their old closeness reassert itself.

'Within the normal sapient range.'

'But?'

She shrugs. 'Her actual speech is less fluid than you might expect. There are certain sounds she finds difficult. It's not that she doesn't understand – her receptive language is fine – but I wonder whether she's slightly less language-oriented than a sapient child.'

'You think she's less intelligent?'

Kate flinches slightly. 'No. Just . . . different.'

'In what way?'

'She often takes longer to initiate interaction or respond to cues from other people. But she's also less restless than other children usually are. There's a . . . stillness about her that can be a little unsettling if you're not used to it.'

'Anything else? What about her ability to process symbolic information?'

'Normal-ish, I suppose.' Kate gestures at the wall. 'She draws. She can read a few numerals and recognises some of the alphabet. And she will listen to stories, although again she sometimes seems a little . . .' Kate hesitates, uncomfortable putting her feelings into words.

'A little what?'

'I don't know. Wary? Perplexed? If I ask her to explain to me what we've just read she usually can. It's really just a feeling but I think there's something different there, some kind of difference in comprehension.' She hesitates again. 'Also, her sense of smell is unusually acute.'

'Interesting,' Jay says, still staring out the window.

Kate looks at him. 'What do you plan to do with her?'

'That's not up to me.'

'Are you sure?'

'I'm not that senior.'

'Not. Or not yet?'

'This one is in Davis's wheelhouse.'

'Surely you have some sway. Or aren't you two messenger buddies anymore?' As the words leave her mouth she regrets the edge of bitterness in her voice.

Jay glances around. 'The only reason he didn't send the police after you was because I talked him down.'

Kate looks out at Eve. 'I'm sorry,' she says.

'Are you?' he asks, a tremor of anger in his voice. 'Really? Because you don't sound it.'

She begins to answer but he lifts his hand to stop her. 'Don't. Just don't.' For a second or two she thinks he is going to continue but instead he just shakes his head and pinches the bridge of his nose. When he speaks again his voice is calmer.

'Jesus, Kate. Why didn't you tell me what you were planning?'

'So you could talk me out of it?'

'Obviously. But perhaps we could have found another way, one that wouldn't have had such drastic consequences.'

'I didn't plan it. It just happened.'

There is a moment of silence.

'I don't know if that makes it better or worse.'

Kate doesn't reply. Finally Jay looks at her, his dark eyes liquid.

'What about us? Didn't it occur to you I might be worried? What you just disappearing might do to me?'

There is a moment of silence.

'That was what you were doing, wasn't it? Leaving me?'

Kate nods.

'Are you sorry?'

She doesn't reply.

Jay looks away for a few seconds. When he turns to her again his face is harder. 'I suppose at least I knew you weren't dead.'

'What do you mean?'

Jay laughs. 'You don't think we didn't know where you were, do you? Davis found you within days. We've been monitoring you ever since.'

Something goes cold in Kate's stomach. 'What?'

'Come on, Kate. You must have realised. Hiding is impossible these days.'

For a brief second something in Jay's stance, his expression, reminds her of Davis, his contempt for the idea he might not be entitled to behave exactly as he chooses. Remembering this is about Eve and not her, she does not retaliate.

'Where is Davis?' she asks. 'Is he here? Does he know we're talking?'

'Of course.' He steps away from the cupboard on which he has been leaning. 'I have to go.'

Kate's legs tremble. 'What? You're not going to take her.'

Jay looks at her. 'No. We're not. But you can't stay here either. Tomorrow you'll both come to the facility and we'll work out what happens next.' He takes a phone from his pocket and places it on the table. 'This is for you. We'll use it to call you.' Turning back to the window he glances at Eve a last time.

'And Kate? We're going to leave a security detail outside, so we know you're safe.'

After Jay leaves, Kate stands in the kitchen. She is cold, in shock. Outside in the yard Eve is digging with a stick: on another day Kate might have gone out and joined her, but instead she just stands, staring, not really seeing her. The house is silent, still, the light almost emptied out of it. She walks through to the front room and looks out; through the leaves she sees the roof of a black car and knows Jay was telling the truth.

At the other end of the house the door bangs.

'It's dark,' Eve says from behind her, her words hesitant, clumsy.

'I know,' Kate says, turning to face her and forcing a bright smile. Eve's vision is better than hers in low light, her large eyes more receptive.

'Are you hungry?' Kate asks. But Eve is already moving ahead of her, through the living room and back to the kitchen.

Eve draws while Kate cooks dinner. Sometimes Kate wonders at the way these routines both sustain and entrap her, the way their daily sameness is itself a kind of love, a kind of being. This house, their life together. Now, though, their presence here seems freighted with sadness, an awareness this is the last time they will be together in this place.

Perhaps Eve senses her mood, because she is difficult to settle, insisting Kate read not one or two but three books, then getting up repeatedly to follow her back through to the living area after her light is turned off, and clinging to her, her body like a tiny seal, when she tries to leave.

In the quiet of the kitchen Kate sits at the table and stares at the phone Jay left. The only noise comes from the occasional car or a truck on the road outside. Had Jay been serious when he said they had known where she was since the beginning? The idea makes her feel sick. And angry. Yet still, it doesn't make sense. If they knew where Eve was, why not come to find her? She stands up, stares out into the darkness. The past two years have not been easy for Gather. Although the company's influence is largely undiminished, it has been rocked by a series of scandals involving its use of private data, failure to regulate hate speech and extremist groups, and violation of lobbying and donation laws in countries around the world, including revelations Gather executives knowingly misled a Parliamentary Committee in the UK and lied under oath to lawmakers in Denmark. To some extent Gather's travails are just one part of a larger story about the growing public anger about corporate power and its abuse, but the company's woes have been compounded by Davis's increasingly bizarre public appearances. Kate has seen the most notorious of them, an interview on an American chat show in which Davis talked in messianic terms about re-engineering human consciousness; watching him laugh abruptly and perform what he had clearly mistaken for charm, Kate was not surprised by the stories the company's board are working to sideline him. At the time she wondered whether this sort of behaviour was an aberration or whether this was the same Davis she had known. Was it simply that he had allowed himself permission to stop pretending? And what did that mean for the project, for Eve?

On the road below a glimmer of light is visible from the car Jay left. She stares at it, wondering how many guards are down there. She mentally reviews her escape plan. All she needs is the bag that sits, ready-packed, under her bed, the envelope of cash sewn inside the lining. She could wake Eve, walk out into the night, begin again.

Yet she knows it would not work. If they found her once they will find her again. And more importantly, any chance she has of holding on to Eve would be lost. From the kitchen she hears the phone ping as a message arrives, but she does not check it, not yet, preferring to stand, staring out at the stars over the dark silhouettes of the trees, the shivering presence of the night.

The car arrives at nine o'clock. Kate has dressed Eve in tights and the burgundy jumper with yellow bobbles she loves. In Eve's room that morning she had considered what to pack. Taking out the rucksack she bought in the charity shop in town a few months ago, she had looked around, her eyes resting on the plastic owl lamp by the window, the stuffed lion on the bed, the patchwork blanket Eve could not sleep without. Sitting on the bed, she picked up Lion and turned his blue-eyed face to hers. The past three years suddenly seemed like a kind of fantasy, an intense dream that was only real in her mind. Squeezing Lion, she thought of Eve's face that morning when she woke, the smell of her hair, and had to close her eyes in order not to cry.

When she hears footsteps outside, Kate picks up the bag and takes Eve's hand, uncomfortably aware of the way the child jumps at the knock on the door. Eve does not fully understand where they are going or why. All Kate has told her is that they are going to visit some people at the place she was born, information Eve seemed to receive and then immediately move past.

'It's okay,' she reassures her as she opens the door. A man in the neat black uniform worn by the Foundation's service staff is waiting outside. He tells Kate the car is ready, his manner carefully neutral.

Eve does not struggle as Kate lifts her into the booster in the back seat, submitting quietly as the buckles are clipped and tightened. But when the car starts she whimpers, and Kate takes her hand. Nobody speaks. Out on the road the car is almost silent, its electric motor barely audible over the sound of the wind against the glass, the hum of the tyres on the asphalt. All morning she has been worried Eve would be afraid of the car or, possibly worse, fall asleep, leaving her confused and ill-tempered when they arrive, but that does not happen. Instead Eve sits quietly in her booster, staring out at the passing scenery, her face unreadable. As Eve has grown, Kate has come to understand all children are unknowable in this way. Perhaps Eve is unbothered by the idea of visiting the place she was born, perhaps she is bothered but does not know how to articulate or conceptualise her concern. Perhaps it is irrelevant to her, or simply not of interest.

As they pull up Eve glances around, and for the first time a look of concern creases her forehead. Kate touches her face.

'It'll be fine,' she says, forcing herself to sound positive.

Jay is waiting when they step out, one hand behind his back. Although Kate knows Eve recognises him she does not show it, instead hanging back warily. Jay approaches and kneels down.

'Do you know what I have?' he asks.

Eve keeps her face averted, unwilling to meet his eye.

'Eve?' Kate prompts her.

Eve shakes her head.

'Would you like to see?' Jay asks.

Eve gives a small nod, and smiling, Jay produces a white stuffed dog and holds it out to her.

'Would you like it?'

Eve looks at Kate for permission, her face full of wonder. Kate nods. Fighting the desire to clutch Eve's hand tighter, she instead releases it. Eve reaches out tentatively and takes the dog.

Jay stands and looks at Kate. The day before, she had found his simultaneous familiarity and strangeness disconcerting; today he seems less like the Jay she knew – sleeker, more guarded – and she has to remind herself to be wary around him.

'Are you ready?' he asks.

Kate forces herself to smile.

'Of course,' she says, and Jay takes Eve's hand and leads her up the stairs.

The facility is almost precisely as she remembers it: quiet, stately, more like some kind of international hotel or upmarket university building than a lab. In the foyer Eve looks up in amazement.

'Do you like it?' Jay asks.

Eve's eyes dart towards him in a way Kate knows means she is listening, but she does not answer. A door in front of them swings open and Mylin appears. She stops and stares at Kate with barely concealed hostility.

'You remember Mylin?' Jay asks.

'Of course,' Kate says. 'How are you?'

'Well, thank you,' Mylin says coldly.

'Mylin's going to take Eve up to the lab,' Jay says. As he speaks he directs Eve towards Mylin.

Kate's stomach gives a lurch. Although Jay assured her no decision has been made about removing Eve from her, the idea of handing her over to Mylin fills her with sudden foreboding.

'Perhaps I should come as well?' she says, her voice wavering.

Jay steps forward. 'I don't think that's necessary. You'll be fine, won't you, Eve?'

Eve stares back at Kate, her eyes wide in her pale face.

'Kate?' Jay says.

'You go,' Kate manages to say. 'I'll see you soon.'

One hand in Mylin's, Eve is led away. As the door closes behind them Jay gestures towards the lift. 'Let's go to the conference room. I assume you remember the way.'

Jay leads her to the conference room in which they first discussed staffing with Davis. Kate remembers how cold that day was, her fingers and cheeks aching from the wind and rain, her sense she was only half-present in her body, that some essential part of her had been lost. As she takes a seat she wonders at how far away that self feels, how close.

'No Davis?' she asks.

Jay shakes his head. 'Some kind of crisis back at the hive.'

Relieved an interview with Davis can be postponed, Kate smiles at the reminder of their private term for Gather's Oakland campus.

'I see the Siberian initiative is moving ahead.'

Jay nods. 'Davis has a lot invested in it. And some of the initial data has been encouraging.'

'They're your animals?'

'Some of them.'

'I've seen the chat-show footage as well.'

He regards her, levelly. 'Davis has been stretched very thin.'

'So, what now?' Kate asks.

'We need to assess her. See what the tests show us.'

'And what part do I have in that process?'

'We need to get your perspective, obviously, but our priority is ensuring we're able to study her effectively.'

'She's not a lab animal,' Kate snaps.

Jay glances at her. 'Of course not.'

'This is why I left in the first place. You want to observe her, study her, but nobody's interested in *her*. What happens to her as she gets older? Is she going to go to school? Get a job? What about friends? She's a child; she deserves a normal life.'

'And you were giving that to her? You of all people should understand what it's like to grow up isolated and afraid.'

Kate falls still. All the air seems to have gone out of the room.

'You know it's not like that.'

'Isn't it? Then tell me what it is like. You stole her, Kate. Your actions put her in danger. And for what? Some fantasy she could grow up like a normal child? What were you intending to do? Enrol her in the local school? Let her join the band?'

'Of course not. But she deserves to have normal social relations with other children.'

'Human children.'

'*Sapient* children.'

'She could have had that here,' Jay says.

'You mean she could have played with the other pet Neanderthals. And how long would that have taken?'

Jay looks uncomfortable.

'What?' Kate asks.

'I should have told you yesterday. After you left, the project was wound up. Davis had us redirect our efforts into the Siberian initiative.'

'What do you mean?'

'Exactly what I said. There were questions being asked about cost and reputational risk, especially after the British election. Davis thought we'd done what we set out to do. We had proof of concept.'

'And you were okay with that?'

Jay stares at her. 'I didn't really have a choice. And besides, my partner had just left me, and there were more than a few people around here who thought I wasn't telling the whole truth about where she'd gone.'

There is a moment of silence. 'I'm sorry.'

'Yes. So am I.'

'She's really the only one?'

Jay nods.

A profound sadness grips Kate. What has she done?

'What will you do with her?' she asks at last.

'I want the best for her, Kate. We all do.'

'What does that mean?'

Jay shrugs. 'Professional support, structured learning. It will be good for her.'

'And what about when she's older? What happens then? Are we going to tell her where she came from? What she is?'

'I think some of those decisions are probably best left until we know more about how she's going to develop. But she'll be supported financially whatever happens.'

Kate takes a breath, imagining Eve at twenty, at forty, at sixty, still living here. Who will care for her when she and Jay and the others are gone?

'And me? Do I have a part in that?'

'I don't know. Would you like to?'

Kate stares at him. She knows this is the test this has been leading up to. 'Of course. More than anything.' She falters. 'I know I went about this all wrong, but what's done is done. I'm her mother, at least in her mind. She shouldn't have to suffer for my mistakes. Or no more than she already has.'

Jay regards her carefully. 'You'd need to agree to some conditions.'

Kate stares at him. 'Of course.'

'Access would be one. And we'd need a guarantee you won't disappear again.' He watches her for a few seconds.

'I've already told you I won't.'

'I think we'd need more than verbal assurances. There would need to be some kind of monitoring.'

'What? Like an ankle bracelet?'

Jay regards her levelly. 'A subcutaneous chip.'

'You're kidding me?' Kate says before she can stop herself.

'No. The chip is non-negotiable. We'll also need access to your online information so we can monitor it.'

'And what do I get in return?'

'You get to remain a part of the project. To be a part of her life.' His voice cold.

After the interview, Kate is led to a room separated from the lab next door by a one-way window. Taking a seat she watches as Mylin and another woman she does not recognise run tests on Eve.

When she arrived the technician in attendance told her they had already taken blood, and conducted a full physical exam; now they have moved on to cognitive tests. While the other woman takes notes Mylin bends over Eve, watching as Eve traces her finger across the screen of a tablet. Eve's mouth is open, her tongue twisted sideways as it often is when she is concentrating, accentuating her heavy brow and jaw. Kate aches at this small reminder of her difference, her vulnerability, the feeling like a yearning, a knowledge of loss. But Eve seems untroubled – no, more than that, she seems *happy*; at one point Mylin leans in and touches the screen as well, and Eve glances sideways at her and smiles, full of shy delight.

Kate is surprised Eve is so relaxed with Mylin, but it is obvious they have struck up a real rapport. After another half hour or so Mylin stands up, and points Eve towards a door. Mylin ushers her through and then pauses to glance towards the glass, and Kate.

Out in the hall Eve launches herself into Kate's arms, almost knocking Kate off her feet. Kate grips her tight, squeezing her to herself, grateful for the weight and warmth of her.

'What did you do?' she asks, lifting her up so they are face to face.

'We played a game,' Eve says. Noticing a round band-aid on her arm, a dot of blood dark in its centre, Kate touches it.

'And this? Were you brave?'

Eve nods gravely, and Kate kisses her. 'Good.'

Behind Eve the assistant is waiting. 'We have lunch for Eve.'

Kate stands up. 'Oh. Good.'

'You can catch up if you like,' the assistant says.

In the doorway, Mylin is watching her.

'Of course.'

Kate pushes Eve towards them, forcing herself to smile. Eve resists, clinging to her arm. Her grip is hard enough to hurt.

'It's okay,' she says, her voice bright.

Eve shakes her head and holds on tighter.

Kate kneels and touches Eve's cheek. 'I won't be long.'

Still wary, Eve allows herself to be led away by the assistant. As the door closes behind them she turns to find Mylin staring at her with barely disguised dislike.

'Is everything all right?' Kate asks.

'She seems healthy.'

'Were they cognitive tests you were doing?'

Mylin nods.

'How did she do?'

'We need to do more, but most of her responses seemed within the range we'd expect.'

'I'm relieved but not surprised. Jay said you'd need to speak to me as well?'

'We will.'

Kate regards Mylin warily. Three years before they had been friends of a sort. 'Is there anything else?'

Mylin's broad face hardens. 'I just wanted to let you know that while I know they've agreed to let her stay with you I'm not happy with that choice. What you did, whatever your reasons, placed Eve in danger.'

Kate stares at her. 'You think she would have been better here? As some kind of lab rat?'

'I think your decision to behave the way you did disqualifies you from the right to have a role in her life. If she was anybody else you'd be in jail.'

Kate is still trembling when she enters the dining room and sits next to Eve. If the assistant guesses what Mylin has said she gives no sign; instead she smiles blandly as Kate grasps Eve's hand and asks about her food, forcing herself to keep her tone light, untroubled.

In the late afternoon they are driven to a house midway between the facility and the city. Separated from the road by a long gravel drive, its timber and glass structure lies low to the land, the light from the windows spilling out into the gathering dusk.

'Is this where we're staying?' Eve asks as the car crunches to a stop.

'For now,' Kate says.

'When do we go back to our house?'

'We're not going to,' Kate says. 'We live here now.'

Kate watches a shadow pass across Eve's face.

'Is that okay?'

Eve doesn't reply.

'Eve?'

Eve looks away without speaking.

With the driver's help Kate gathers their things. A few seconds later Jay's car swings up the drive. Eve hangs back behind Kate as Jay climbs out.

'Come on,' he says. 'I'll show you around.'

He opens the front door and ushers them in.

'Would you like to see your room?' he asks Eve once they are inside.

Taking her hand, he leads her down the corridor that runs along one side of the building. The room is plain, but inviting: a bed with a printed quilt cover, a desk with shelves and a lamp decorated with cut-out bears and foxes, a collection of painted Ice Age animals hanging from a mobile in the window.

Eve stares at it in amazement. Finally she turns to look at Kate and Jay. Kate realises she is asking permission because she cannot believe it is hers.

'Go on,' she says. 'It's okay.'

Moving slowly, as if she still cannot quite believe it, Eve goes in, circling the room carefully, touching its contents one by one.

Jay watches, smiling. Then he looks upward. Kate follows his gaze. A small black hemisphere sits on the ceiling in one corner. A jolt of nausea hits her.

'Is that a camera?' she asks.

'Yes. It will let us observe Eve in non-clinical conditions.'

Kate stares at him in astonishment. 'You have to be joking.'

Jay keeps his eyes on Eve. 'I'm sorry. It wasn't my decision.'

Kate grabs his arm and pulls him out into the hall. Eve looks back warily, but Kate smiles reassuringly. Looking up, she sees another camera.

'How many more are there?'

'Three. One in the living area, one in the kitchen, one in the garden.'

'So, only five?' she asks bitterly. 'And who will have access to the footage? You? Mylin? Davis?'

'There will be strict limitations on access.'

'And that's supposed to reassure me? Come on. You know this is bullshit. Nothing they'll get on these cameras will have any research value. Davis and his Silicon Valley cronies might think privacy is a thing of the past, but Eve's not a lab animal or a prisoner. She has rights.'

'It's just for the time being. We'll reassess in a few months.'

She stares at him. 'You mean once you're sure I'm not going to disappear again?'

Jay turns to look at her, his handsome face tight with anger. 'Perhaps.'

Kate shakes her head. 'Jesus, Jay. What happened to you?'

He snorts. 'I could ask you the same thing.'

Across the next week Kate cannot rid herself of the awareness her every action is being observed and assessed. Occasionally Eve reacts to her mood, but for the most part she seems surprisingly untroubled by the transition to the new house. At the rear of the building the bush crowds close, scribbled gums and fountains of grass giving way to pale-trunked trees, and despite the winter chill Eve roams happily among the boughs, gathering leaves and stones. Twice Eve is conducted back to the facility for more tests, returning cheerful, and one afternoon Jay comes to watch her, standing in the living area or the kitchen and gazing out the windows at her; after their conversation on the night they arrived at the house, Kate can hardly bear to be near him.

On the third day a truck arrives with their possessions. Arrayed in the house they look mean and cheap; seeing them Kate feels ashamed of them, of her own decisions. But as she tries to arrange them in Eve's room she finds herself growing angry, irritated by the unthinking superiority of Jay and Mylin and the others, their incomprehension of the contours of other lives. Love does not only happen in nice homes, between nice people, it is not always expressed politely.

Back in the living area, she takes out the phone Jay left her and messages Yassamin to suggest she and Sami visit. When she tells Yassamin they have moved, Yassamin is surprised.

WHAT!!??!!

Explain when see you.

Kate places the phone down and smiles. Yassamin's exuberant and informal messages always seem at odds with the dignity of her manner in person. When Sunday comes around Eve is excited about seeing Sami, peppering Kate with questions about when they will be there so often that Kate is relieved when Yassamin's battered blue car winds its way up the drive.

Sami has fallen asleep on the drive up. 'Thank God,' Yassamin whispers theatrically, as she unbuckles him from his child seat, 'I thought he'd never stop talking.'

'Hello, Sami,' Kate says as Yassamin lifts him out of the car and places him on the ground. 'Eve's been so excited about having you visit.'

Sami leans against Yassamin's leg, ignoring her. His black hair is long, his eyes even darker than his mother's.

Kate places a hand on Eve's back. All morning she has been full of excitement about Sami's arrival, but now he is here her anticipation has been replaced by a sudden shyness.

'Why don't you show Sami your new room?' she prompts.

Eve shakes her head, refusing to move. Her tiny body tense.

'Sami?' Yassamin says, removing the boy's hand from her jumper and pushing him towards Kate and Eve. He takes a step or two forward, then stops. He looks up at Kate, and for a moment she is startled by the odd directness of his gaze, the way he seems quite unafraid of her. Then he steps forward and takes Eve's hand. To Kate's relief Eve relaxes, and a second later the two of them dart away towards the house.

'Shall we go inside?' Kate asks.

Yassamin nods, but does not move, instead standing, staring, at the house.

'What happened? And how did you end up here?'

Kate hesitates. 'It's a long story.'

They have only been inside a minute or two before Sami returns. Pulling on Yassamin's sleeve, he begins pestering her for her phone. Yassamin ignores him, but he does not stop. 'Maman, please, maman.'

'Perhaps Eve can take you outside, show you the garden,' Kate says.

'Yes,' Yassamin says. 'Go play in the garden.'

At first Sami resists, but when Yassamin stands and walks out he follows her, still pulling on her arm.

'We can watch them from here,' Kate says.

The garden is a carefully defined rectangle of grass dividing the rear of the building from the bush behind. Released from the house, Eve crosses the lawn towards the scrub, glancing back once or twice to watch Sami from beneath her mane of hair. Finally Yassamin pushes him away and tells him to go play with Eve.

Kate sneaks a glance at Yassamin as Sami wanders across the grass; the other woman looks tense.

'Don't go where I can't see you!' she calls after him, but Sami doesn't turn around.

'They'll be fine,' Kate says.

Yassamin looks around. 'Yes, of course,' she says.

'I'll get us some tea,' says Kate.

They sit watching as Eve and Sami pick their way through the undergrowth just beyond the lawn.

'How is he doing in childcare?' she asks. Yassamin swallows her tea, thinking.

She shrugs. 'The same. He never wants to go, and when I arrive to pick him up he doesn't want to leave.'

Eve is showing Sami the tree where she saw a possum the day before. Kate knows without hearing her what she is saying.

'That's good though, isn't it?'

Yassamin shrugs. 'I suppose.'

'Have you seen his father since you moved back to the city?'

Yassamin takes a sip of her tea but does not look around. 'Once or twice.'

'How was it?'

She shrugs.

'And Sami?'

Yassamin shakes her head.

'And Sami?' Kate persists. 'Does he ask about him?'

Yassamin shoots her a wary look. 'Does Eve?'

Kate hesitates, then shakes her head. 'Not really.'

Yassamin turns away, her expression unreadable. 'He asks often.'

'And what do you tell him?'

'That he can meet him when he's older.'

'And can he?'

Yassamin shrugs. 'Perhaps.' For a few seconds she does not speak. 'And your partner? Have you seen him?'

Kate pauses. Until now she has always been careful not to

tell Yassamin more than she needed to about her relationship with Jay.

'I've gone back to work. He's there. It's complicated.'

'And this house? Is it part of the job?'

Kate nods. Yassamin regards her steadily.

'What is it?' Kate asks.

Yassamin shakes her head. 'Nothing,' she says. 'I'm tired. Work is difficult. And Sami is exhausting. I'm pleased you are doing so well.'

Kate hesitates, stung by the edge of judgement she hears in her friend's voice. 'Things aren't always how they seem,' she says.

After Yassamin and Sami leave, Eve is mulish, standoffish.

'Did you have fun playing with Sami?' Kate asks, but Eve ignores her, playing instead with her plastic toy.

'Did you show him the big tree?'

Eve does not look around. Not for the first time Kate is aware of the force of character in her, her obdurate determination. Perhaps, she thinks, this refusal, this wilful seeking of personal pleasure, is the basis of all human nature.

Over the next weeks and months Jay and the team run a battery of tests on Eve. Some are physical: scans of her skull and brain, measurements of reaction times and muscle and hormonal levels. Others are cognitive, designed to explore potential differences between her Neanderthal mind and their sapient minds.

Kate observes these tests with considerable unease. Although Jay and the others are guarded in their opinions around her, she knows that at least some of the team believe the structure of Eve's brain means she will lack the complex social awareness of a sapient child, and more particularly the ability to imagine her way into the mental states of others. And indeed, as the weeks pass, it becomes clear this is at least partly true. While a sapient child of her age would be likely to understand that the adults around her are capable of being mistaken or holding false beliefs, Eve is troubled by the concept. Faced with a test in which a cartoon character does not know somebody has moved her toys from one basket to the next, Eve often fails to understand why the character does not immediately go to the basket in which the toys now are. And while all of them believe this failure is almost certainly developmental, and she will eventually acquire this understanding, it suggests her acquisition of other, more sophisticated forms of social comprehension may be slower as well.

Her capacity to manage social relationships is similarly less developed. Tests of her cortisol level and eye movement confirm Kate's belief that while deeply bonded to those she knows well, she is uncomfortable with strangers, although whether this is because of subtle differences in the size and structure of her frontal lobe or because she has been so isolated is less easy to determine. And although not far outside the normal range for a child her age, her fine-motor control is less precise.

It is possible this is linked to her language development. As Kate has already guessed, Eve's expressive language is slower and less developed than might otherwise be expected. In part this seems to be a function of the physical structure of her throat and mouth, which make the production of certain sounds difficult. But it also seems to be connected to the way she processes and organises language: although her comprehension is good, she seems to rely on a series of non-verbal cues involving scent and touch, and to be less focused on verbal communication than a sapient child.

These deficits are offset by other abilities: her general intelligence and problem-solving skills are all at the high end of the range for a child her age, confirming Kate's sense of the speed of her mind. Likewise her eyesight and visual memory are both remarkable: in set tasks where she is given thirty seconds to look at a grid of objects and remember them and their order, her performance is off the chart. Similarly, as her powerful musculature suggests, her physical coordination and strength are considerably more developed than those of a sapient child of the same age. And although it is difficult to quantify, she is less volatile than sapient children, better able to focus for long periods of time.

Kate is not sure how to feel about these discoveries. At first she is unbelieving, even though they mirror some of her own suspicions, and in those meetings she is invited to attend she finds herself disputing the methodology and findings, even beyond the point where she herself knows the data is sound. After that she feels grief, not just for Eve, but for herself. It is unbearable to think of her so vulnerable, or of her being unable to participate in the way other children might. But in time this passes, and she realises Eve is not a condition but herself.

Meanwhile Jay and the rest of the team set about devising a program to help Eve extend her abilities in those areas where she has deficits. At Kate's insistence they also formulate a plan to allow her to develop herself in those areas in which she exceeds the normal sapient range. 'Why should we limit her education with sapient standards of normality?' Kate argues. 'By that reasoning *we* should be being trained to improve our visual memory until it equals Eve's.'

Although this process is complicated by Mylin's overt antipathy towards her, Kate finds she enjoys these sessions with the team, and the chance to contribute to their work. And so, at the end of their fourth month she catches Jay alone, suggests to him there might be a more formal role she could play.

'I can contribute,' she says. 'You know that.'

Jay regards her carefully. 'Davis would need to agree,' he says. 'And we'd need to do it in a way that isn't disruptive for Eve.'

The next Monday Kate arrives at the lab to find Davis seated opposite Eve at the low table they use for her tests and lessons. At the sound of the door Eve looks around and hurtles towards her, flinging herself into Kate's arms. Kate lifts her up, embracing her, and looks at Davis, who has stood up.

'I didn't know you were here,' she says.

'It was a spur-of-the-moment thing.' He takes a few steps towards them and Kate has to resist the urge to back away.

'She's getting tall,' he says.

'Yes. Although you'd know that from the videos.' Kate says, immediately regretting the sharpness of her tone. But if Davis notices he gives no indication. 'Where is everybody?' she asks, looking around.

'Team meeting.'

Kate feels a prickle of apprehension. Davis looks at Eve in Kate's arms. 'You've bonded with her. As I knew you would.'

Kate hesitates. 'I'm sorry?'

He regards her, his bland face seemingly emotionless. 'We did a psychological assessment before we approached you and Jay. It indicated your emotional state was such that you were highly likely to form close attachments with any children produced by the project.'

'You mean you hired me because you thought I was . . . what? Vulnerable? A potential mother?' She speaks carefully, aware Eve is in her arms, listening.

Davis smiles. 'Of course not. But your psychological state certainly played a part in our choice of you and Jay to head up the project.'

Kate stares back at him, wondering why he has decided to tell her this. Is it ego? An expression of his messianic belief in his own genius? Or is it a way to remind her of his power over her? 'You know I've asked to rejoin the program?'

He nods. 'I do.'

'Are you worried I might be a distraction?'

He regards her dispassionately. He has changed, somehow, she realises. The affectlessness he possessed when they first met has given way to something harder, closer to madness. Or has he always been like this and she is only noticing it now because he has power over her? A few weeks earlier he was the subject of widespread condemnation after a Twitter meltdown in which he accused a progressive Congresswoman in the United States of doing deals with big oil after she criticised the focus of the Foundation's activities.

Suddenly he smiles. 'We only want what's best for Eve. That's all we've ever wanted.'

A fortnight later Jay summons her to his office and presents her with a proposal. She will return to the Foundation three days a week. On these days Eve will accompany her to the labs or, more often, remain at home with a carer selected by the Foundation. When Kate demands to be involved in the choice of carer it is made clear that will not be happening. Despite the offer to provide her with work and housing, the Foundation – or more likely, Davis (and perhaps Jay) – seems intent on ensuring her responsibilities are limited, as a security measure or a punishment, or both.

In the end the Foundation selects a behavioural psychologist with experience working with children. The weekend before her first day Jay brings her to meet Kate and Eve. It is not the first time Jay has been here on the weekend: since Kate's return he has made a point of visiting two or three times a week, often bringing gifts for Eve, as if determined to be a part of her life. Kate does not know how she feels about these visits: although she resents both his assumption she will welcome them and her inability to object to them, there is no question Eve has grown fond of Jay, often asking about him and when he will visit again.

Kate opens the door as Jay pulls up; he waves but she does not respond, instead focused on the woman who opens the passenger door. Kate has already googled her, meaning she knows what she will look like, yet she is surprised by the other woman's relative youth as she steps out, the easy athleticism of her long limbs. Seeing Kate standing there, the other woman smiles.

'This is Cassie,' Jay says.

Cassie smiles warmly and extends a hand. Beneath her long ash-blonde hair her face is friendly, open. 'It's very exciting to finally meet. Jay has told me a lot about you,' she says. Her Californian accent a reminder of Kate's years there.

Kate takes her hand. Behind Cassie, Jay is watching her, his face carefully composed. 'Yes,' she says. 'I've heard a lot about you as well.'

Once they are inside, Cassie stands and looks around, her face giving nothing away. Kate is uncomfortably aware that despite the Foundation-arranged furnishings the house still feels bare, only half-lived in. Once when she and Jay were first together he joked she lived like she was always ready to stage her own disappearance; he had laughed, but in the moment before she realised he was joking she had felt herself tense, all her years of being afraid others might see who she was, where she came from, coming rushing back.

'What a great house,' Cassie says.

'Apparently the architect has won awards.'

'I'm not surprised,' Cassie says, but before she can say more Jay interposes himself between the two women.

'Is Eve around?'

'Of course,' Kate says, moving towards the door to the yard. 'She's outside.'

Cassie and Jay follow and stop beside her.

Eve is playing a game with sticks and leaves beneath the tree, her tawny hair bright in the pale sunshine. Cassie hesitates, just long enough for Kate to see she didn't quite believe what she had been told before she came here.

'Have you been with the Foundation long?' Kate asks.

Cassie smiles. 'Three years. I was working on the project in Canada. With the Inuit.'

'And they moved you here for this?'

Cassie's eyes dart towards Jay, as if seeking his permission. 'No,' she says. 'I came for another role. Davis and Jay recruited me for this.'

'Have you worked with children before?'

Cassie nods. 'Yes. I specialised in work with kids, but I also worked as a nanny right through university.'

'We chose Cassie as much for her personality as for her qualifications,' Jay says.

Kate folds her arms.

'I'm excited to be doing this,' Cassie says. 'For scientific reasons, obviously, but also because of who she is, the chance to be near her. It's astonishing.'

'Perhaps Cassie could meet her?' Jay says.

Kate glances from him to Cassie and back. Then she places a hand on the door and, sliding it open, calls out to Eve.

'Eve? There's somebody I'd like you to meet.'

On the far side of the lawn Eve's shoulders immediately tighten and she does not look up. Instead she concentrates on her game with renewed energy.

Cassie glances at Kate. 'May I?'

Kate hesitates, then nods.

Cassie crosses the lawn and crouches down beside Eve. 'Hi Eve,' she says. 'My name's Cassie.' When Eve does not respond Cassie leans back and sits, cross-legged. 'What's that you're doing?' she asks, quietly. Eve still refuses to respond.

Kate cannot move. She knows that Eve will withdraw if pushed. But she is also concerned Eve will seem difficult, sub-normal, that Cassie will mistake her manner for pathology. Perhaps sensing this, Jay places a hand on Kate's arm. She flinches, then relents.

Long seconds pass. Cassie does not move, just sits, quietly, watching Eve move her sticks and doll around. And then, without speaking or looking at her, Eve turns, and presses one of the leaves into Cassie's hand, before returning to her game. Kate touches her throat, her heart too full to speak.

One of Cassie's first initiatives is the creation of a playgroup for Eve. Because of the danger Eve's appearance will arouse suspicion if she spends extended time in the wider world, Cassie proposes they work within the organisation by identifying staff who have children a similar age to Eve.

'You don't think they're more likely to guess the truth about her if they're already involved in the Foundation's projects?' Kate asks.

'I think we have to assume that will happen,' Cassie replies. 'But working internally means anybody involved will be bound by the non-disclosure clauses in their employment agreements.'

A week later Cassie has a list of six possible candidates, all within a year of Eve in age. 'We'll have to assess them, obviously,' Cassie says, 'and run some background checks on their parents. But they look promising.'

In the end only four are deemed suitable: one of the original six – the oldest girl – is disallowed after an analysis of her mother's social-media postings suggests she is likely to pose a security risk, while another is found to have a tendency to resort to physical violence with younger children. ('It's not just about protecting Eve,' Cassie tells Kate. 'There's also the issue of Eve's unusual strength creating the possibility she could harm him.') After briefings with the parents the others all agree, though, and so, as the winter gives way to spring, two days a week are given over to a structured program of group activity and play.

Kate and Eve arrive early for the first session. Cassie has organised for one of the rooms to be converted into a play area for the session, arranging toys and art materials and beanbags in particular zones. Eve has spent enough time in the facility to understand she is allowed to play with them, so after a quick glance at Kate and Cassie she goes over to the collection of dolls in one corner and begins to play.

Cassie stands beside Kate, watching. 'She's going to be fine,' Cassie says. 'The others are all great kids.'

Kate nods. The first day she left Eve with Cassie she could not concentrate on her work, and although she successfully resisted the desire to call, at the end of the day she left early and raced home, heart pounding, pushing her car so far over the speed limit its systems felt the need to caution her. When she arrived Eve was standing in the drive with Cassie, and as Kate got out of the car Eve charged towards her and threw herself into Kate's arms. Perhaps Cassie saw the anxiety in Kate's face, because she stepped forward and stroked Eve's hair.

'We've had a great day, haven't we, Eve?' she said, her eyes meeting Kate's and holding them. Over the weeks, Kate's initial suspicion of the younger woman has given way to wary regard and an understanding that, whatever her wider agenda, Cassie genuinely cares for Eve, but Kate still had to fight the fear she was being supplanted.

'They've all agreed to the study?' Kate asks as they wait for the rest of the playgroup to arrive.

Cassie nods. The other parents have not been told about Eve. Instead they have agreed to their children taking part in a longitudinal study into language development. 'They have. And they've all signed the relevant non-disclosures.' She points to the roof. 'We're going to record the whole thing as well.'

Kate is about to reply when the door behind them opens, and a man Kate recognises from one of the other labs looks in. He has a thick ginger beard and carefully sculpted hair and holds a girl of about Eve's age by the hand.

'Is this the playgroup?' he asks.

Cassie smiles. 'Hi Daniel!' she says. 'And Rose! How are you?'

The three other children – a boy, Felix, and two more girls, Heti and Zelda – arrive soon after, accompanied by their parents. Cassie has been careful to ensure none of them already know each other, meaning they are wary at first, but gradually the four sapient children drift together. Eve does not join them, instead continuing to play quietly on her own. Kate waits. It is obvious she knows they are there, but does not feel able to approach them. Finally Cassie intervenes, taking Eve by the hand and leading her across. Kate watches, fists clenched, her heart leaping.

'This is Eve,' Cassie says, crouching down beside the other children. 'She doesn't know anybody. Would you all look after her for me?'

There is a moment's silence, then Rose nods. Cassie places Eve's hand in Rose's, and Rose solemnly instructs her on the game she and the others have been playing.

'She's yours?' a voice says behind her. Kate turns to find Daniel standing there.

'Yes,' she says, forcing herself to smile.

'Eve?'

She nods.

'How old is she?'

'Three and a half.'

Daniel glances at Eve again, his surprise obvious. Cassie has chosen the children so they are all within a year or so in age, but Eve is considerably more powerful and physically developed than any of the others.

'And Jay. He's her dad, right?'

Rose whispers something to Eve, and Eve laughs shyly. Kate smiles.

'He is. Although we're not together.'

Daniel looks at her, his blue eyes careful. 'I'm sorry. The first years can be tough, can't they?'

Kate nods. 'They can.'

Rose leads Eve closer to the others and then releases her hand to return to the game. Eve stays where she is, looking down and away. Kate forces herself to smile.

The second session is easier. Although Eve still spends much of the time playing alone, she also joins in group activities and, gradually, with the games of the other four. At first it is mostly parallel play, but by the third session she and Rose and the boy, Felix, begin to play together. Watching Eve run and shout, or her shy pleasure in playing with the blocks and dolls leaves Kate full of love.

Despite herself, Kate also finds herself drawn into conversation with the other parents. At first it is mostly coincidental, glancing meetings during drop-offs and pick-ups, but one day she accepts an invitation to have lunch with Daniel and Heti's mother, Seepaj, in the dining area. Kate is friendly but distant, wary of Daniel's desire to draw her into his social circle, his curiosity about Eve, but as she walks back to her office afterwards she finds she was grateful for a chance to compare notes with other parents. It is only later that it occurs to her this may have been Cassie's intention all along.

Meanwhile she finds herself drawn back into her work. For obvious reasons she has been moved off the main project; instead she has been attached to a virtual team working on the development of synthetic organisms capable of consuming methane with a view to slowing the release of greenhouse gases from the permafrost and the ocean bed. The work is technical but absorbing, and although Kate tries not to think too much about it, charged with urgency. Each week brings worse news about the hastening changes in the north, images of sinkholes and rivers collapsing through the earth, of the melting corpses of ancient animals rising from the ground, as if the past is intruding, ghostlike and uncanny, into the present, and time is hastening, hastening, hastening.

Spring becomes summer, then winter returns, snow with it, whistling down from the mountains and covering the lawn outside. Kate takes Eve outside, watches as she races across the narrow patch of lawn, her dark footsteps crisscrossing its white oblong. Afterwards, inside, she heaps wood into the fireplace. Somewhere in the distance she hears a peculiar, wheezing cry, and a moment later a sort of yip in reply, the sound raising the hackles on the back of her neck, not just for its strangeness but for its unsettling familiarity.

On the rug by the fire Eve is drawing, her crayons spilling colour onto the page in the flickering light. Immersed in her task she seems oblivious to Kate's scrutiny.

The cry does not come again. Opening her screen, Kate finds a story about thylacine sightings. A shiver runs down her spine. Could that be what she has heard? And if it is, have they come from the facility? Glancing at Eve again, she feels a sort of vertigo, a feeling the world is shifting beneath her.

The snow passes, replaced by freezing rain and low mist. Despite its elegant design the house leaks heat, warmth bleeding away into the dank darkness outside. In the afternoons Kate takes Eve walking, pushing through low bushes and spiky shrubs, their branches glistening with droplets of freezing water; as she brushes against them they lose their shape, splash down against her.

Eve seems at home in this wet gloom: she moves quickly through the trees, her hair thick, fiery in the half-light. Once or twice she looks around, checking Kate is watching, that she has not left her behind; each time Kate smiles back.

Back at the house she sees a missed call from Yassamin. Although Yassamin and Sami have come to the house several times since that first visit, in recent weeks Yassamin has taken to suggesting Kate and Eve visit them in the city, an idea Kate has rejected, uneasy about the potential for disturbing the delicate equilibrium of her and Eve's life.

Pressing the button she calls Yassamin back. She answers quickly, greeting her.

'I wanted to check you're all right,' says Yassamin. 'I saw there had been snow.'

Kate reassures her they are fine.

'And your work? It goes well?'

'Yes,' Kate says. 'Very well.'

'It is Sami's birthday in a few weeks,' Yassamin says. 'I thought Eve might like to come.'

Kate hesitates. 'I don't know. Eve finds large groups difficult.'

'Perhaps you could come another weekend, then? Sami would love to see Eve.'

'Perhaps,' Kate says. 'Perhaps.'

They talk for a little longer, exchanging stories about work, the two children, until eventually Yassamin says she has to go; Sami is shouting in the next room. Placing the phone down Kate stares at the window, her reflection. The house is almost silent, the only sound the distant dripping of water from the trees and gutters. She has grown used to their isolation, but sometimes she wonders what will happen when Eve is older. How will she find friends? Develop relationships?

As she boils the pasta for Eve's evening meal she continues to consider the question, reminded again of her own childhood, her mother's moods and need for attention, how difficult it made it to make or maintain normal friendships. How much of who she is has its origins in those years? Would she have been different, less unyielding, more able to trust if her mother had been different? Or would she have been this way anyway? Once she would have rejected her inability to decide. But being with Eve has made her understand these questions are never simple: we are never either the teller or the tale; we are both, and neither.

Later, adrift in the warm glow of the lamp by Eve's bed, Eve's small body pressed against her as she reads to her, she watches the solemnity with which Eve listens and wonders, not for the first time, how much she understands. Not the narrative, the sequence of events as it is related, but the meanings that move beneath the surface of the story. Can Eve make sense of the pictures? Interpret the emotions they are supposed to communicate and provoke? Can she infer motivations, purpose? Is her mind capable of symbolic meaning, of making sense of metaphor?

Of course it is difficult to know with a child so young, but as Kate watches her touch the picture and turn the pages, wanting to know what happens next, it is difficult not to believe that Eve understands. One day she reads her a picture book about a lying bear and is surprised when Eve erupts into laughter at the end, immediately recognising the bear's frantic overcompensations for his untruth for what they are.

At other times, Kate is less certain. Out on the track one day they come across a raven lying dead on its back, its glossy black plumage rumpled and dull, its eye filmy. Ants are already describing lines across its beak, inside its mouth.

Kate is uneasy. A group of ravens nest in one of the trees behind their house, and most mornings they spend an hour or so tracing long arcs in the air above the lawn, their wings creasing the air in stealthy beats as they pass overhead; more than once Kate has come upon Eve sitting in the kitchen, watching them, her face intent. One day she asked Kate what they were, and since then she has called them 'raffins' – sometimes they are 'Eve's raffins', other days they are 'Mummy's raffins'. How will she react to finding one of them dead like this?

'Raffin?' Eve asks, in her throaty voice.

Kate nods. 'The raven is dead, sweetie.'

Eve doesn't reply, just stands, staring down at the rumpled shape. The moment stretches on. Finally Eve nods, steps past the bird and heads on up the path. She does not look back.

That night Kate wonders what had passed through Eve's mind in that moment. Grief is well known among animals, especially primates, and there is evidence at least some animals understand the idea of death, its blank irretrievability. Yet what does it mean to 'understand' death? She is not sure she understands it herself, except as a sense of blank absence.

Yet still, Eve is happiest outside, moving through the trees. Out there her physical strength grants her confidence. But it is more than just her physical prowess. When she is in the bush she seems more alive, her body attuned to her surroundings, preternaturally alert. More than once Kate has watched her ascend a hill, moving fast and low, as fluid as a cat. Her hearing and sense of smell are similarly heightened; frequently when they are out she will fall still suddenly, raise her head, sniffing or listening for something Kate cannot hear, her body tensed. Sometimes she will glance back at Kate and smile, her wide face full of delight or excitement; other times she will run on, oblivious, focused on whatever it is she is doing.

They are walking like this one day in April when Kate pauses on an outcrop at the top of a ridge. To the south, cloud is gathering. This lonely island is not her country – its dark stone and wind-scoured topography are nothing like the softer landscapes she knew as a child on the mainland. Yet after seven years here she has come to understand something of its beauty, its finality. Once, years ago, she read a poem about the islands to the south – Macquarie, Heard, Kergelen – and was brought to a halt by the description of them forming 'full stops to sentences about the end of the world'. Perhaps something similar is true of here, she thinks, this place suspended at the end of things. Or perhaps everywhere is like that now, as the world rushes on, towards disaster.

Turning, she looks around for Eve. They are high, and although she knows she has grown complacent about Eve's capacity to assess risk, she does not like the thought of Eve unsupervised above the drop. Unable to see her she takes a step sideways and, as her foot touches the ground, something shifts beneath it, and she slips sideways.

There is an awful moment when she hangs suspended, her balance lost but her body not yet falling, a moment in which she sees with horrible clarity the space around her, the body-shattering rocks below, the moment stretching on and on, until all at once she feels space give way beneath her. Twisting sideways, she tries to right herself, swinging herself away from the edge, but only far enough to avoid the plunge into the air. Overhead the sky wheels past, and she slips down the face of the rock, crashing past ferns and lichen, striking rocks and on, down the hill face, until she lands, heavily, and is thrown outward across a ledge. For a few seconds she is too stunned to move, too shocked to feel anything. But then she tries to sit up, only to cry out as pain stabs up from her leg, sharp, blinding. She drops down again, closing her eyes against it. Then she moves once more, stifling a sob as she turns over and looks at her leg.

It is not obviously twisted or bent, but each time she moves it the pain is almost overwhelming, and now the initial shock of the fall is passing, she is aware of a deeper, more persistent pain. When she was a child she broke her wrist falling off a swing: she remembers the subterranean ache of it, and knows, without needing to be told, she has broken a bone. She smiles grimly, consoling herself that at least the pain means she hasn't damaged her spine, but as she does she remembers Eve, and looks up, following the line of broken branches up to the ledge ten metres above her. Eve is standing, staring down, her wide face pale. Kate tries to move but pain stabs through her, and she lets out a cry. Opening her eyes again, she sees Eve has pulled back, away from her.

'Eve,' she says, trying to keep her voice calm and steady. 'Are you okay?'

Eve hesitates and then nods slowly. Kate takes a breath. 'That's good. Now, do you know the way back to the house?'

Eve nods again.

'And you could find your way back here?'

This time Eve has to think about it: 'Yes.'

'Okay. I need you to go back and find my phone. Call Jay. Tell him I've broken my leg and I need help. Then do what he tells you. Can you do that?'

Eve nods.

'That's good. Don't be frightened. And don't forget: call Jay. And make sure you listen to what he says.'

'Can't you come?'

Kate shakes her head. 'I can't. So, you have to get him, and bring help.'

Eve's face is pale, terrified.

'I know you can do it,' Kate says. When Eve doesn't move she smiles again, as convincingly as she can. 'Now, go.'

A moment passes and then Eve backs away and disappears. Kate slumps back, whimpering as she closes her eyes in an attempt to block out the pain.

Although the day was clear when they set out, as the morning passes clouds feed in, bringing cold air and specks of rain. Trapped on the ledge, Kate stares out across the valley, trying not to think about what will happen if the weather really turns. Only a few months ago a pair of hikers went missing not far from here, their bodies turning up a week later. At the time Kate had been careful not to tell Eve the story, something she is glad of now, but still, it is an unwelcome reminder of her vulnerability. Closing her eyes, she does the sums again, trying to calculate how long it will take for Eve to get home, to speak to Jay, but she finds it difficult to keep the order of events straight in her head.

Sometime after noon the wind begins to pick up, the temperature dropping again, and soon after, it begins to rain. At first the cold brings her back to herself, making her predicament more acute, but within a few minutes she is shivering, her teeth chattering as she tries to huddle in closer against the wind, and soon after that she finds herself slipping again, losing minutes, or possibly longer.

Hours pass, and then, as she fades back into consciousness, she hears movement above, a voice, and looking up sees Jay scrambling down towards her.

'Kate, thank God,' he says, kneeling beside her. 'Are you okay?'

'My leg,' she says. 'I think it's broken.'

Jay follows her gaze. 'Don't worry about that. Let's just get you out of here.' Behind him a woman in the white overalls of a paramedic drops down, and Kate leans back, closing her eyes again.

Between the cliff face and the hospital she slides back into unconsciousness, time slipping past her. When she opens her eyes she is in a corridor, Jay beside her. For a second or two she does not know where she is, then fear knifes through her.

'Where is she?' she asks, grabbing Jay's arm. 'Where's Eve?'

'She's fine,' he says. 'Cassie is with her.'

Kate leans back and stares at the ceiling.

'That's good,' she says.

Over the next few hours she is examined and x-rayed, before being moved into surgery. When she wakes again she is in a bed, Jay beside her. When he smiles at her she feels a rush of love that surprises her, and reaching out takes his hand, grateful for its warmth, his presence.

They discharge her the next day, the wait for her doctor's approval delaying her departure so long that it is dark by the time she and Jay reach the house. Eve and Cassie step out the door as they arrive;

silhouetted in the light from within, their icy breath a pale nimbus. Eve is already at the car by the time Jay opens Kate's door. Kate winces as Eve wraps herself around her. Ignoring the wash of pain, she draws her close. 'I'm so glad to see you,' she says, pressing her face to her head and breathing in the smell of shampoo in her coarse hair. 'Have you been good for Cassie?'

Eve nods.

'I'm sorry I frightened you. But I'm so proud of you.'

She can feel the tension in Eve's body.

'Will it be okay?' Eve asks, staring at her leg.

Kate nods. 'Eventually. But only thanks to you.' Shifting in her seat, she slides her leg out and takes her crutches from Jay. 'Now we have to get you to bed. It's so late!'

Kate's leg heals slowly. For much of the time she is stuck in the house, incapable of driving, walking more than short distances. The presence of Cassie in her and Eve's life means this is easier than it would have been a year earlier, her days with Eve allowing Kate time to work and convalesce.

Yet while Kate has learned to work with Cassie she has never really warmed to her. This is partly because she dislikes the younger woman's manner, not just her wide-eyed American enthusiasm, but also the carefully correct way Cassie behaves towards her, the constant implication Kate is somebody who needs to be managed. At first Kate assumed this to be simply another manifestation of the generalised mistrust of her by those associated with the original project – she knows Cassie and Mylin are close – but in recent months she has begun to wonder whether there is more to it than that. On several occasions she has caught Cassie and Jay in conversation when they thought themselves unobserved, and been struck by the way they stood close to each other, Cassie's unguarded laughter. And while the grateful affection she felt for Jay on the day of her accident has faded, there is no question he is more relaxed with Kate, suggesting he is happier.

Meanwhile, however, there are other problems. Although the release of de-extinced species continues apace, in October Davis is sidelined into an honorary role at Gather after a much-publicised disagreement with the board. According to the press releases he is pleased with this outcome, and the opportunity to devote more time to the Foundation, but it is widely understood he has been put on notice, and the board will no longer tolerate his public excesses.

Kate is made uneasy by these realignments, and by the growing sense the Foundation's work is being overtaken by external events. In the Arctic images of woolly rhino and mammoth roaming across the empty landscape are increasingly blotted out by videos of melting ice and fires sweeping through the grasslands, while governments in Europe and elsewhere are falling to leaders who see advantage in division and fear.

In the week after her cast is removed Kate finally agrees to take Eve to visit Sami in the city. Although Yassamin is keen for her to visit them at home, Kate declines, instead suggesting they meet in a playground on the city's outskirts. On the day appointed she bundles Eve into the car, relieved to see Eve is happy and excited at the prospect of seeing Sami. It is mid-morning by the time they arrive. Kate selected this park for the meeting because of its relative seclusion, and as they pull up she is pleased to see the only other car is Yassamin's. Climbing out of the car Kate unclips Eve; by the play equipment on the park's far side Yassamin waves, and while Kate locks the car she begins to walk towards her. Yassamin is wearing oversized black sunglasses; against her dark hair they make her look like Jackie Onassis, but when she reaches Kate she takes them off and embraces her warmly.

Kate is relieved. Although Yassamin visited once while she was recuperating, the visit was awkward and marred by Sami and Eve's constant – and uncharacteristic – bickering. While Sami and Eve climb and play the two of them sit ȯn a bench and talk. Yassamin is happy: the boss who had been making her life difficult has been moved and replaced with a man she likes much better. 'He is very handsome as well,' she says. 'Although obviously that is irrelevant.'

After an hour or so Yassamin suggests coffee, but Sami and Eve both refuse to leave, standing next to each other and shouting 'Nooooooo!' in a parody of childish misbehaviour. Yassamin laughs, and suggests Kate stay with the children while she drives to a cafe a kilometre or so back down the road.

With Yassamin gone Kate settles back on the bench to watch the two children. Although Sami is several months older and a head taller than Eve her compact body is visibly more agile and powerful, and she has a physical confidence he cannot match. Yet despite Eve's shyness, her wariness when it comes to expressing herself, when she is with Sami she forgets her reserve, laughing and playing without concern. By contrast Sami seems to require constant approval, his neediness a stark contrast to Eve's containment. Even now, as they play, he turns to her constantly, checking she is watching, that she has noticed him.

After a few minutes Sami runs towards her, asking for food. Kate glances around. Seeing nobody she decides the two of them will be safe, and heads back to the car. But as she is walking back she realises a group of children have appeared, and are gathered at the far end of the play area, their backs to her. She begins to hurry, searching for Eve, but she is nowhere to be seen. Then there is a cry of distress.

'Hey!' she shouts. The children do not turn, but she has time to see one of them – a boy with blond hair – roll to one side and back, his arms scrabbling towards his armpits, his face contorted in a grotesque parody of an ape, and beyond him, Eve huddled on the equipment, her face turned away.

'Hey!' she shouts again. 'What do you think you're doing?'

This time two of the children turn, startled expressions on their faces. One of them – a boy with black hair – seems to be considering darting away, but before he can Kate shoves them aside and sweeps Eve up. Pushing her hair back, she searches her face for evidence of harm.

'Are you okay?' she asks. Eve cowers away from her.

'Eve?' she presses.

Finally Eve nods, and Kate turns back to the children. Perhaps still surprised by her interruption, they have not fled, although most have backed away. For the first time she sees Sami off to one side, his manner telling her he was not one of the tormenters, but nor did he defend Eve.

'What were you doing?' she demands, staring wildly from one to the next. There are four of them: the blond boy, a smaller girl who stands with her mouth open, the boy with the black hair and a skinny boy with ginger hair.

'Well?' she demands.

'Just playing,' the girl says resentfully. Kate stares at her.

'Well, it didn't look like you were *just playing*.'

The girl looks down.

'And you?' Kate asks, leaning towards the blond boy. 'What have you got to say for yourself?'

He stares back, unmoved. His eyes are clear, blue, his hair white gold and fine where it sweeps up from his forehead. 'We were just mucking around,' he says, his expression daring her to contradict him.

Kate stares back at him. He is six, possibly seven, little more than half her height. Yet she feels his cool pleasure in his own power.

'Is that what you call it?' she asks, surprised by the cold fury in her voice.

'Jeez, lady, don't get so worked up,' says the ginger-haired one.

There is a ripple of laughter. Kate feels something shift.

'You should be ashamed of yourselves,' she says, adjusting her grip on Eve, who is clinging to her. The blond boy's gaze does not waver, but some secret amusement passes between the ginger-haired one and the other two.

Aware the situation is slipping out of her control, she extends a hand to Sami to indicate he should follow, and steps past them. But almost at once she hears one of them whisper, 'Oo-oo-oo, monkey girl.'

Enraged, she swings around to find the blond one staring at her, his face lit with amusement. Behind him the ginger-haired one is laughing openly.

'You little shit!' she explodes, but as she does she hears a shout from behind her.

'Hey! What's going on?'

She turns to see a heavy-set woman with frizzy brown hair approaching from the other side of the park. The woman places a solicitous hand on the ginger-haired boy's shoulder.

'Are you okay?' she asks him.

The boy tries to look rueful and nods.

'Did she hurt you?'

'She shouted at us,' says the blond one, his voice clear, careful. The woman swivels to stare at Kate. Her small eyes are hard.

'They'd cornered my daughter and were picking on her,' Kate says, aware even as she speaks of how weak her words sound. The woman regards her coldly.

'And where were you when this was happening?'

Kate feels her dislike of the woman tip over into anger. 'I could ask you the same.'

'Yes, but I wasn't the one abusing children in a playground.'

Kate is about to snap back when Eve whimpers and presses her face into Kate's leg. Realising her display of anger has frightened her, Kate chokes back a retort. Perhaps mistaking her silence for defeat, the woman smiles unpleasantly. Kate grabs Sami's wrist.

'Come on,' she says, and without looking back drags the two of them towards the car park, but when they reach it she realises Yassamin is not back, and she cannot put both children in her car. She stares ahead, resisting the impulse to go back, wipe the look of bland superiority off the woman's face, although in a way it is not the woman who has enraged her but the entire situation: the cool certainty of the children, their tormenting of Eve, their – correct, as it turns out – belief they will get away with it. Not for the first time she feels the pull of misanthropy, of the consoling hatred of the human race, its cupidity and cruelty, its heedless destruction of that which it doesn't understand. Trembling with silent fury, she heads on, towards the road, hoping Yassamin is not far away. As they walk she squeezes Eve's hand. 'I love you,' she says fiercely. 'You know that, right?' But even as she speaks she does not know whether she is saying it for Eve's sake or her own.

HOMO GENOCIDUS

Kate is in the supermarket car park when her phone rings. A Sydney number she does not recognise. She considers ignoring it, but at the last moment presses the button, holds the phone to her ear.

'Is this Kate Larkin?' asks a woman's voice.

She hesitates. Her years of hiding still shadow her. 'Who's this?'

'I'm sorry to call out of the blue,' the woman says, the words coming in a rush, as if she is uncomfortable with what she is calling about. 'I wasn't sure I'd be able to find you. It's about your mother, Claire Larkin?'

Kate feels a tremor pass through her. 'Yes,' she says.

'I've got bad news, I'm afraid.' Then a pause. 'She died this morning.'

Kate doesn't speak, just stares out across the empty grass towards the highway.

'Doctor Larkin?'

'Yes,' Kate says.

'Would you like to call me back?'

'No.'

'I really am sorry to have to tell you like this.'

'It's all right,' Kate says. 'I'm glad you did.'

'We wondered whether you might like to make arrangements for the funeral. And to deal with her things.'

'Yes,' Kate says eventually. 'Yes, of course. What do you need me to do?'

Back in the car, she grips the wheel and stares ahead. She is at once clear and outside herself. In some part of her she understands she is in shock. She has not seen her mother in nearly twenty years, and even before the last time they spoke the process of disentangling herself was almost complete, or at least as complete as it could ever be, but her death does not feel like a release. Instead she feels as if the world has shifted under her, and she is unmoored, adrift.

Later, she will realise it was a mistake to drive, that she cannot remember the trip home. Eve is in the front yard when she turns up the drive, playing one of the elaborate physical games she seems able to spend hours absorbed in. Kate smiles and greets her as she climbs out, forcing herself to keep her voice level so she seems bright and untroubled.

'Did you get the jelly?' Eve asks. Despite all the years of speech therapy her deep voice is still slightly slurred. Kate glances down at the bag over her shoulder. It is as if the person who left the house an hour before to visit the supermarket was a different individual to the one who has returned.

'Yes,' she says. 'Come inside. I'll open it for you.'

Eve runs ahead of her through the door. In the months since her twelfth birthday she has grown rapidly, so that at twelve-and-a-half she is almost as tall as Kate, and broader across the shoulders by half. Last time she was weighed she was almost ten kilograms heavier as well, testament to the powerful muscles that shift and flex beneath her skin.

Kate has found this transformation profoundly unsettling. For as Eve's body has accelerated into puberty, it has become increasingly difficult to ignore the biological gulf between the two of them. She is no less beautiful – more, if anything, Kate often thinks – yet she is also obviously non-sapient, her face and body constructed on a different scale, out of different clay. These disparities are not the cartoonish ones of popular culture, nor even those Kate feared: her brow is lower and heavier than that of a sapient girl of her age, her nose and cheekbones wider, but not grotesquely so, especially not when seen as part of her face and body as a whole. Instead what strikes Kate is the strength and power of Eve, the way her fox-brown eyes and tawny hair give her the look of a forest creature, wild and sleek. Yet while her body and face have changed, she herself has not, or not in the ways one might expect of a human adolescent. Although her moods have grown more volatile, especially when she is tired, for the most part she remains childlike, gentle and playful and seemingly content to spend long periods absorbed in her own world.

'What flavours did you get?' she asks, pulling at the bag Kate unloads onto the kitchen bench. For weeks Eve has been obsessed with jelly, demanding Kate make it as often as possible.

'Pineapple,' Kate says. 'And grape.'

Eve's shoulders sag.

'What?' Kate asks, trying to keep the note of testiness out of her voice.

'You said you'd get raspberry.'

'They didn't have raspberry.'

Eve stares at her with sudden petulant fury.

'I'm not a magician,' Kate says. 'If they don't have it, they don't have it.'

Eve lets the box drop to the counter but as she backs away her elbow strikes the other bag and knocks it sideways. Vegetables and tins and packages spill out and clatter down, a bag of lentils splitting open and ricocheting across the floor.

'Jesus, Eve!' Kate snaps. 'Be careful!' Even before she has finished speaking Kate regrets her words. 'I'm sorry,' she says. 'I didn't mean to snap. I'm just tired.'

But Eve is already backing away from her, tears welling in her eyes.

'Eve . . .' Kate begins, but Eve shoves past her. Kate calls after her, but the only reply is the sound of Eve's door slamming.

Kate stares after her for a few seconds, then turns back to the kitchen and the wreckage strewn across the floor. She bends to pick up a tin of tomatoes and a bunch of celery, then stands up and places them on the bench. Through the window over the bench the sky is cloudless, its blue tinged with smoke. Reaching up, she touches her face and realises she is crying.

The next afternoon she is on a plane to Sydney. The aisle seats were taken, so she is seated by the window, watching the ground below. Once this landscape was hers, but it is more than a decade since she has been to the mainland, and as the dark hills of the Great Dividing Range spool by beneath she cannot help but be struck by the silence of this spine, the long curve of the Earth.

Jay has agreed to mind Eve until Kate returns. For the past two years he and Cassie have been living a few kilometres from Kate and

Eve in a house they bought not long before they got married. Despite their new domestic arrangements and the fact Eve now sees tutors as part of a home-schooling program, both have remained a part of Eve's life.

When Kate rang Jay he was solicitous. Even after all these years the two of them still fall into the habits of intimacy with surprising ease.

'How did they find you?' he asked.

'Apparently she gave them my name and details.'

'So, she knew where you were?'

'It seems so.'

'Oh, Kate, I'm so sorry.'

'I think I have to go up there, sort out her things.'

'Would you like to leave Eve with us? We'd be happy to have her.'

'Could you stay here instead?' she asked. 'I think she needs the continuity.'

Jay was silent for a moment, no doubt thinking through Cassie's reaction.

'Of course,' he said at last. 'Whatever you need.'

After she hung up she knocked on Eve's bedroom door, then went in and sat down on her bed. After convincing Eve to put down the game she was playing she told her she had to go away for a while, and explained why, keeping her words clear and simple. To her surprise Eve burst into tears. Startled, Kate leaned closer and put an arm around Eve's powerful shoulders.

'What is it?' she asked.

'Are you sad?' Eve had asked. Kate had opened her mouth to speak and then found she had nothing to say.

'I suppose,' she said at last. 'I mean yes, of course. But I haven't seen her for a long time and ...'

'And you didn't like her?'

Kate stiffened, suddenly uncomfortable. Eve has asked about her mother before, and she has always been careful not to tell her too much. 'As she got older I found her very difficult to be around. Eventually I decided not to see her anymore.'

Eve stared at her, clearly unsettled.

'But she knew where you were?'

'What do you mean?'

'Because they found you.'

Kate nodded. 'Yes. I suppose.'

Eve hesitated. Kate can tell she was thinking, worrying. 'Was it because of me?'

Kate leaned back to look at Eve, startled. 'What?'

'Were you were ashamed of me? Is that why you stopped seeing her?'

Kate stared, shocked Eve might think of herself in this way. 'No! Of course not. This all happened long before you were born.'

Eve nodded, sniffing. 'Was she sad?'

Kate swallowed. 'I don't know. I suppose so.'

Eve didn't reply. Not knowing what else to do, Kate leaned in and hugged her, pressing her close, grateful for the warmth and solidity of her, hanging on as if she might fall.

The airport is busy when she disembarks, the press of people surprising her. But as she hurries down the hall towards baggage collection she cannot help notice how down at heel it seems, its seats worn, the shops crowded with unsold things or – in two cases – seemingly unattended, the security grilles half-lowered, the spaces behind them unlit. After so long largely confined to the space of the facility and the outskirts of the city, it is a shock, but other travellers seem not to notice, hurrying by, heads bent over devices or eyes distant behind glasses. When did this happen? Is the unravelling this disrepair suggests so slow people do not notice it? Or do they just try to ignore it, losing themselves in the virtual world of their screens? On the wall, screens show footage of flooded streets, people huddled on rooftops. It could be Mozambique or Myanmar or any one of a dozen places. Kate stares at one, watching the faces of the people wading hollow-eyed through chest-deep water; they look exhausted, alone.

Outside in the car park she calls a car, and, climbing in, stares out the window in an effort to forestall conversation with the driver. As they wind northward she stares at the passing buildings, struck by the changes to the city. In Rosebery and Zetland, apartment blocks line the road. Yet despite their profusion many are unfinished, their shells open to the elements and covered with torn sheets of orange plastic, a legacy perhaps of the most recent economic crisis, while here and there other spaces stand empty, long grass poking through the broken concrete of empty blocks adorned by fading signs advertising abandoned developments.

The sun is setting by the time she reaches the hospital, the light fading. To the west the sky glows deep red, a legacy of the recent fires in Malaysia and Indonesia. At the front desk she explains she is here to collect property, surprised to hear herself stumble over the words 'my mother', and the receptionist directs her to the ward, where a distracted-looking nurse opens a drawer cabinet and produces a plastic bag, its side decorated with the logo of a department store.

Kate takes it without opening it.

'How did you find me?' she asks.

The nurse looks blank. 'I assume she had you down as next of kin.'

'Did she say how she had my number?'

The nurse shakes her head. 'I'm afraid not.'

'Was there someone here? At the end?'

'I'm not sure,' she says kindly. 'I can ask the others if you like.'

Kate shakes her head. She is not sure she wants to know. 'No,' she says. 'It's all right.' Kate hesitates before asking: 'Do you know where she was living?'

The nurse glances at a screen. 'We have an address. That's all.'

'Can you give it to me?'

The nurse looks at Kate. Finally, she nods. 'Yes, I suppose so.'

Outside the hospital Kate sits down on a seat in the garden and opens the plastic bag, recoiling from the stink of piss and stale cigarette smoke. It contains a handbag, a phone, what looks like an old tracksuit. Taking out the handbag she opens it. Inside is a jumble of junk – a pen, a broken lipstick, its base scratched and worn, a couple of receipts – as well as a red snakeskin purse and a set of keys. Opening the purse she finds a five dollar note and a couple of cards. Putting the keys to one side she places everything else back in the plastic bag and heads towards the street in search of a taxi.

The address the nurse gave her is in one of the old tower blocks in Waterloo. As the taxi pulls up Kate looks up at it. In the years after she left for California this entire area was redeveloped, the old public housing swept away and replaced with new buildings and a Metro station. Yet its facelift is already sagging, its garden beds dry and dead, the facades faded and peeling.

The lifts are out of order, so she has to use the stairs; by the time she is halfway up she is grateful the flat is on one of the middle levels, and not at the top. Pausing by the door, she takes out the keys. Choosing the one that looks most like a house key, she lifts it to the lock, but before she can slip it in the door to the flat next door opens and a woman appears. She is small, her black hair cut short and her compact body squeezed into a green floral dress.

'Oh!' she says. 'I thought you must be Claire.'

Kate shakes her head. 'No, sorry. I'm her . . . her daughter.'

The woman narrows her eyes. She has an alert, intelligent face. 'Kate?'

Kate nods, surprised. 'That's right.'

'Has something happened? Is Claire all right?'

Kate pauses. 'No, I'm afraid not. She died yesterday morning.'

The woman blinks twice. 'Oh,' she says. 'I'm sorry.' She takes a step forward. 'I'm Kina,' she says.

'You knew her?'

'A little. What happened?'

'She had a heart attack. They said she never regained consciousness.'

'That must have been a shock for you,' Kina says.

'Yes,' Kate replies. 'It was.'

The smell hits Kate as soon as she opens the door. Covering her face with her hand, she goes through to the kitchen. The room is small, bare, the sink cluttered with dirty glasses and used mugs; half a dozen empty vodka bottles stand on the draining rack, and empty wine bottles crowd the small table against the wall. Seeking the source of the stink Kate opens the bin and almost gags. Glimpsing a greasy takeaway box still filled with chicken amidst the mess of papers she yanks the bag free and, tying it shut, carries it out to the landing.

Back inside she opens the bedroom door. The room is almost empty, the only furnishings an old mattress on the floor, a chair under the window and a white metal clothes rack in the corner with a jumble of dirty garments beside it. Beside the mattress an overflowing ashtray sits alongside a pair of vodka bottles; under the chair another bottle lies on its side. At some point her mother has made an attempt to liven up the space by pinning an old scarf to the window, but the drooping fabric only emphasises the poverty of the whole.

Stepping back she glances behind herself at the living area, a wave of despair washing over her as she takes in the miserable furnishings and disarray. On the stained sofa against the far wall a quilt is bunched at one end; opposite it a television stands on a chest of drawers. Bottles and ashtrays cluster on every surface. She takes a breath, trying to steady herself, but before she can she hears a sound from the landing, and races back to the front door to find Kina holding the bag she left outside a few moments before.

'Can I help you?' she demands.

Kina backs away in surprise. 'I thought I would take this down to the waste room for you,' she says.

Kate stares at her, and Kina places the bag back down. 'I'm sorry. I was just trying to help.'

'Please, don't apologise,' Kate says, already regretting her outburst. 'It's not your fault. It's just been a long couple of days. I just . . . The apartment . . . have you been in here?'

Kina looks past her down the hall. 'Yes. Once or twice.' She pauses, as if considering what to say next. 'I had to call the police a few times,' she says at last.

Kate closes her eyes. She wants to leave, but knows she cannot. 'I'm sorry about that.'

Kina smiles. 'It wouldn't be the first time the police have been here.'

Kate takes a breath, grateful for the other woman's kindness. 'Still, I know what she could be like. It can't have been easy.'

Kina regards her carefully. 'I think she got worse as she got older. Especially after she was attacked a few years ago. I'm not sure she ever really recovered.'

'Attacked?'

Kina nods decisively. 'She was walking home one night. Apparently it was three men. They took her bag and phone, hurt her badly enough to put her in hospital. I think they wanted to keep her there but she checked herself out.'

Kate stands, unspeaking, unsteady on her feet.

'She didn't tell you?'

Kate shakes her head. 'But she spoke about me? She had my details?'

Kina nods. 'She said you were working in Tasmania.'

Kate wonders how she knew that. Did she search for her online? 'That's right.'

'You weren't in contact with her?'

'Not for a long time.'

'I remember her saying you were angry with her, that you couldn't forgive her for things that happened when you were a child.'

Kate looks up. 'She said that?'

Kina shrugs. 'She said a lot of things when she'd been drinking.'

'Did she say anything else?'

Kate can see her deciding how much to tell her. 'Nothing that matters,' she says at last.

Kate stands very still, unable to move. She has heard her mother's apologies, her self-pitying desire for absolution too many times. None of it was true. Finally she breathes out, realising she has been holding her breath this whole time.

'The flat. It's rented?'

'It's public.'

'I don't have any of her details. Is there somebody I have to notify?'

Kina stands, staring at her. 'You need to speak to the department. I can find the number.'

'Thank you,' Kate says.

Closing the door, she slumps down at the kitchen table. She had thought herself defended, that she had left all this behind. But now she is here she knows she has not. The state of the flat, the chaos of her mother's affairs – already she can glimpse what lies ahead: the unpaid bills, the overdue accounts that will need closing, the debts that will no doubt come to light. As she looks around the squalid room, Kina's words ring in her mind: *She was walking home one night. Apparently it was three men. They took her bag and phone, hurt her badly enough to put her in hospital.*

Kate has heard these stories before. When she was a child her mother would often proffer accounts of people following her or hurting her as explanations for injuries or lateness. The first time Kate recalls it happening was a Saturday afternoon when she was in her first year of school, and she had been left at her friend Emily's house. When Claire dropped her off, she told Kate she would be back later, but at some point Kate realised it was getting dark, and her mother had not returned. Emily's parents didn't say anything, but she can remember them standing in the kitchen, talking in low voices, and knowing that it was about her. Eventually Emily's mother served dinner, the four of them sitting in an uneasy quiet around the table, and later they let Kate and Emily watch television. It was almost eight when the doorbell rang, and Claire appeared. She was dishevelled, her lip bleeding and cheek bruised. When she saw her, Emily's mother gasped – Kate remembers the way she put her hand over her mouth, like a character in a play – and let her in.

Claire stumbled into the room, blinking in the light. Grabbing Kate she embraced her, kissing her and telling her she loved her, over and over again. 'I was so scared, so scared,' she said, her breath sickly and sweet. Finally she let Kate go, and straightening, began to talk, explaining that she had been attacked, and although she had escaped she'd lost her handbag and purse. 'I think they took it,' she said. 'All my money, everything.'

She had heard her mother apologise before, many times, but that night it was different. Perhaps it was the presence of Emily's parents, perhaps it was simply that it was late, and Kate was tired. But as Claire spoke Kate could not help but notice the way she swayed from side to side as she spoke, the looping, frantic nature of her story, the way it kept changing, the way she slurred her words. Nor could she help being aware of Emily's parents' silence, the way they looked at her as they said goodbye.

On Monday Emily would not speak to her, and neither would her other friends. Nor was she invited back to Emily's house. On the street a few weeks later she came around a corner to find Emily and her mother walking towards her; seeing Kate, Emily's mother placed a hand on Emily's shoulder and steered her across the street.

Even now, Kate has trouble disentangling which of her mother's stories were truth and which were lies. When she is angry she tells herself there is no point believing any of it, that what little of it was true wasn't worth knowing or, as she once said to Jay, 'if her mouth was moving, she was lying'. Half a lifetime later she is still able to surprise herself by coming across new evidence of her mother's compulsive deceits. Just six months ago, she stood on the threshold of Eve's room and found her mind snagging on the time when she was four, and they had to leave all her toys behind and move because their apartment building was being demolished, and realised that made no sense. What had happened? Had her mother not paid the rent again? Or was it something else, some conflict with a neighbour or a former lover?

Harder in many ways has been forcing herself to understand that her mother's drunken professions of love, her weeping apologies and promises to change or get sober were just empty words, that in the end the only person her mother cared about was herself. Jay always said she had to let her anger go, but what he could not understand was that without the anger she was afraid she would have nothing left.

Nor has she ever really been sure how much of her own bullshit her mother believed, to what extent her lies and fantasies consumed her. When she was thirteen she went away on school camp – the trip paid for by the school – and arrived back to discover that her mother was not waiting to pick her up. Her friend Lily's mother was worried, and offered to drive her home, but Kate assured her it wasn't a surprise, that she had always intended to catch the train.

It was dark by the time she got home, and as soon as she got out of the lift she knew something was wrong. For the past six months her mother's boyfriend, Paul, had been living with them, but the night before Kate left for camp he and Claire had fought, and Paul had stormed out. Kate had assumed he would be back, but as she pulled her bag down the corridor she saw a pile of what looked like his clothes heaped against the wall.

The apartment was dark but the front door was open. Kate stopped in front of it, staring in. The floor inside was wet and a trickle of water had leaked out onto the landing, soaking the carpet so it squelched beneath her feet.

Uneasy, she called her mother's name, then Paul's, but there was no answer. Finally she placed her bag against the wall, and went in. She trod carefully, quietly, afraid that if somebody had broken in they might still be there, waiting. Outside the living room she stopped and scanned the room; seeing no one, she took another breath and moved on. By the door to her mother's bedroom she stopped. It was half-closed. She lifted her hand and, before she could lose her nerve, pushed on it, her heart leaping in her chest at the sound of it against the carpet.

Nothing moved. The room seemed to be empty, though it was difficult to tell in the darkness. Taking a breath, she followed the stream of water towards the bathroom. Inside, the room was empty but the shower was running, water spilling across the floor, its surface reflecting the yellow light that shone through the window set high in the wall. Frightened now, she turned and ran into the kitchen.

At first she thought it was empty as well, but then she caught sight of someone slumped against the stove.

'Mum!'

Claire jerked away, her eyes unfocused, confused.

'Mum?' she repeated, moving closer and kneeling down. Although the kitchen was dark, some light fell through the window, enough for her to see that her mother's hair was dripping and her sodden dressing gown clung to her pale skin.

Her mother flinched again, then turned to stare at her. Her eyes were wide.

'Kate?' she said, disbelievingly. Kate recoiled from the rank stink of vomit on her breath.

'It's me, Mum,' Kate said. 'What's happened? Are you okay? Where's Paul?'

Claire stared at her again, then looked away. 'Not here,' she said, almost to herself.

'Why are you wet, Mum? Why's the shower on?'

Her mother looked at her, and for a moment Kate saw something else there, something cunning and cruel. 'They were outside,' her mother said. 'I had to hide.'

'Who was outside?'

'The men.'

'I don't understand.'

'They wanted to come in. I wouldn't let them.'

'What men? Do you mean Paul?'

'Not Paul. Other men.'

Kate looked around. 'Are they still here?'

Claire closed her eyes again and lolled back. 'I don't know,' she said, her voice slurred and sleepy. 'I think they're gone.'

Her mother hiccoughed, and began to snore. Kate stood up, suddenly disgusted by the gross physicality of her.

'I'm going to turn the shower off,' she said, but Claire didn't answer.

When her mother appeared the next morning she seemed to have no memory of the night before, instead sitting next to Kate and peppering her with questions about her camp and school. When Kate could take no more she went back into her room and took out her homework. She had a high, thin headache and had barely slept: after getting her mother to bed the night before she had spent several hours trying to dry the carpet and tidy up. Her mother had clearly barely eaten in the week Kate was gone; instead the bins were filled with empty bottles and cigarette butts.

Paul was gone as well. Not just his clothes, but the television he had brought with him and his collection of DVDs. Kate wasn't sorry – if anything she was relieved, grateful she would not have to avoid him in the bathroom or listen to his dirty jokes or feel his eyes on her when he was in the room. Paul had a way of sitting still and staring at her that made her skin crawl. But through it all the thing she had not been able to put aside was the image of her mother staring at the empty doorway, the look of cunning on her face, the growing awareness that whatever it was her mother had thought had happened had not actually happened, that she had invented it, or worse yet, imagined it. Had she meant to punish Paul somehow? Or perhaps to show him and Kate how wounded she was in some desperate bid for sympathy? Or were the intruders phantoms she half-believed were there?

Seated there, in the ruin of her mother's apartment she realises she will never know.

She spends the night in a hotel opposite the train station. Once she could have called a friend, but she has long since lost contact with everybody she knew up here. She knows it should worry her, to be so alone, that her lack of social connection echoes her mother's, yet it doesn't, or not in any way she can easily describe.

She also knows she is not alone in this. A few years earlier, before the baby and Davis and Eve, she had received a call from a woman who began by saying, 'Kate? Hi, it's me, Vanessa,' as if they were picking up a conversation from the day before. Kate recognised her voice, but it was several seconds before she realised she was a school friend Kate had not seen in more than a decade.

Like Kate, Vanessa had been an outsider, though in her case it was by choice. Her parents were always easy to spot at school events: her father – immediately recognisable by his mane of grey hair and meticulously tailored vintage suits – was a painter, and was almost thirty years older than Vanessa's mother, who composed music for films. In retrospect Kate understands their bohemian cool was sustained by family wealth, yet at the time she mistook their sprawling, shabby house and separateness from the world of the school for a principled rejection of convention.

In her last few years of school Kate took to spending long periods of time at Vanessa's, sleeping over most weekends and doing homework at her kitchen table rather than going home in the evenings. At the time she assumed Vanessa's parents were just being kind, although now she suspects they knew enough about Kate's circumstances to understand that Kate needed help. And although Kate and Vanessa weren't particularly alike in temperament or interests they became close, falling into a friendship of convenience that was, in many ways, genuine.

Kate had only been back from America for a few months, and had few contacts in Sydney, so they agreed to meet for a drink. Kate arrived early, worried she might not recognise Vanessa. But when she appeared she knew her at once.

Seated at a table in the corner of a bar in Newtown they had no trouble finding things to talk about, moving from old friends to their own lives. Vanessa had been living with a man she had met at university, but they had separated a year ago, and now Vanessa was living alone.

Finally Kate asked about her parents. She knew they had separated not long after she and Vanessa finished school, her mother moving away somewhere, leaving her father alone. A look of pain passed across Vanessa's face, and she looked down at the table. Finally she shrugged.

'My mum is living up in Blackheath, she said. 'But my father died last year,' she said. 'Not long after Ben and I broke up.'

'I'm sorry,' Kate said. 'I didn't realise.'

Vanessa looked at her. Her eyes were bright, the grief still close.

'No reason you should.'

'Was it quick?'

Vanessa shrugged again. 'Not really. He was eighty-five, his body just gave up.'

'I'm so sorry. I always liked him.'

Vanessa nodded. 'You think because you know it's coming it will be easier, that you'll be prepared. But you're not. It's like one day you're somewhere you know and the next day you're standing on another shore looking back at this world.'

Kate didn't reply. A moment later Vanessa collected herself and smiled, her manner suggesting the subject was now closed. Half an hour later she left and Kate never heard from her again.

She wakes early, eats alone. A quick search leads her to a funeral company a suburb away; after making an appointment for later in the morning she settles in to trying to tie up her mother's affairs.

The process is strange, the business of death rendering the loss itself almost banal. On one call she is put through to an actual human being, a woman with a broad Australian accent who delivers a checklist of things to look into in a bored, businesslike voice, then pauses and asks how she's coping, and the simple humanity of the question almost undoes her.

At the funeral parlour she is interviewed by a woman whose performance of fake sympathy sets her teeth on edge. Clearly unwilling to believe Kate is genuine in her claim to know almost nothing of her mother's life – or perhaps pruriently hoping for some admission as to the reasons for it – she keeps circling back to the question of whether the smallest chapel will be large enough, and pressing Kate on the question of numbers and speakers. Finally Kate sets down the tablet and pushes it back towards the woman.

'She was quite isolated,' she says, her voice hard.

The woman stares at her, and for a brief moment Kate glimpses the mix of stupidity and belligerence that lurks behind her simpering manner. Then the woman smiles and picks up the tablet.

'Of course,' she says.

Back at the apartment, though, she finds herself unready for the rush of emotion that greets her as she goes through her mother's things.

She has come equipped with plastic bags and cleaning products, but once she is inside she finds herself overcome by the wretchedness of the place. The kitchen is the worst: its cupboards almost bare, save for the bottles stuffed in here and there, some finished, others half-empty. In one drawer she finds two empty bottles of vodka and half a dozen pieces of cutlery, in another three plates and a chipped bowl. In a box in a drawer she finds a half-eaten pizza, the pieces dessicated and dry with age.

When she is done she steps out onto the balcony. This complex is supposed to be mixed use, a combination of public housing and high-cost development, and through the windows of the building next door she can see people moving around, talking and laughing, a young boy doing his homework, a pair of teenage girls in headsets dancing. Families, she thinks, normality. Not something she ever knew, not something she can ever provide. She feels weightless, untethered, unsure why she is here or where she is going.

After she locks up she heads back towards the hotel. The sky is yellow, the air heavy with smoke. It is August, and there are fires, though that is no longer new. A solitary bird flies fast against the sky. Sometimes it seems the whole world is burning. A few days ago she watched a report on one of Davis's projects, a vast park in Lithuania he had hoped to re-wild with wolves and auroch and giant sturgeon, as well as mammoth and other creatures. The mammoth are beautiful: vast russet mountains that tower over the landscape and sway slowly as they walk, the wonder of them undiminished by the decade that has passed since they were first created. The first specimens were raised by African elephants, whose social structures the mammoth were thought to share, and though that was successful, as their numbers have grown they have formed their own clans, some larger than those of the elephants, some smaller.

What the report didn't reveal is that Davis's efforts seem to be making things worse rather than better. Jay is careful in his assessments, but she knows the reforestation programs have not been working, and while some of the resurrected fauna seem to be thriving, other animal populations in the regions Davis's programs are being implemented are not recovering. If anything, rates of mortality have risen. In Canada, moose and deer have been dying in their millions, their bodies scattering the tundra, while in the Pacific, seals and walrus have been dying in waves as well, seals lying down on the rocks and not waking, the starving walrus struggling onto beaches to fight and perish in their thousands. Elsewhere, other populations are simply disappearing: insects, reptiles, amphibians, fish. Sometimes the causes are clear: habitat loss or pesticide or warming waters; more often they just seem to vanish.

This sense of accelerating collapse haunts her. Online somebody has started something called the Extinction Diaries, a site on which the details of these disappearances are catalogued. Sometimes there will be video, images that dance across the screen, ghostly reminders of the lost; more often there will simply be a photo or two; sometimes there will be nothing more than a name. Despite herself Kate has taken to checking back, daily, sometimes more.

There is something numbing about this process, a sense that with each new diminution the world slips further out of alignment. Yet while Jay and Cassie and many of her colleagues feel the same, few of them talk about it, except in the most guarded terms, and out in the street or the supermarket it is as if nothing has changed. Do people not feel it, the way death shadows them? This sense the world is coming apart? This sense they are all a part of it?

Back at the hotel she calls Jay, asks to speak to Eve. When Eve comes on, her voice is soft, faraway.

'What have you been doing?' Kate asks, and as Eve details her day, Kate's heart clenches. She only wants this to be finished, to be back there. And when Eve is done, Jay picks up again.

'How is it?' he asks.

Kate swallows and stares out the window. 'Difficult.'

'But you knew that.'

'It's worse than I expected. It's just such a waste.'

'It's not your fault.'

She pauses. 'I know. How's Eve?'

There is a brief pause. She knows Jay is looking at Eve.

'She's well. Busy.'

'Has she been doing her lessons?'

'Of course.' A moment passes. 'What is it?' Jay asks.

'Do you think she's happy?'

'I do.'

'But what will happen to her? Once she grows up? Once we're gone?'

There is a long silence. They have talked often, both within the team and privately, about her education, about her future. For years now they have cleaved to a strategy devised when she was young, in which she is taught privately and then assisted into some kind of role with the Foundation. Yet this is not a plan, not a blueprint for a life. Who will love her, befriend her, share her days? And what if there is no world left to grow up for? When Eve is asked she says she wants to be a scientist, or a ranger in one of the parks, but Kate knows these ideas are not really real to her.

'I don't know,' Jay finally says. In his voice Kate can hear the same pain she feels when she thinks about Eve's future, about her part in making it. 'We just have to do all we can to make sure she's ready for it.'

Kate nods. 'I have to go,' she says.

The memorial is scheduled for ten o'clock, the first of the day, and as Kate steps out of the car the funeral director is waiting for her by the door. Kate greets her quickly, not lingering to talk, then goes through into the foyer.

There are only a handful of attendees. Kina, a pair of older women Kate does not recognise, a confused-looking man with rheumy eyes and white hair in a dark suit and sneakers. Kina notices Kate and waits while one of the older women finishes saying something before excusing herself and crossing to where Kate stands.

'Thank you for coming,' Kate says.

'Of course. I saw you finished cleaning out her apartment.'

'If there's anything you want, please let me know.'

Kina nods. 'I will.' Before she can say more the funeral director approaches to say they are ready to begin, and in a straggling line the five of them head in.

The service is brief, almost businesslike, the celebrant speaking in generalities she has clearly mouthed many times before. When she spoke with the funeral director on the day after she arrived Kate was adamant she did not want to speak: there was nothing for her to say; she and her mother had not had a relationship for twenty years, but as soon as the moment when she could have spoken passes she knows she has made a mistake, that she should have found some form of words to describe her feelings, that whatever else she was, her mother was still her mother. She is surprised to feel tears fill her eyes as the coffin slides away, but afterwards she only wants to be away, and is relieved when the others show no sign of lingering.

On the way to the airport she remembers a conversation the year before. Hugh, one of the researchers employed on the wider project, had taken her aside after a meeting at the facility.

'I need to ask you something,' he said. 'About Eve. She is what I think she is, isn't she?'

Caught off-guard, Kate hesitated. Hugh watched her intently. Seeing there was no point denying it, she gave a quick nod.

To her surprise, Hugh smiled. 'I googled you, saw you'd been involved since the beginning. It didn't take long to put two and two together, although I'll be honest with you: I didn't really believe it until just now, and I'm still not sure I do.'

'You mustn't tell anybody,' she said.

'Of course not,' he said. 'How did you end up caring for her?'

'It's a long story. I was part of the team that carried out the genesis but when . . . when I saw her I realised what we'd done – that she wasn't an experiment, she was a child, a person – I left and took her with me.'

'And they let you do that?'

She shook her head. 'No. When they found me I had to fight to keep her.'

He regarded her thoughtfully for a few seconds. Then he turned and looked at Eve, who was waiting a little way ahead. 'She's extraordinary. I've seen her out in the bush near the facility. There's a . . . a stillness to her. An alertness.'

Kate followed his gaze. Perhaps feeling herself observed, Eve turned to look at them, her face wary in the way Kate knew so well.

'She's more comfortable out there than in the city, or with people.'

'You think that's genetic?'

'I don't know. Sometimes, I suppose. But other times I think it's just her. Or her and me. Or just everything.'

'Is she the only one?'

Kate hesitated. 'As far as I know. Why?'

Hugh looked thoughtful. 'It must be very strange, to be alone like that. There are animals I've seen, birds mostly, that are the last of their kind. Endlings, we call them.' He paused, as if something was troubling him. 'Does she know?'

Kate looked aside. Cassie and the other psychologist have long argued it is better to wait until Eve is older to tell her the truth, partly because they believe she will be better prepared emotionally, partly because of a fear she might find in it an excuse to impose limitations on herself.

'No,' she said after a moment.

There is a small silence. 'Is that fair?'

'What would it change if she knew?'

'Possibly everything. And there are practical considerations. What if something happens to you, and she gets sick? Or she wants to have children?'

Kate does not reply at once. Finally she just says, 'Or it would just make her feel even more alone.'

As she boards the plane she is still thinking about Hugh's words. Once, she would have believed everybody had a right to know where they came from, that withholding this sort of information was a kind of abuse, but now she is not so sure. Would it make things better for Eve to know the truth? Or worse? And what would it really change?

Yet simultaneously she knows her reluctance to share the truth with Eve is as much about her own fears as it is about concern for

Eve's wellbeing. What if Eve is angry? What if she blames Kate for not telling her sooner, or for her part in creating her?

Without realising why, she begins to cry again. She feels unmoored, lost, but she knows what she must do. And when she arrives home she tells Jay, and together the three of them sit down.

Kate takes Eve's hands, squeezes them tight. Her eyes are bright with tears, her heart so full she thinks it will burst. 'There's something we have to tell you.'

I WAS A TEENAGE
NEANDERTHAL

In the weeks after Kate and Jay tell her the truth about herself Eve cannot make sense of it. What can it mean? Who is she? Is this why she feels so different? So alone? Despite Kate's efforts to coax her out she retreats to her room, watching videos and searching the web for information.

The details online are scattered, contradictory, meaningless. They – her; the gap between the two seems incapable of collapse – were either less intelligent or as intelligent as modern humans, could probably talk, or couldn't, buried their dead and created art or were primitive brutes incapable of symbolic thought. These propositions are debated and contradicted over and over. Behind them are other suggestions. They were violent, brutal, cannibals. They were simply less successful, were outcompeted. They were exterminated. There is a story she returns to more than once, of the last population of her kind, trapped on the edge of the Iberian peninsula. A dying community. Sometimes she tries to imagine their lives. What was it like to be so alone? Did they know they were the last?

And then there are the images. So many are grotesque, hulking monsters. But even those that are not monsters bear little resemblance to her. One evening she calls up a virtual tour of the Natural History Museum, steps into its Hall of Mankind. The figures that populate it are so lifelike it is unsettling, but though she recognises their thick hair, the large eyes and wide noses from her own mirror, she cannot bear to approach them.

Disturbed by Eve's behaviour, Kate insists she accompany her to the facility in order to speak to the psychologist. Until recently Eve enjoyed their sessions; now the psychologist's desire to explore her feelings leaves her bored and resentful, aware of the way the woman watches her, her anatomising gaze, and after one particularly frustrating session Eve simply refuses to go back. In the car Kate presses her to know why, asking her whether she is okay, but Eve just stares out the window at the passing scenery and ignores her.

Is she the creatures she sees online? Ugly, hulking, misshapen? When she is alone – on her bike or moving through the forest – she feels strong, fast, free in motion. Yet she also sees her body in the mirror every morning and evening, its broad shoulders and heavy musculature misshapen, lumpen. Is this what others see? Although her mother has forbidden her to go there alone, one afternoon when Kate is at work she rides her bike to the shopping centre on the city's edge, and for a time can feel all eyes on her, cannot shake the sense they are watching her, mocking her.

One night, alone with her screen, she stumbles on a movie about cavemen, sits watching the grunting, fur-clad figures lope through the sun-blasted landscape of the Los Angeles hills. It is absurd, yet she cannot put it out of her mind, images of the bestial cavemen and women returning to her again and again.

After that she seeks out other movies, not just about cavemen but about robots and monsters and patchwork people, all the uncanny golems of the Gothic imagination. Across that winter and into the summer she watches everything she can find, looking for guidance in films: *Frankenstein*, *Splice*, *Blade Runner*. Every time the story is the same: the thing created is monstrous but also tragic, its desire for life a violation of the natural order. Is this why her mother and Jay keep her away from people, why they are so careful to control her movements, even at the facility? Would she be shunned, tormented, driven out? She watches the villagers pursue the Monster through the streets, torches aloft, and cannot move, her hands gripping the screen. Under their trilbies the men's faces are no different from those of the people she glimpses at the Facility, but it is not them that frighten her the most. Instead it is the snarling dogs she cannot take her eyes off; as they strain at their ropes she can almost feel their hot breath, the snap of their jaws.

Finally, a year after she learns the truth, an alert leads her to an article about a cave discovered in Gibraltar, its entrance concealed thirty metres below the water. The team that locates it have been exploring the Mediterranean, combing its bed for remnants of towns and settlements lost when the water rose at the end of the last Ice Age, and came upon it by accident. Clad in wetsuit and wearing scuba gear, the lead archaeologist crawled upward, through a shaft, into a space sealed from the air above, a bubble in the rock, its air fifty thousand years old.

This was one of the last places her ancestors survived, eking out an existence in these caves, yet as the diver shone her light upward she saw marks on the wall, etched lines and crosses, and over them the dark mark of charcoal.

Armed with photos, the diver left, but when her team returned they found a wealth of remains – bones, charcoal, carved bone, entire skeletons, all layered one on top of the other. And perhaps most incredibly, at the back of the cave, a wall adorned with dozens of handprints outlined in ochre.

At first there was debate: these markings on the stone must be the work of modern humans, equipped with brains capable of creating art, minds lit by fire and an awareness of the presence of meaning in the world. But the remains in the cave were definitely Neanderthal, and dating proved the marks were of the same vintage. Even in the face of this evidence the notion the handprints are the work of Neanderthals has been vociferously resisted by many in the scientific community.

Yet the details of the debate concern her less than the images, which have been assembled into a virtual re-creation of the cave, complete with a journey up the shaft through the water. Setting aside the screen for Kate's goggles, Eve moves through the cave, staring at the scratches on the wall, the charcoal marks, their mute incomprehensibility. What do they mean? What was it they needed to record? Are they a map? A drawing? A set of ritual shapes possessed of other significance again? The impossibility of knowing eats at her, echoed by the feeling she almost understands, that she holds the key in her mind, that their meaning, like a word or a name half-remembered, lies somewhere just out of reach.

But it is only when she is done, and she walks deeper into the cave and finds the handprints, that she finally understands. For there, in that pale-walled gallery, where once firelight flickered, illuminating this record of so many lives, of so much time, she lifts a hand and places it on one of them, suddenly aware that it fits, time telescoping in a rush like wind.

The next summer arrives early, the baking air heavy with smoke. Early in December she is woken one morning by a rumble like distant thunder and finds her room moving around her, the lampshade overhead swinging. Whimpering, she slithers off the bed, her gut sick with fear, and braces herself against it. On her shelf a book topples over with a heavy thump, sending a cup of pens and textas and paperclips spilling onto the floor. And then, almost as soon as it began, it is over. Eve takes a breath – it seems to have lasted forever and no time at all – and runs for the door. Kate is in the hall, staring around. Her face is pale, her eyes wild. Eve hurls herself into Kate's arms.

'It's okay,' Kate says. 'You're all right.'

Pressing her face into Kate's neck Eve drinks in her mother's smell and nods. Her legs are shaking, the sense of wrongness that gripped her in her bedroom still not dissipated.

'What was it?' she whimpers. 'What happened?'

'I think it must have been an earthquake,' Kate says.

'Will it happen again?' Eve feels sick at the thought of it.

Kate strokes her hair. 'I don't know.'

In fact, it happens three more times. After the second, Eve realises she can feel the tremors coming before they arrive, the intimation of their approach like the foreboding of an impending storm. Knowing they will simply make her take more tests she does not tell anybody, holding this small act of defiance to herself. At first nobody seems to know what is causing the quakes, but after the third, Kate tells her scientists believe they are caused by the crust shifting as the Antarctic ice sheet buckles and breaks, a process that should take place over thousands of years but is instead rushing forward. Later, outside in the heat, Eve closes her eyes and tries to imagine the ice, its cool blue, the ancient silence at its core, but she cannot.

*

Although it is several years since Eve met regularly with the other children from the playgroup, they have kept in touch. At the urging of the Foundation, Rose and Heti were home-schooled, and for a time Eve attended classes with them several days a week. Eventually Heti's mother took a job on the mainland and Rose began working with a different group of home-schoolers, but for several years after that Rose and Felix continued to visit intermittently. Felix stopped coming the summer he turned eleven, although he and Eve chat online sometimes, but even now, a decade after they began playgroup together, Rose still visits for a few days every holidays. Whether Rose submits to the arrangement out of duty or some less easily defined sense that her relationship with Eve connects her to her past, she seems happy to spend days at a time watching movies on their screens or wandering in the bush. Last winter she brought makeup and combs, and while Kate worked she showed Eve how to style her hair and apply lipstick and mascara; Kate blinked back tears as the two of them appeared, giggling with delight, Rose already long-limbed, her hair piled high on her head in an awkward imitation of the 1960s, Eve's coarse, red-brown hair in a high ponytail, sparkling powder sheening on her wide cheekbones, pink lip-gloss bright against her pale skin.

Rose comes twice more after Eve learns about herself. Both times Kate sits down with Eve before she arrives, emphasises the importance of keeping the truth to herself. But when Kate suggests Rose come again this summer, Eve says she does not want to see her. In the moment after she speaks a silence falls.

'Really? Why?' Kate asks.

Eve does not move. She had not realised she was going to refuse until she did, but her mother's reaction is oddly thrilling. 'I don't feel like it.'

Kate pauses, but Eve just stares back. Now she has made it real the thought of not seeing Rose is like a hollow pain, but she ignores it.

'Perhaps you can come to work with me instead,' Kate says.

Eve shakes her head. 'I'm not going to the facility anymore.' She hesitates. 'And I don't want Cassie to come here, either.'

'But you'll be alone.'

Eve snorts. 'Good,' she says.

Afterwards, in her room, she opens her screen, calls up Felix and Rose and Heti's accounts and deletes them from her contacts. Setting the screen aside, she stares at the wall, unsure whether she wants to laugh or cry.

Left alone in the heat, she takes to riding long distances. Sometimes she sees bushwalkers, their figures strung out on the hillsides as they push through the scrub, or children playing. One day she rides for two hours, right to the outskirts of the city. Standing under a tree she gazes down at the buildings along the wide space of the river, the dark weight of the mountain behind them. Although it terrifies her she goes back the next night, and the night after that, guiding her bike down the silent avenues, staring at the people on the streets and in the windows. Sometimes cars stop beside her, their occupants turning to gaze at her through the glass. In the dark with her helmet on she is anonymous, but still, there are times when a passenger starts or stares, and the feeling is like a knife in her belly.

As the days shorten and the winter begins to bear down, she spends more and more time out on the road. One morning in April she rides her bike into a shopping centre on the city's fringes and circles around the car park, watching the cars pull in and out. She is about to leave and head out towards one of the bush tracks when she hears somebody call her name behind her. Startled, she turns to find a dark-haired figure jogging after her. She hesitates, confused, but then he calls her name again, and all at once she recognises him, the knowledge falling into place like a key. He comes to a halt in front of her.

'Sami?' she says.

He grins. 'Eve! It *is* you!' he replies triumphantly.

'What are you doing here?'

'Shopping. You?'

'Nothing. Riding.' She cannot take her eyes off him. Three years earlier, when Sami turned twelve, he began to act out, skipping school and disappearing for long periods. When Yassamin tried to discipline him he went to stay with his father. At first Yassamin thought it was just a phase, that he would be back before long, but he has not returned. Seeing him again she is not sure she would have known him if he had not called her name: though she now sees the shadow of the boy she knew in him, he is taller, thinner, his black eyes liquid. Even his manner is different: distracted, twitchier, his childish cheer infected by a sort of restlessness. Yet when he smiles, the Sami she knew – foolish, playful, needful – is there again.

'Is your mum here?' she asks, and Sami shakes his head, his face darkening. 'Nah. I'm with Dad now. I thought you knew.'

Eve nods, but before she can ask him anything more she notices a figure behind him. Like Sami he is dressed in dark clothes, yet where Sami is soft-faced he is all angles, narrow black jeans protruding from a battered army jacket.

'This is Lukas,' Sami says.

If Lukas is surprised by her appearance he gives no sign of it. Instead he stares at her with a directness she finds uncomfortable. Eve looks down, embarrassed. 'Hi,' he says.

'Are you still living where you were?' Sami asks.

Eve nods. She feels thick-limbed, awkward, painfully aware of her stumbling speech. 'Yes, same place,' she says, gesturing behind her. Sami follows her gaze, his stare distant, unfocused.

'Up on the mountain road?'

'Just past there.'

Sami nods. 'There's a party up that way tonight. You should come.'

Eve looks uncomfortable. 'Where? In the forest?'

'Up one of the old logging trails. I can send you the details.'

Eve can feel Lukas staring at her. Her mother's warnings about outsiders replay in her mind. 'I don't know,' she says.

'Come on,' says Sami. 'Meet us.'

Eve takes a step back. There is something childlike in Sami's face, a lack of focus. It makes her anxious, but still, it is exciting.

'Perhaps,' she says.

She rides back along the highway, ignoring the cars and trucks as they roar by. She cannot stop thinking about Sami's invitation. She has come across the traces of parties in the forest before – discarded bottles and empty cups and still-smouldering fires, the stink of spilled beer and piss and marijuana – and she once watched one from the trees, marvelling at the fire dancers and the thump of the music, but she has never stepped into their circle, never joined them. Yet seeing Sami again has made her wonder whether there is something she is missing out on, whether her isolation is really loneliness.

Kate is out when she arrives home. She locks her bike in its place under the overhanging eave, steps into the house. Once, when she was younger, Kate made a point of never leaving her alone, meaning the house was never empty: even when Kate was working and it was quiet Eve knew she was there, her silent presence filling the house.

But recently Eve has come to enjoy her mother's absence, the sense she is unscrutinised.

In her room she pulls off her jacket and lies on the bed. Closing her eyes, she reaches inward, calls up Sami's smell, the warm friendliness of him. It was good seeing him again even if he seemed different. Is that because he is living with his father? She once asked why Yassamin did not like Sami's father and Kate had been deliberately vague in the way she is when she does not want to talk about something.

Opening her eyes, she rolls onto her side and stares out the window. The cloud is low, grey.

Her phone pings. *Are you coming?*

She stares at it for a few seconds. Then types. *Yes. Tell me where.*

Getting away is not easy. First, Kate lingers in the living room, staring at her screen and making notes. Then, even after she says goodnight and closes the door to her bedroom, Eve can hear her moving around in her room. After she finally goes quiet Eve waits another fifteen minutes, watching the seconds tick by on the clock Jay gave her when she was eight, before slipping out the door, down the hall, and into the night.

Out on the road the night is immense, the only sound the whirr of her tyres on the asphalt, the soft shifting of the trees and the occasional screech of a possum. She is nervous, but also excited. For a moment she tries to imagine what Kate would do if she caught her – the idea of her mother's anger and concern pleases her, then almost immediately upsets her, and she leans forward to pedal harder, as if by so doing she can outride the feeling.

Near the turnoff to the trail, she dismounts. In the distance she can feel the low throb of music, the occasional murmur of voices, but otherwise it is silent. Rolling her bike along the verge she looks around, her heart beating fast. Have they already left? Has she missed them? And then, up ahead, a figure detaches itself from the liquid dark of the trees and steps forward, his face pale in the moonlight.

In the darkness behind Sami is the red glow of a cigarette, the shadowed outline of Lukas's face.

'I thought you weren't going to turn up,' Sami says.

'My mum wouldn't go to bed,' Eve says.

'Doesn't she know you're here?'

Eve shakes her head.

'That's okay?' Sami asks, and Eve nods, although she is trembling.

'Cool,' Sami says.

Eve stows her bike out of sight among the trees and they turn up the trail. Sami walks beside her, talking rapidly, but Eve is nervous and distracted by the acrid reek of Lukas's cigarette. She feels edgy, agitated. Halfway there they hear a whoop from behind, and three figures race past hooting and shouting. As the last one passes he slows and turns to them, his pale face and wispy beard glowing, and lifts a hand, shouting, 'Wild, brother!' Sami slaps his hand in response, then steps aside as the man extends his hand to Eve. She is momentarily confused but then realises what is expected of her and strikes his palm in return. A wide grin creases the young man's face, and to her surprise Eve finds herself smiling as well. He hollers again, and leaping in the air twists away, already bounding up the path ahead of them. Sami turns to her, grinning, excitement arcing between them like electricity.

Lukas looks back down the path towards them. 'Come on,' he says.

The music grows louder as they approach, sound booming through the forest, but it is not until they step out into the clearing that the full extent of the crowd becomes apparent. There are maybe a hundred people, some dancing, some standing around a giant bonfire, others watching a group of fire dancers twirl flame above their heads. Eve hesitates, ready to bolt from the booming music, the smell of so many bodies, but before she can Sami grabs her hand and pulls her into the press of bodies.

It is dizzying, terrifying, too much all at once, and as she stumbles on, people turn to her, grinning and talking, their faces looming out of the dark. She keeps her eyes down, but still, more than once she glimpses their startled expressions as they catch her eye then freeze and stare or look away, pretending they have not noticed her at all. At one point a bearded man with blue eyes beneath close-cropped hair fixes his gaze on her, detaching himself from the people he is talking with to stare after her, and for a few seconds Eve tenses, afraid he is going to chase after her, grab her. By the time they reach the fire she is shaking.

Next to her, Sami is snaking his head back and forth in time to the music, his eyes darting this way and that as if he were looking for someone. He glances at her and grins.

'Everything okay?' he asks, his face bright in the firelight.

Eve forces herself to smile and nod.

Sami grins. 'I told you it'd be great.'

Lukas appears beside Sami, three beers in his hands. Sami and he exchange a look, then Sami reaches into his pocket and pulls out a plastic bag full of pills. Angling his body away from Eve, he shakes one out and slips it into Lukas's hand. Lukas lifts it to his mouth and swallows it in one quick, clean motion and washes it down with beer.

'What's that?' Eve asks, leaning towards Sami.

He glances at her, and for a brief moment she sees somebody else behind his eyes.

'Nothing,' he says. 'Just pills.' Then he smiles, and the old Sami is back.

Eve stares at him. 'I want one.'

Sami laughs, surprised. 'Nah, Eve. I don't think so.'

'Why not?'

He straightens, and glances at Lukas, who stares at the two of them as if they were of scientific interest only.

'I don't know. What about your mum . . .'

'I don't care.'

Sami regards her for a second longer. Then he shakes out two more pills and hands one to Eve. She sweeps it up and swallows it in one quick motion, wincing at the bitter chemical aftertaste. Lukas hands her a beer and she gulps it down, then coughs, disgusted by the sharp yeasty rush of it.

Sami is staring at her.

'What now?' she asks.

He grins. 'Dunno. Let's see who's here.'

At first the pill doesn't seem to do anything. She follows Sami and Lukas through the crowd, nodding hello to the various people who greet them as they pass and pausing here and there to look around. For a while they watch the fire dancers, their bodies sweaty in the frigid air as they leap and twirl. The flames on their sticks shift and fly, leaving patterns of sparks in the sky, shifting and parting as they rise. At some point Eve realises the lights seem brighter, the sound louder. Turning, she stares through the crowd, sees people smiling at her, realises she is smiling back. Beside her, Sami catches her eye and grins, and a wave of feeling washes through her, filling her chest and hands. She closes her eyes, losing herself in it for what might be a minute or only a few seconds, and when she opens them again Sami is holding her hand.

'We should dance,' he says. She nods, following him across the broken ground to where dancers are moving in front of the speakers, hands above their heads as they shift and sway. Lifting her arms, she feels the same wash of feeling all over again, the music moving through her, filling her, so her body seems all sensation. For a time she loses Lukas, and then Sami, but then they are there again, and she embraces them, delighted.

After a time they find themselves on the edge of the dancers, and as if by mutual consent they move away and sit in a space beneath the trees. Another girl has joined Lukas; she has dark hair in dreadlocks, and she smiles at Eve. Sami produces a bottle of water and takes a swig, then hands it to Eve, and she drinks, surprised to discover she is thirsty. Whatever it is the drug is doing to her is changing, she realises, the intensity dissipating, replaced by a desire to talk. Next to her Sami is staring around, his head bobbing in time to the music. Eve places a hand on his arm and he turns to her, his face filled with a look of uncomplicated happiness that makes her realise how guarded he has always seemed.

'Thank you for bringing me,' she says, and he grins.

'You're having fun?'

'So much,' she says.

Later they dance again, and she takes another pill, then the three of them and the girl – whose name seems to be Marina – decide to head up into the forest.

'There's a house up there we can stay in,' Lukas says. Eve and Sami and Marina laugh and talk as they follow him and the light of his torch up a path, and then there it is, a timber structure standing in a small clearing. Lukas produces a key and leans into the door, pushing it open, and they all stumble in. Lukas's torch dances about the space, revealing bunks, a wooden floor, a camp stove, then there is a soft whoosh and a match flares into light, followed by a lamp.

'They should have LEDs,' Sami laughs, and Lukas nods.

'This stuff has been here for years,' he says.

'How do you know about this place?' Eve asks, and for what seems the first time all night Lukas looks at her.

'Lukas spends most of every weekend up here in the forest,' Sami says.

Lukas keeps his eyes fixed on Eve as Sami speaks. Uncomfortable under his scrutiny she looks away.

'I found it a few months ago. There are others further up,' he says.

Across the room Marina has taken her coat off and is lying back on one of the bunks.

'Have you got more pills?' she asks.

Sami laughs and pulls the bag from his pocket. 'Loads,' he says. 'Do you want one?' But Marina waves it away.

'Maybe later.'

They settle in, talking and dancing to songs on Sami's phone. At some point Eve finds herself talking to Lukas and Marina, when Marina takes a handful of her hair and strokes it.

'You have beautiful hair,' the girl says, and Eve smiles, blushing.

'Eve has always been beautiful,' Sami says.

Marina looks at him. 'What do you mean?'

'Our mums were friends when we were kids. I used to go visit her in the mountains.'

Marina looks amazed. 'And you're still friends now?'

'Nah,' Sami says, his old playfulness returning. 'We just met up again today.'

'Still,' Marina says.

Later Eve finds herself lying next to Sami on one of the bunks. She has taken another pill, and whatever they are doing to her has changed again.

'Do you ever see Yassamin?' Eve asks. Sami turns away and stares at the bunk above them.

'Not really. Do you?'

Eve shrugs. 'She still visits from time to time. Do you miss her?'

Sami stares up at the mattress above them, thinking. 'I don't know. Not really. She was on me all the time, telling me what to do, hassling me. It was too much.'

'And your father?'

'He's an arsehole, but I can stay out of his way.'

Eve glances across at the others. 'And Lukas?'

Sami looks at Lukas and makes a face. 'What about him?'

'How do you know him?'

Sami shrugs again. 'From school. He only moved here when he was thirteen. His parents . . .' He hesitates.

'What?'

'His parents were lawyers or something. They bought a place down here. But last year, they had a car accident. They were killed.'

Eve looks up. Lukas is staring at her. Worried he has heard, she looks away. 'So, he's alone?'

Sami nods. 'He was supposed to go live with his aunt in Melbourne but he wouldn't go. Instead she comes here every few weeks. The rest of the time he's on his own.'

Eve looks at Lukas, who is talking to Marina again. What must it be like to be alone like that?

'Is that allowed?'

Sami closes his eyes and laughs, lost somewhere in the wash of the pills. 'I don't know. He says he's going to go to university when he's finished school.'

'To do what?'

Sami laughs. 'Lukas? What do you reckon? Politics.'

Eve falls quiet, thinking. 'And you?'

Sami hesitates. 'I don't know. I'll work something out.'

All at once Eve feels a great tenderness for Sami, and turning to him she embraces him, pressing her face into his neck, the warm smell of him strong, undercut by the sharp stink of sweat, the chemical reek of the pill. He moves closer too, pressing his face into her before bringing it up so they are staring at one another. This close his face looks weird, an alien geography of bone and angle and eye. And then she closes her eyes and presses her mouth to his, slipping deep into the kiss, his body hot and close to hers, the two of them moving as one.

She is not sure how long it lasts, only that in the ebbing wash of the drug, as Sami slips into sleep beside her she leans close to him and whispers that there's something she needs to tell him, the words almost unbelievable when she speaks them into the world, and that while she half-expects Sami to pull away or recoil, he doesn't, just presses her face to his neck and says, 'Cool.'

She wakes with no memory of falling asleep. The hut is cold and smells of ashes and timber. She feels soft, sad, and in her confusion about where she is she feels certain she has made a mistake, said something she should not have. Sitting up, she looks around. The space is dim, the only illumination the pale light leaking in through the dusty pane of glass above the door. On the other side of the room Lukas and Marina are asleep, faces turned towards the wall. By the stove Sami is pulling on his shoes. Seeing him, she remembers her words as they fell asleep last night, and a sick dread rises in her. She sits up and he glances around. He looks edgy, uncomfortable.

'Are you going?' she asks.

He nods. 'I need to be somewhere.'

'Where?'

'It doesn't matter.'

'Can I come with you?'

He shoots her a wary look. 'No,' he says.

'Did something happen?' she asks.

Sami shakes his head. 'Nah, nothing,' he says. Eve begins to protest, but as she does she notices Lukas and Marina are awake. She turns back to Sami, but he is already on his feet.

'Sami,' she says. 'Wait.' But he just pushes past her and out the door, into the chill of the morning.

'What was that about?' Marina asks but Lukas ignores her.

'Are you okay?' he asks Eve, but she waves him away, and grabbing her coat races out the door after Sami.

She emerges in time to see Sami disappearing down the track. She knows she should call out or go after him, but she cannot bear the thought of him rejecting her again. Her cheeks burning she stares up at the pale sky. It is cold, the air thick with the smell of damp earth and leaf. She does not understand. Why did Sami leave? Was it what she told him? Or was it simply that he could not bear to be next to her anymore? Either way it is unbearable, a reminder of her hateful clumsiness, the coarseness of her skin and hair, her ugly face with its jutting brow and splayed nose. Who wouldn't find her monstrous?

And then something else occurs to her. What if he found her hideous all along? What if the whole evening was a kind of joke, a trick? What if they were laughing at her even now? She feels nauseous at the thought of her own body, its repulsiveness.

She walks faster, pushing forward, shoving her way through the undergrowth, heedless of the way it scratches and pulls at her. At some point she slips, unable to stop herself from sliding down the hillside, landing clumsily in a bog. But she does not stop, just pushes on until finally, unable to go any further, she drops to her knees by a creek and weeps.

Only when she is done does she sit up, look around. Cloud moves against the sky, but down here in the forest among the ferns and the trees it is cool, the forest quiet save for the fading cries of the birds, the whisper of the trees. Standing up, she begins to walk again, trudging along the stream in search of the road or a trail or somewhere she can use to find her way back to the road.

Kate is standing in the kitchen staring out when Eve turns into the driveway. She dashes out the door and down the drive towards her.

'Oh thank God,' she says, pressing Eve to her. 'You're all right.' Pushing her back, she grasps Eve's arms, her grip ferocious, hard.

'Where have you been? Why haven't you answered your phone? I thought something had happened to you.'

Eve doesn't reply, just jerks away, but Kate doesn't let go. Thrown off balance, she takes a step or two after Eve.

'Eve? What's wrong?' she says, but Eve just shakes her head.

'It doesn't matter,' she says.

'It does matter,' Kate says. Eve glances down at Kate's hand on her arm. A wave of anger washes through her and she twists away, pushing Kate back. Kate stumbles, losing her footing and landing hard in the dirt.

'I said leave me alone!' Eve storms past her and into the house. Kate follows her, catching her in the kitchen.

'Eve!' Kate says, her voice sharp. Eve slams the door and the bowl by the door tumbles to the floor. Looking down Eve sees it shatter, the sound releasing something in her, so she grasps the corner shelf on which it stood and casts it forward, sending the things piled on it smashing to the floor. Elated, she sweeps her arm out, sends a pile of papers flying, then lunges forward and pushes the table so it flips, thumping onto the floor with one of the chairs beneath it.

She steps forward, her breath coming raggedly, but as she does she sees Kate standing in the door, her face pale. There is a moment when she wants to charge at her, scream at her, exult in the terror she sees on Kate's face. But something holds her back, the hesitation enough for her exaltation to turn to shame, and instead she turns and flees back through the house and out, into the forest again.

It smells of smoke out in the trees. All year it has been like this, the land convulsing as the forests burn and the ice melts. Yet as Eve shoves her way through the trees she is not thinking about the fires or the way the world is unravelling all around her, but about her own isolation, her own shame. When she arrived home all she could remember was the way Lukas and Sami had looked at her, but now that humiliation is overlain by the memory of Kate's expression, her all-too-apparent fear in the face of Eve's fury. What made her behave that way, what dark violence made it possible to give in to her anger like that, to take such pleasure in destruction? She has read enough to know this violence is part of what makes her mother's species what they are, that it is part of what happened to her own. The desire to dominate, to kill, to give in to their most primal urges infects human society, disfiguring it at every level. Even the fires she can smell, the disruption of the forest can be seen as an expression of that same violence, enacted on a planetary scale. Yet until now she had not realised it was there in her, that she too was capable of such unchecked aggression. Is it possible she is not only no better but actually worse? Is it possible she is indeed a monster? And if she is, what does that mean?

Down by the creek it is quiet, the air still. She sits, stares out over the water, its depths crystal clear. Three fish hang suspended, their bodies rippling as they swim against the current, dappled light moving across them. Eve stares at them, struck for a moment by their beauty, their silvery otherness. What do the fish think, what is their world composed of? What other rhythms make up this landscape? If she were to dive down, swim beside them, would she understand their world, could she lose herself in that motion, become a fish? Or would she still be her awkward, hulking self?

MELTWATER

That year it feels as though winter will never arrive, the autumn lingering, unbroken, through May and June and into July. The plants and birds are thrown into confusion: in the branches, parrots and pardalotes cry plaintively into the darkness of the evenings instead of heading north to their winter homes; in the trees near their house rosella chicks call urgently in their nests, a late brood that will surely die when the cold eventually arrives, as it must. Even the trees react unpredictably, the natives flowering spontaneously, months out of season, the exotics either keeping their leaves or turning in the most half-hearted way, their confusion lending the wooded approaches to the city a curiously piebald look. In the mountains, fires smoulder, the smell of smoke and ash never far away.

Nor is it just the birds and plants that are unsettled. Late May brings a run of days in the mid-thirties, hot as summer, the blue water on the beaches dazzlingly clear in the weak winter light, the holiday mood made brittle by the shared sense that, delightful as the weather is, something is deeply awry. Eve feels it too, a sense of hastening, a dislocation deep in the fabric of things.

And then, in mid-June, it changes. For a day it feels like a storm is approaching, low cloud hanging overhead, the warm wind shifting uncertainly. Late that evening Eve walks along the path behind the house into the forest: in the darkness the landscape seems fitful, anticipatory. Overhead the leaves whispering, the limbs of the trees creaking like the timbers of a ship at sea.

Perhaps the animals feel it as well, because the usual cries and hoots are absent. But where the path divides she hears a rustling, and, quick as thought a fox steps onto the path in front of her. It is close – no more than three metres ahead – and at first it seems not to have seen her. But then it turns, and for a brief moment their eyes meet and she feels its awareness focus on her.

She stands, frozen in place. Like her it is a visitor here, an alien, but that does not mean she sees anything like recognition or affection in its gaze. Instead she glimpses another mind, one absorbed in the business of its life, to which she is at best an irrelevance. Then it turns, its attention passing over her and away, and stepping back into its vulpine world jogs away down the path and into the undergrowth.

Kate is already in bed when she returns, the house silent. In her room she opens the window above her bed and lies down, the scent of the night air filling the room as she waits for sleep.

The change arrives sometime around three, a brief silence preceding a sudden blast of wind, the sound of branches whipping, a gate banging in the distance. Perhaps responding to some shift in the air pressure, Eve wakes in the moments before it strikes, and for a few minutes she lies listening to the wind, the passing of the warmth filling her with a curious sadness. And later, when she sleeps again, she dreams of the forest, the sleek shape of the fox moving through it.

In the morning it is bitterly cold, bruised cloud filling the sky, pale light limning the distant horizon. Kate is at work, and Eve stands by the glass doors in the kitchen as she eats, watching leaves and sticks swirl in the strange, sepulchral light. There are reports of snow to the south, suggestions it might reach the city soon, and by nightfall the air is littered with drifting flakes, their substance ringing the streetlights, an inverted penumbra in the dark. As she slips into sleep that night the silence has depth, texture.

When she wakes the next day, the land outside is white, lost beneath drifts of snow. Stepping out, she looks around, the transformation making her feel giddy, delighted. Down by the gate Kate is visible, checking the letterbox; she waves and Kate waves back, then Eve heads back in and flicks on her screen to check the news.

She is scanning the weather reports when she hears a sound outside. Not quite a cry, more like a release of breath, a soft clutter. She stands up, goes to the window above the sink. A moment before Kate was there, yet now she is gone. Crossing to the door she opens it and steps out. At first she sees nothing unusual, but then she peers around the corner of the building and there is Kate lying on the ground, the snow around her undisturbed by anything but footprints, as if Kate has simply fallen.

'Mum?' she shouts. 'Mum!' and runs towards her.

When she reaches her, Kate is on her back, her head twisted sideways, limbs rigid, eyes rolled back in her head. For a brief, shocking moment Eve thinks she is dead, then she sees her hand trembling.

Her heart clamours. Two years ago on one of her excursions through the city streets she saw a man have a fit in a doorway down near the waterfront. It was Friday night, revellers passing on every side, and by the time she stopped, a small group was clustered around him, obviously aware they should do something but unwilling to approach.

She knew she should get off her bike and help, but she was frightened to touch him, unsettled by the sense he was not himself, that his body had become other, alien, a thing that could not be trusted. Some of that same revulsion surfaces as she kneels beside Kate, a moment of recoil before she forces herself to reach out and touch her.

Kate does not respond. Her hair is unravelled, and a line of saliva runs down the crease beside her mouth. Eve shakes her, repeating her name, willing her to re-enter her body. When at last Kate's eyes flicker, consciousness returning, Eve clutches her arm.

'Mum, are you okay?' she says, her words coming too fast.

But Kate doesn't answer, only stares around in confusion. Eve gets to her feet.

'Wait here,' she says. 'I'll be right back.'

She races inside and grabs her phone. Jay and Cassie are in California, and the staff at the facility are half an hour away. Putting the phone on speaker she tells it to dial an ambulance, then she grabs a throw off the couch and races back outside, tries to cover Kate with it. The computer voice asks her for the address, the patient's condition. Eve looks at Kate, the specks of snow dusting her hair and face.

'I don't know,' Eve stammers. 'She just collapsed.'

'Is the patient conscious?'

Kate's eyes are open and turned to the tenebrous sky.

'Yes, or sort of. Please, just send somebody; I don't know what to do.'

There is a moment's silence, then the system speaks again. 'An emergency vehicle has been dispatched. It should be with you in fifty-two minutes. If there is any change in the patient's condition, contact us on this number.'

With one hand Eve opens the tracking app, registering the location of the ambulance.

'They're coming, Mum,' she says, sinking back onto her haunches and staring towards the road. 'It's going to be okay. It's all going to be okay.'

Casualty is crowded when they arrive, its low space a jumble of beds and blue-clad staff. As she follows the paramedics along the corridor Eve fights not to panic, keeping her eyes down and forcing herself to shut out startled stares of the people they pass. Inside the cubicle she stands beside the bed, one hand clutching Kate's arm as if she might lose her if she let go. Kate is awake and talking, but unsettled and confused. Several times she calls out Eve's name, but even when Eve reassures her she is there Kate is distracted, as if she does not recognise her.

It is almost an hour before a doctor arrives. When she sees Eve she hesitates, surprised, before recovering and introducing herself. Eve mumbles hello. Earlier she caught two of the nurses staring in her direction and whispering to each other; when they caught Eve looking back at them they turned away.

With one last surreptitious glance at Eve the doctor turns to Kate. She begins by trying to establish the general situation – what happened? Does Kate remember anything? Is there any history of fainting or epilepsy? – before shining a penlight in Kate's eyes and asking a series of questions about the name of the prime minister and Kate's plans for the weekend. Eve leans in as the doctor works, careful not to get in her way but worried she might miss something; several times the doctor glances up, clearly unsettled by Eve's appearance.

'What's wrong with her? Is she going to be all right?' Eve asks as the doctor puts her penlight away, uncomfortably aware of the clumsiness of her speech.

The doctor glances at her. 'It's difficult to say. We need to run some tests.'

Eve remembers a researcher at the facility who suffered a massive stroke, and simply disappeared one day. 'Could it be a stroke?'

The doctor shakes her head. 'I don't think so. But until we're clearer I'd rather not speculate.'

Eve spends the day in a succession of waiting rooms, the hours passing in a shapeless blur of worry. Evening is closing in by the time somebody arrives to tell her Kate has been moved into a room. When Eve arrives Kate is sitting up in bed; her face is pale, scoured but otherwise normal.

'They said you were outside,' Kate says.

'I've been here all day,' Eve says. 'Has the doctor been?'

Kate shakes her head. 'Not yet.'

'Do you remember anything about what happened?'

Kate shakes her head. 'I remember being outside. Then I was here. In between . . .' Kate shrugs. Eve feels the space she has conjured open in front of her, a void into which she might slip, an intimation of erasure. She takes her mother's hand, surprised at how fragile it looks in her powerful fingers, the vulnerability of her skin.

'It'll be okay,' she says, her voice unsteady. 'It'll be okay.'

Except it isn't. As the doctor explains when she finally appears, the scans have revealed a tumour in Kate's brain. They will have to speak to the neurosurgeon, but its position means surgery is unlikely to be an option. Kate holds Eve's hand as the doctor explains the situation.

'How much time do I have?' Kate asks, her voice wavering on the final word but still clear, direct.

The doctor hesitates for a moment. 'It's difficult to say. But you need to prepare yourself for the idea you may not have long.'

After the doctor leaves, Kate does not speak, just sits, one hand on Eve's, her eyes fixed on the view of the city lights through the window. The quiet of the room is immense. Finally Kate turns to her and squeezes Eve's hand, her jaw set and eyes bright with tears.

'Well,' she says. 'There we are.'

It is after eleven before Eve leaves the hospital. With Kate's help she has summoned a car, and on the drive home she stares out into the darkness. She feels drained, her eyes sore from tears. Although it still shines whitely on the verge and in the fields, the snow is already melting, and the road is covered with an icy slush. Everything is clear, silent, the windswept streets devoid of life.

The specialist who arrived in the early evening showed them images of the lesion, which nestles in the centre of Kate's brain like an egg, bloated and swollen. As he ran his finger over the image on the screen Eve asked him how long it had been there, why Kate hadn't known, and the specialist paused to look at her before saying there was no way of knowing: they grew quickly, and people often had no warning until it was almost the end.

Afterwards, Kate told her she had been feeling tired for several months. She had thought it was just age, exhaustion, but in fact it was the tumour, the future that was already set contained within it.

It is almost midnight before Eve arrives home, the house dark and cold. She flicks on the lights and then the heater, settles herself beside it. She knows she should eat, but she is too tired to think, too tired to speak. The world seems alien, her connection to it so tenuous she is not sure it is there at all, even when she flicks on her screen and slips into the electric non-space of the virtual.

For months now the news has been about West Antarctica, the possibility the ice sheet has reached a critical point, but as she calls up the news she sees the story has moved rapidly in the hours she has been away, and the sheet really is collapsing. And when she sleeps she dreams of shifting ice, the yaw and tectonic creak of it, the way it slithers down into waiting ocean, dark as grief.

When she wakes, the last of the snow has gone, the sky clear except for a scurf of grey above the ridge. As she dresses she stares out the window, the yearning to be outside and away from other people so intense it frightens her.

In the kitchen Kate's phone sits on the counter, forgotten in their frantic departure the day before. Staring at it, Eve is struck by how far away yesterday seems, how irrecoverable. Before she left the hospital one of the nurses realised Kate did not have her phone, and so took Eve's and punched her number into it. 'Call me,' she said, placing it back in Eve's hand. 'I'll tell you how she is.' Taking out her phone Eve selects the woman's number and listens to the whirr of the ring, the click when she answers. At first the nurse's voice is wary, but when she realises it is Eve she softens.

'She had a good night,' she says. 'She's a lot brighter this morning.'

After she hangs up Eve sits, uncertain what to do next. She knows she needs to ring Jay, tell him what has happened, but something holds her back. It is almost two years since he took up his new position at the Foundation's headquarters in Oakland, and though he calls Eve from time to time she cannot shake the feeling he has moved on somehow. Finally she gives in and calls him, choosing the relative anonymity of voice over video, her voice breaking as she tries to answer his shocked questions.

'I should come,' he says. 'You need help.'

'No,' Eve says.

'At least let me arrange for somebody from the Foundation to drop past.'

'No,' Eve says again, her voice breaking. 'I'm fine. I can handle this alone.'

There is a long silence. 'Okay. But if that changes just say.'

Back at the hospital Kate is awake and dressed, seated on the side of her bed. Seeing Eve, she smiles.

'Why are you up?' Eve asks, hurrying towards her. 'I thought the doctor said you'd have to stay for a few days.'

Kate stands up. 'I feel fine. I'm not going to lie in this bed all day doing nothing.'

As she speaks her legs buckle under her. Eve jumps forward to catch her.

'Are you sure? Perhaps we should get a nurse?'

Kate shakes her head. She is pale, drawn, her grey hair tangled and dirty. 'I want to go for a walk,' she says. But once they are out in the hall she has to sit down almost immediately. Leaning back against the wall, she closes her eyes.

'You need to go back to bed,' Eve says.

Kate nods slowly without opening her eyes.

The next week passes in a blur. For the first two days they are told the neurosurgeon will arrive to see them soon: first that afternoon, then the next morning, then again on the second afternoon, but it is not until the morning of the third day that he finally appears, apologising for his absence. His manner is careful, precise, although the whole time he is with them he keeps glancing across at Eve. Apparently the tumour is too deeply rooted for surgery or radiotherapy. Kate says nothing at this news, just nods and asks about chemo, at which point he becomes evasive, telling them there are problems with supply, but they will do what they can.

Once he leaves Kate begins to get dressed, her movements quick, almost ferocious.

'What are you doing?' Eve asks.

'You heard him. There's nothing they can do here.'

Eve stares at Kate. 'What if it happens again?'

'We'll deal with that if it happens.'

Eve does not reply. Kate looks away. 'Let's go find a car,' she says.

Back home, Eve helps Kate to her room, acutely aware as she settles her in her bed of how much weight Kate has lost in the past week, the speed with which her muscles have begun to waste. As always the room smells sweet with Kate's perfume, the smell of her body. When she was a child Eve would often crawl into Kate's bed, pull the quilt over her head and fall asleep, cradled in it. Yet now the scent is undercut by other odours: the cloying sweetness of hospital soap, the chemical tang of the drugs, and beneath it all something else, a thin odour like rotting grass that Eve knows without being told is the tumour.

Kate falls asleep almost immediately, only waking for long enough to drink a cup of tea before slipping back into sleep. But the next morning when Eve rises Kate is already up, dressed and seated at the table.

'I thought we might finish the weeding,' she says.

Eve nods, not sure what to say.

Over the next few weeks a strange sort of normality reasserts itself. Although she is weak, and tires easily, Kate seems well enough.

Yet Eve knows she is not. As the days bleed by Eve wonders over and over whether there was some sign in the weeks leading up to Kate's fit, whether she should have noticed. Kate had been tired, but Eve now suspects there were other signs as well, signs she missed. Several times Kate had lost things in the house: her screen, her keys, a book she had been reading, and twice she had set off to buy groceries and forgotten to pick up things she had meant to buy.

But as she stares at her mother lying in the bed, she cannot help but wonder whether the ghost of it was there in her speech as well, whether her tiredness had been about a need to concentrate harder than she otherwise might have. Eve has always been aware of her sensitivity to the non-verbal cues of others, to the unspoken shadings of affect and sublimated feeling others seem unaware of; how could she not have realised something was wrong?

But that is not all. Whenever she is least expecting it she catches the smell of it, the foul waft of the sickness, its scent clinging to her, rubbing off on her sheets and the furniture, clinging to the air. At first Eve finds it difficult to ignore, its putrid undertone making her feel ill. But one night while Kate is watching something on the television with a blanket over her legs Eve lies down beside her and, closing her eyes, presses her face to Kate's chest. For a few seconds all she can hear is the beat of Kate's heart, the pulse of her blood, but then she smells the sickness leaking in. This time, though, it is not foul, it is just there, part of Kate, part of them. Without speaking Kate lifts a hand and strokes Eve's head, and for a few seconds Eve feels herself slip away, the isolation that surrounds her disappearing into the shared space of the two of them.

Still, as they move through the weeks, it is as if the world has divided, and two different realities inhabit every moment. In one version there is Eve and Kate, together in the house, their lives entwined yet untroubled. In this reality it sometimes seems Kate's time in the hospital was nothing more than a bad dream, already half-forgotten. Yet this reality is haunted by another in which Kate's extinction hovers just out of sight, unable to be approached or imagined yet eclipsing everything. Which of them Eve inhabits changes, hour by hour, minute by minute.

What Kate feels is not clear to Eve. Some days she wants to talk, to tell Eve things about her past, or to plan for Eve's future. Jay calls most days, either to talk to Eve or to Kate. The last time anybody heard from Davis he had relocated to a safehouse in New Zealand; in his absence Jay and the others in senior positions at the Foundation are doing what they can, but as disasters proliferate they too are being overwhelmed.

'I've arranged for you to be accommodated at the facility,' Jay tells her one night, his voice in her ear almost too close to hear. 'So if anything happens you just call them, they'll look after you.'

Eve stares at the dark shadows of the trees outside. 'Why can't I stay here?'

'Because you'll be safer with them.'

'I'm safe here.'

'Please, Eve. I know this is difficult, but you have to start thinking about the future.'

'I don't want to talk about it,' she says.

Yet as the days lengthen, the past and future seem to fall away, until there is only the two of them, the endless present. One afternoon

Eve returns from a walk to find Kate burning papers on the concrete in the yard.

'What are you doing?' she asks.

Kate stuffs another bundle of papers into the flames. 'Just getting rid of a few things.'

'What things?' Eve asks, and Kate looks at her.

'Just stuff,' she says, and as she speaks Eve realises she is erasing her past, hiding those parts Eve might find upsetting or inconvenient. That night she wonders what Kate gave up for her, why she never had another relationship, suddenly aware of how little she really knows about the woman she calls her mother.

Their shared existence is so consuming it is almost possible to shut out the news, which grows worse every day. Everywhere the water is rising, a centimetre or sometimes more a day, inundating roads and flooding subways, crawling across beaches to swallow wetlands and parks. Offshore huge currents have developed as the meltwater disperses itself. On the east coast of America a string of hurricanes have forced the rising sea higher again, poisoning the land and sweeping away communities. Miami, New Orleans, Long Beach, all gone. To Eve these are just words, names of places she has only glimpsed second- or third-hand on her screen, yet still, the sight of the exhausted figures huddled on rooftops or trudging along roadsides fills her with foreboding.

In October the heat returns, a string of days in the high thirties and low forties, and with it fire, followed by wild winds and storms. Kate and Eve watch them rumble across the hills, relieved by the hot spatter of rain when it arrives.

And then, on the day after the weather breaks, Kate has another seizure. Eve is in the yard when she hears her call her name, her voice high and panicky. Racing in, she finds Kate standing in the middle of the kitchen staring at her hand, which is jerking uncontrollably. Kate looks up, her mouth opening to form words that do not come, then falls sideways like a tree, her head narrowly missing the edge of the kitchen counter. Eve dives forward to catch her, but she is not quick enough. Dropping to her knees beside Kate she cradles her head and shoulders. Kate stares sightlessly at the ceiling, her face and body twitching.

'Mum!' Eve cries. 'Mum!' Her voice sounds awkward, overloud.

The seizure passes quicker this time; in fifteen minutes Kate is able to speak again, although her words are slurred and halting.

'I'll call an ambulance,' Eve says, but Kate presses a hand to Eve's and shakes her head.

'No point,' she says.

Eve does not know what to say. 'Are you sure?'

Kate nods.

'What, then?'

'Bed. Help me.'

Eve lifts Kate, shocked by how light she has become, and bears her down the hall to her bed. Laying her on the side, she tells her not to move.

Seated beside her on the bed Eve rings the doctor. But by the time he arrives two hours later Kate is coherent again.

'I had a seizure,' she says. 'I'm fine now.'

Eve sees at once that the doctor thinks there is little he can do. He tells Kate to rest, asks about painkillers and care. When Kate tells him she has Eve, he glances at her, his scepticism obvious.

'Nobody else?'

Kate shakes her head. 'Nobody else.'

He leaves Kate with a prescription and tells her to call him again if she needs help. As he leaves he catches Eve in the hall.

'I don't know what she's told you,' he says, 'but she doesn't have long. And you're going to need help. Are there people you can call?'

Eve leans away from him, her back pressed against the wall. Aware of how uncomfortable she looks she nods, the movement jerky, almost violent. For a few seconds she thinks the doctor will not accept her assurance, that he will press her further, but after a moment's hesitation he seems to decide to believe her.

'Call me if you need me.'

Kate is already asleep when Eve gets back to her room. A triangle of sun across her chest, her face in shadow. For a minute or two Eve stands, watching the rise and fall of her breath, drinking in the familiar scent of her.

Late in the night Eve is woken by the sound of Kate moaning. She stumbles through the darkened house to find Kate curled on her side in bed, whimpering in a low voice, her breath coming fast. Eve leans in, her face close to Kate's.

'Tell me,' she says. 'What is it?'

Kate doesn't reply, just shakes her head. The bed is wet with sweat.

'Does it hurt?'

Kate nods.

'Shall I get the doctor again?'

Kate shakes her head. 'In the morning. The prescription.'

Eve squeezes Kate's hand. She does not know what to do.

By morning Kate's pain has subsided enough for her to ask for a cup of tea. When Eve places it beside her Kate touches her arm.

'I'm sorry about last night,' she says. 'I didn't mean to frighten you.'

'It's okay,' Eve says.

'It was wrong of me to ask you to do this alone. We have to get help. Jay said he can arrange for the Foundation to send somebody.'

'No! I don't want anybody else here. I can do it myself.'

Kate strokes Eve's arm. 'I don't think you realise what it's going to be like.'

'Please,' Eve says, her words coming with sudden ferocity. 'Let me do this.'

Kate looks at her for a long moment. Finally she gives a small nod. 'Okay,' she says.

'The medicine. How do I get it?'

Kate picks up the prescription the doctor left.

'You need to take this to a chemist. Ask them to fill it.'

Eve nods, uncertain.

'Can you do that?'

'Of course,' she says.

Kate takes Eve's hand. 'Be careful,' she says.

Eve climbs onto her bike and heads towards the city. These past weeks she has been so busy with Kate she has not taken her usual trips through the streets, and she is shocked by the change. The parks and streets are ringed by cars and vans, their boots and backs packed with bags, children and hollow-eyed men and women inside them, as the first wave of those displaced by flooding and rising water begin to move inland, towards higher ground. Finally she stops outside a chemist on the outskirts of the city. Now she is here she is nervous, unsure she can go through with it, but finally she takes a breath, leans her bike against the wall and goes in.

It is quiet and cool inside, the only sound the echo of music, the soft hum of the air-conditioning. Unsure where to go she walks down one aisle and the next, sweat prickling on the back of her neck, then stops in a corner and stares around in confusion.

'Can I help you?' says a woman's voice, and she jumps. A woman in a white uniform standing beside her.

She swallows. 'I need to fill a prescription,' she says, painfully aware of the awkwardness of her speech.

The woman smiles and points. 'Up the back.'

Eve mumbles a thank you and hurries up between the racks to the counter at the back. Spotting a young woman she goes towards her and places the prescription on the counter, careful to keep her eyes down.

'It's for my mother,' she says.

The woman picks up the prescription. She is young, dark-skinned, with glasses and a delicate fuzz of black hair on the sides of her cheeks.

'These are controlled substances,' she says. 'I can't give them to you without ID.'

Eve looks up in a panic. 'I don't have ID,' she says.

The woman looks away in surprise. Placing the prescription back on the counter she slides it towards Eve. 'I'm sorry,' she says. 'It's the law.' Her voice slow, careful, as if she thinks Eve will have trouble understanding her.

Eve's cheeks burn.

'It's fine,' she says, snatching back the prescription.

Outside she slumps against the wall, fighting back tears. She wants to look after Kate but she has failed at the first hurdle. She has no ID, does not exist in any official sense. A car door opens in front of her and somebody climbs out, gives a startled gasp. Eve looks up and sees a middle-aged woman standing there, caught in the act of opening the back door of her car for her children, who slump in booster seats inside. As Eve meets her gaze the woman takes a step back and pushes the door slowly closed. Scrambling to her feet, Eve runs towards her bike and speeds away.

A few blocks away she skids to a halt by a small patch of bush, dropping her bike across a fallen log. She knows she should call Jay or the facility but she cannot bear the thought of giving up so easily. With a cry of frustration she kicks the log once and then again, then she picks up a fallen limb, hefts it over her head and hurls it into the trees. Finally she picks up her bike and pedals off down the road, desperate to lose herself in motion. Only when she is within sight of the city does she turn around, but as she begins to head back up the hill she passes two men loading boxes into a van. She stares at them, but when one of them catches her watching them she looks away and rides on, only to have him call out her name.

Confused, she stops and looks back. She cannot place the thin face and tousled hair. Then the intensity of his gaze triggers a flash of recognition.

'Lukas?'

He smiles and steps forward. 'Eve! What are you doing here?'

She hesitates. 'My mother is sick. I'm supposed to be getting medicine.'

Lukas pauses. 'I'm sorry,' he says. 'Is it serious?'

Eve looks away and nods, tears filling her eyes.

When Lukas speaks again his voice is gentler. 'Is she at home?'

Eve nods again.

'That's probably good.'

Eve hesitates. 'Why?'

'A lot of the hospitals are having problems with staffing and stocks of drugs.'

Eve doesn't reply. Lukas takes another step towards her. His face wears an expression Eve does not recognise: guardedness, but also sympathy. Eve remembers what Sami said that night in the forest about his parents dying, his refusal to be taken into care.

'Is there some kind of problem? Can I help?'

Eve shakes her head. 'I can't get the medicine because I don't have ID.'

If Lukas is surprised by this news he doesn't show it. 'Would you like me to help?'

Eve blinks. Gives a short, hard nod.

Lukas loads her bike into the back of the van and drives back towards the shopping centre. His friend doesn't speak as Eve climbs in next to him, but she can feel him watching her. Once they are there he and Lukas climb out and have a short, hurried conversation while Eve sits in the van. Once or twice they glance at her. Finally Lukas comes back and leans in the window.

'Tomas is going to head back into town. If you give me the prescription I can fill it and then I'll drive you home.'

Remembering her mother's many warnings about bringing strangers to the house, Eve is about to resist, but she doesn't. Instead she just nods.

He returns a few minutes later. Eve cannot help but notice the way he glances from side to side as he emerges through the sliding doors, as if wary of being observed. As he climbs in he hands her a small package, the paper rustling stiffly as her powerful hand closes around it.

'I filled the repeat as well,' he says. 'They didn't really want to do it, but I don't know how much longer they'll have stock. You need to get the doctor to write more prescriptions. I can help you fill them.'

Eve doesn't answer. She cannot think that far ahead.

When they arrive back at the house Kate is standing in the kitchen in a dressing gown. She opens the door as Eve and Lukas climb out of the van.

'Who's this?' she asks.

Lukas extends a hand. 'Lukas,' he says.

'He's a friend of Sami's,' Eve says. 'He helped me get the medicine.'

Kate regards him warily as she shakes his hand. 'I suppose I should thank you, then,' she says.

Lukas shakes his head. 'I'm just sorry you need it,' he says.

'Would you like to come in?'

Lukas looks at Eve. She smiles.

'Only if you don't mind.'

'Of course,' Kate says.

In the kitchen Kate sits down while Eve makes tea. Out of the corner of her eye Eve watches the way she closes her eyes, the wash of pain as she arranges herself on the chair. Her hair looks dirty, the threads of grey through it more noticeable.

'I couldn't get the prescription filled on my own,' Eve says. 'They wanted ID.'

Lukas glances at her. 'I said to Eve you should get another prescription as soon as possible. Nobody wants to say it but things are going to get very bad very quickly, and medical supplies are already breaking down.'

Kate nods, although something in her expression makes Eve wonder whether what Lukas is saying seems real to her. Perhaps she no longer believes in the future.

'I'll talk to the doctor.'

Lukas hesitates. 'If you don't mind me asking, why doesn't Eve have ID?'

Kate stares at him over her cup. 'It's a long story,' she says.

Lukas doesn't reply, but Eve can feel him looking at her.

She takes another sip of tea.

When Lukas leaves, Kate asks Eve to help her to the door. 'Lukas?' she calls after him as he is opening the door of the van.

He looks back.

'I appreciate you helping Eve and me like this.'

Lukas nods, his expression guarded. 'Let me know if you need anything else.'

Kate stares at him thoughtfully for a few seconds. 'We will. And please visit if you have time.'

Once Lukas is gone they turn back towards the house. By the door Kate unwinds her arm from Eve's grasp, steps free. In the dark glass of the sliding door Eve sees their reflections, transformed by the past weeks: Kate grown old, frail, Eve rangy, powerful, her thick hair coiled above her wide-browed face. For a moment Kate turns, looks back down the hill towards the road. Over recent days she has looked shattered, uncomprehending, riven by her diagnosis, but as she stares across the space outside the house it is not shock or grief Eve sees in her expression, but something more like determination.

The medicine makes things easier. But two nights later the pain returns, and Eve wakes to the sound of Kate moaning and sobbing. Running to her room she finds her twisted on the bed. Eve gives her a spoonful of the medicine, then another, but it does not seem to help.

'What do you want me to do?' Eve asks her. 'Should I call the doctor?'

Kate whimpers and shakes her head, and so Eve climbs in next to her, cradling her until she sleeps.

In the morning she wakes to find Kate still asleep in her arms. Getting up, she goes through to the kitchen and calls Lukas.

Lukas brings food and supplies, pocketing the cash Eve gives him without speaking. He is businesslike, efficient, but also careful somehow. When she first met him, that sense that he was always calculating, always thinking bothered her; now it is almost reassuring.

Once he has left, Eve makes a cup of tea for Kate, then disappears to her room. She scans the feeds on her phone, sees the chatter has not changed: so many people frightened, fighting, looking for somebody to blame. She heads to Kate's room to offer food, only to find Kate still asleep. Behind her the window is open; the pale light falls on her face, silvering it.

Eve closes the door quietly behind her, heads out. She is tired, exhausted by lack of sleep and anxiety, so she follows the path upward, into the trees.

The following weeks are brief yet endless. The weather is bright and blue, although nobody seems to know how long it will stay like this. On the feeds the talk is all of collapse, shifting tides of fear and denial. From time to time Kate seems to rally; one day after she has not left her bed for three days Eve rises to find her seated in the kitchen, her screen open in front of her. When Eve enters she smiles, and for a brief second Eve sees her as she was, only a few weeks ago. In her bed that night Eve lies awake, wondering how she failed to notice, what might have happened if she had realised earlier, if she had pushed Kate to see a doctor more often, if, if, if.

Eve does not leave the house except when she has to, preferring to spend time with Kate out on the lawn, in the sun.

She knows Kate is concerned about her, about what will happen to her once she is gone. But one evening, when Eve is watching her screen, Kate appears in the doorway. Eve takes off her headphones.

'I've been talking to Lukas,' she says. 'He was telling me about his farm, this compound he's been building up in the hills.'

Eve doesn't answer.

'He's right, you know. It's all slipping out of control. I don't know what's going to happen, but you're going to need help.'

'I'll be okay.'

'You don't know that. I know Jay has made arrangements with the Foundation, that they have contingency plans, but perhaps you need a backup plan, somewhere you can go if something happens at the Foundation, and that falls through. I have money I can leave for you, but I don't know how long that will last.'

'Please,' Eve says. 'I don't want to talk about it. I'll be fine.'

'Fine how? There are no jobs, things are coming apart. What happens when you can't pay for food? Or power? I can't leave you alone. I need to be sure you're in contact with the Foundation, that they can help you. And that there will be somebody else if they're no good.'

Eve does not reply. She does not want to think about the future Kate is describing.

Over the next few weeks Lukas becomes a regular visitor to the house, bringing food, news. Every time things are worse. Overseas there are stories of riots, governments falling. It is as if everything is gathering momentum, slipping downhill.

'It's over,' he says one day.

'What is?' Eve asks.

'The government. The world. All of it. We need to be ready.'

'I don't know what that means,' Eve says.

'Nobody does,' Lukas says. 'That's part of the problem.'

'What will you do?'

'I have my place, up in the mountains. I think we can make do there. Grow food.'

Eve remembers Sami talking about Lukas's parents, the accident. 'You own it?'

Lukas glances at her, his old antagonism briefly visible again. 'I do.'

Eve nods. 'When will you go there?'

Lukas relaxes. 'I don't know,' he says. 'But soon.'

In the last fortnight, time becomes elastic, the days blurring into each other. One afternoon Yassamin visits, sitting with Kate through the dusk and into the night. Several times Kate wakes, and they talk, and laugh. In the days that follow the seizures come more often. Her speech is slurred, the effort of speaking making her work and strain, as Eve once did, and there are moments when she seems distracted, confused. At other times she seems just like herself, only more so. In those moments it is as if some magic trick or transformation has taken place, as if the more Kate's body fails the more vividly she inhabits it, the presence within burning brighter, faster. Perhaps we are all just spirit, Eve thinks more than once, the body simply a vessel, something that can be pared away. Yet with each new seizure Kate gets weaker, her capacity for speech slipping away until one day they seem to stop, and instead she lies still, the only sound her breathing, until just before dawn one morning that too falls still, and quite suddenly, she is gone.

Eve does not know how long she lies next to Kate after she realises she is gone. It is still dark outside, the wind moving in the trees. Lukas is supposed to be coming later, but there are hours between then and now she does not know how to fill. Finally she gets up, goes out to the kitchen.

Lukas arrives mid-morning, pulling up in the drive with a box of groceries. Something in her face must tell him what has happened before she speaks, because he crosses to her, enfolds her in his arms, the gesture surprising her, seemingly surprising him.

'What now?' he asks, once he releases her, but Eve cannot answer.

But later, with Lukas's help, she begins the process of working out who to tell, and calls Jay, Yassamin.

When she is done Eve walks outside. The air is hot and dirty, the smoke from the fires inland and on the mainland burning her eyes, her throat. She does not know what will happen now. Things are chaotic, not just here, but everywhere, the panic of the past months giving way to violence, fear.

On the day before Kate's burial she walks a trail that used to lead through the forest to the beach. The water has already risen high enough to cover the sand and poison the trees, which stand bare and dead, their branches winding skywards.

The tideline reeks, the stink of rotting seaweed mingling with the smell of rotting birds. But finally she rounds a headland and comes upon a small patch of bone-white sand. She gathers shells: the sculpted curve of clams, the reddish ridged coarseness of scallops, with their purplish interiors. Back in the trees she picks up lumps of ochre, and from the stiff spray of the scrub she takes the striped feather of a kookaburra and the white feather of a cockatoo.

Back in the house, she decorates Kate's body, tracing lines on her hands with the ochre, stringing the shells and feathers around her neck. Kate's body has grown stiff, the skin waxen, its matter pulling back so her face seems too tight, like a mask – whatever Kate was, now fled. One by one Eve pushes the feathers into Kate's hair, letting her hands linger on it; when she is done she ties the flowers together, just as Kate taught her on their lawn, so many years ago, and winds them around her neck. She is crying as she works.

Lukas helps her organise the funeral. It will just be her, him, Yassamin, a handful of colleagues from the Foundation. No Jay, no Cassie, no Sami. They stand on the back lawn, wind whipping around them, the smell of smoke in the air. There is no priest or celebrant: instead they take turns speaking, stepping forward one by one. When it is Eve's turn she finds she cannot, and instead stands, overwhelmed, until finally Lukas and Yassamin step forward and, placing an arm each around her, draw her away.

They bury her wrapped in a blanket, lowering her into a grave dug by Lukas. As the dusty earth covers Kate's swaddled form, slowly erasing the faded patchwork, Eve feels something give way and realises this is what grief feels like. Shock, absence, and something else. Not the wrenching pain she imagined but something deeper, less easily articulated. She feels as if she is being unmade, forgotten, her past slipping away.

Afterwards, when the last of them have left, Eve is surprised to realise Lukas is still sitting outside in the darkness. He is smoking, the acrid stink oddly comforting.

'Thank you for being here,' she says. 'For everything.'

'I wish I'd had a chance to get to know her better,' he says.

Eve looks at him, surprised. 'Thank you.'

Lukas looks out at the tree. 'I saw the photos of your father on the screen. You don't look much like him. Her either.'

She glances around. In the darkness his eyes glitter, the tip of his cigarette glowing. 'I'm adopted.'

Lukas smiles a strange, secret smile, his expression suddenly reminding Eve of his manner when they first met. Not for the first time Eve wonders how much he has guessed.

'When I met you with Sami, I didn't like you,' she says.

Lukas exhales a cloud of cigarette smoke. 'I know.'

'You didn't like me either,' she says.

'What makes you say that?'

'You don't like anybody.'

He laughs. 'No. But that's because most people aren't worth liking.' He drops his cigarette and grinds it into the ground with his boot. 'Have you thought about what you're going to do now? Because you need to. We've been protected up until now because we're reasonably isolated, but that won't last. What's happening in America and Europe and on the mainland, it's going to start happening here as well. People are scared, the systems are failing.'

'My mother arranged for me to go to the facility, stay with the Foundation. She says I'll be safe there.' She trails off.

'But?'

Eve shakes her head. 'I don't want to go. Not without her. I don't belong there.'

Lukas watches her. 'You can't stay here.'

'Why not?'

'You won't be safe on your own. Not once things start getting really bad.'

'Then, what?'

'Come with me.'

'To your farm?'

He nods.

'And what will we do there?'

'Try to make do. We won't be alone: there are others up there as well.'

She looks around. The house so familiar, yet already not. 'I don't know.'

'Of course. I understand. But don't leave it until it's too late to decide.'

Eve nods, but does not reply. She can feel the ground shifting beneath her.

A week passes, then another. Eve stays in the house, alone, un-speaking. Occasionally she hears cars moving past on the road outside, once or twice she sees smoke rising on the horizon. She feels empty, hollowed out.

In the night, she wakes. Something has woken her but she does not know what: all week she has felt time collapsing, the past bleeding into the present, the future already here. She sits up, looks around. Through the window the lights by the road have gone out. There is an audible click, and the house falls silent, the fridge spinning down. And just like that the world is over.

THE FOREST

Eve is working in the vegetable garden when she spots movement at the bottom of the hill. Pushing her trowel into the dirt, she stands up, sees a figure beneath the tree by the gate.

Whoever it is has their back to her, but something about the way they are standing, their uneasy, feral posture is familiar. Dusting off her jeans she begins down the hill. It is quiet, the only sound that of the wind in the grass, the shifting branches of the tree, but still, she is almost upon him before he finally turns.

She stifles a gasp. He looks older than the last time she saw him, his face gaunt, black hair shaved close to his scalp.

'Sami?'

He smiles. 'Hi, Eve.'

'What are you doing here?'

He darts a look over her shoulder and shoves his hands deeper into his pockets. His right eye is bruised and blackened, and he has a raw contusion on one cheek.

'I thought Lukas might be around.'

She hesitates. There are rules about visitors. 'Does he know you're coming?'

Sami folds his arms and shakes his head.

'He's out at the moment. Do you want to come in?'

Sami glances up the drive towards the house, then nods jerkily. 'Sure.'

It is warm in the kitchen, the sun bright through the high window. Sami stiffens as he enters, staring at the loaf of bread sitting on the table.

'Are you hungry?' she asks and he nods.

She fetches a bowl and ladles some of the soup they made the night before into it. Sami spoons it hungrily into his mouth.

'Where have you been?' she asks while he eats.

He shrugs. 'In the city.'

'Doing what?'

He slurps down another spoonful. 'Surviving.'

She doesn't reply. She has heard stories about the chaos. Lukas says martial law has been imposed, but that doesn't mean a lot.

'Is your mum here as well?'

Eve looks away and shakes her head. 'No.'

Sami puts down his spoon. 'Did something happen?'

Eve pauses. 'She died.'

Sami stares at her. 'Oh. I'm sorry. When?'

Eve looks past him, her face impassive: she had hoped her grief was mastered but here it is, as raw and immediate as ever.

'The winter before last. Just when everything was falling apart.'

Before Sami can reply they are interrupted by the sound of the front door opening, and footsteps in the hall. A moment later Lukas appears. He greets Eve and then comes to a halt, staring at Sami.

For a long time neither speaks. Finally Sami extends a hand. 'Hey, man.'

Lukas shakes his hand, his face hard.

'How did you find us?'

Sami shrugs. 'I asked down in the town. They told me how to get up here.'

'Who did you ask?'

Sami looks vague. 'I don't know. Some guy with a beard.'

Lukas turns to Eve. 'Did you know he was coming?'

She shakes her head. 'Not until now.'

He turns back to Sami. 'So, what brought you?' Eve tenses at the note of aggression in his voice.

'I thought I could stay for a while.'

'We work here, Sami. All this—' Lukas extends an arm, taking in the vegetables in the larder, the stove, '—we made it ourselves.'

'I can work,' Sami says.

Lukas looks at him. 'And there are no drugs.'

Sami nods. 'I know that. I'm clean.'

Lukas stares at him for a few moments.

'Jesus, man,' Sami says, pulling up his sleeve. 'Look.'

Eve winces. Sami's forearm and bicep are blotchy and ulcerated, the skin scarred and discoloured. But the damage is old, a legacy.

Something quickly suppressed passes across Lukas's face. He looks towards the back door. Eve can see he is thinking. Finally he shakes his head. 'All right. You can sleep in the room at the back. Eve can find you some blankets.'

Eve leads Sami to the back of the house, shows him the room. They have been using it for storage, boxes and bags and old equipment stacked along the wall. But by the other wall is a mattress, which Eve pulls down and sets out for Sami. He looks around, an assessing expression on his face. She has never pressed Lukas about what came between him and Sami. 'Some friendships don't last,' is all he has ever said, although Eve knows there is something else there, some betrayal.

'How many of you live here?' he asks.

'Twelve.'

'And Lukas is in charge?'

'No. We talk about things. Make decisions together.'

Sami snorts. 'But it's Lukas's place, isn't it? So if Lukas says no, that means no?'

Eve hesitates, surprised by the anger in his voice, how close it is to the surface. 'I suppose.'

'Then Lukas is in charge.'

She looks away. She does not feel comfortable with this conversation, or Sami's tone. 'We should go outside,' she says. 'I have work to finish.'

Out in the garden she crouches down and goes back to transplanting the potatoes. Sami hovers by the fence, his hands in his pocket, glancing around. Eventually he comes and stands close behind her.

'I'm sorry about your mother,' he says. She pauses. There is something awkward in his tone, as if he is searching for some point of connection. She remembers him as a boy, his restless energy and inability to be still. With a quick movement she shoves the trowel into the ground. 'Thank you. How is Yassamin?'

Sami shrugs. 'I don't know. I haven't seen her for a long time.'

'But she's okay?'

Sami hesitates. 'I think so.'

Eve feels a little rush of relief at the news that Yassamin is all right. The disasters of recent months have come thick and fast.

'Is she still in her apartment?'

'I suppose so,' he says, his voice flat and expressionless.

'Lukas says it's bad in the cities.'

Sami looks down. 'Yeah. It is. You have enough here, though, by the look of it.'

Eve doesn't reply. The past year has not been easy, and they have had to learn many things the hard way.

'Trust Lukas to land on his feet,' says Sami.

That evening Sami joins them in the dining room. He is the last to arrive, and while they wait the others pepper Lukas and Eve with questions about him. When Sami walks in, though, they fall quiet, waiting while Lukas introduces him to those who have not met him, pointing to them and listing their names: Carla and Malla, Virat, Octavia, Tomas and Sophie, Otis and finally Callum, then pulls out a seat so he can sit next to him.

Dinner is soup and bread, simple but filling. Sami eats quickly, avoiding Eve's eye, but he cannot avoid the questions of the others. Where have you been? How is it down there? Is it true, have you seen, did you hear, they roll on and on. With every answer Sami grows more confident, more voluble, more like his old self. Finally somebody asks how he knows Lukas, and for a brief moment the two of them look at each other, something wordless passing between them, before Lukas looks away.

Sami grins. 'We went to school together.'

Carla laughs. 'Hard to imagine Lukas at school. When I met him at university he was already so serious.'

Lukas leans back in his chair and folds his arms, his eyes fixed on Sami.

Sami laughs. 'He was just the same.'

*

After they have eaten the others linger in the dining room for longer than usual, chatting and laughing and enjoying the novelty of Sami's presence. But by nine the last of them make their excuses and retire to their rooms to read or sleep. Once the last of them is gone, Eve goes outside to check on the animals, grateful for the time alone. She returns to find Sami sitting on the step.

'I heard you go out,' he says.

'I wanted to make sure the goats are okay.'

'You look after them?'

'We all do.' She pauses. 'They asked you a lot of questions.'

Sami nods. 'They did.'

'You didn't mind?'

'I survived,' he says, then grins. 'I could murder a cigarette, though.'

'You could ask Lukas.'

Sami laughs. 'I'm not sure he'd give away one of his stash for me.'

Eve supresses a laugh. 'Probably not.'

Sami looks up at her, his black eyes liquid in the half-light. 'It's good to see you, Eve,' he says.

She smiles. 'It's good to see you as well.'

Later, alone in her room, she listens to the sounds of the night. The distant lowing of the animals, the murmur of Malla's voice from the next building, the soft creak of the bed in Tomas and Sophie's room two doors away. What must it be, to have somebody to lie with like that, to share that private world? Sometimes she hears the sound of bodies moving with bodies, the stifled cries of release, so close to pain, and feels the gulf of an absence she is afraid to name. Touching her lip, she remembers that night with Sami, the feel of him close to her, wonders whether he remembers it as well.

*

She wakes in the pre-dawn darkness to the sound of a car door in the distance, voices she does not know. Pulling a jumper on over her nightdress she hurries out into the hall and finds Sophie standing there, her legs bare beneath a stretched T-shirt.

'There's someone at the gate,' she says, her face pale. Eve pushes past her and heads towards the door. Tomas is standing on the edge of the veranda, staring down; as she emerges he glances around, then back. The gate is open. Outside it, a pair of utes are parked on the track, their headlights illuminating the four figures advancing up the driveway.

'Who are they?' she asks Tomas.

He shakes his head. 'I don't know,' but before he can say more the screen swings open behind them and Lukas appears, pulling a T-shirt over his head, boots loose on his feet. He stares down the drive, his face set.

'Fuck,' he hisses under his breath.

He grabs Tomas's arm, pulls him towards himself. 'Wake the others,' he says.

Tomas nods and takes off towards the other buildings. Lukas turns to Eve. 'Stay back,' he says. 'I'll handle this.'

Eve waits until he is halfway down the drive and then steps down off the veranda and circles around so she can see what is going on. Lukas stops a little way from the gate and the men approach him. Two of them have rifles slung over their shoulders, and although their stance is deliberately loose, almost casual, there is no mistaking the threat contained within it. The largest of them grins.

'Jesus,' he says. 'This place wasn't easy to find.'

Lukas stares at him. 'Is there something you want?'

The man nods. 'My name's Drago. We're with the Security Council. We're making an inventory of resources.'

'What kind of resources?'

Drago smiles. 'Just the basics. Food. Weapons. Numbers of residents.'

'I'm not sure those are any of your business,' Lukas says. As Lukas speaks Eve is suddenly aware of the contrast between his lean frame and the heavy build of the four men.

'The Council is handling security for the Provisional Government. There have been a few unfortunate incidents. We just want to make sure there aren't more.'

'We haven't had any trouble here,' says Lukas.

Drago stares at him for a moment. 'No?' he says at last. 'No saying what the future holds, though, is there?'

There is a long silence. Lukas does not move. 'If that's everything, perhaps you should go,' he says at last.

Drago begins to reply, but then he notices something over Lukas's shoulder. Eve turns to see that Sami has emerged from the house and is standing with Tomas and Virat and Carla.

Drago stares at Sami for a second or two. Then he smiles unpleasantly and returns his attention to Lukas.

'We'll be back in a few days. We can chat more then,' he says.

Lukas doesn't reply, just stands, staring, as Drago and his companions turn and walk back towards the utes.

Lukas waits until the utes are gone, then turns and stalks back towards the house. Eve and the others follow him in. In the kitchen he ties his shoelaces, his motions swift, almost violent.

'Who were they?' asks Octavia.

Lukas finishes tying his shoes.

'I don't know.'

'Do you think this Security Council they say they work for is real?' Tomas asks.

Lukas turns and stares out the window.

'Perhaps. Does it matter?'

'But why come now? And so early in the morning.'

'Because they wanted to catch us off guard,' says Tomas. 'See how many of us there are.'

'Exactly,' Lukas replies.

'They had cars,' Carla says. Lukas nods, his face troubled.

'That means they have access to petrol,' Tomas says. Since last summer fuel has been almost impossible to come by. The backup generator runs on diesel, but heavy work now mostly relies on securing the loan of a horse. The question of what they will do when it comes time to plough the field again is one they have all discussed repeatedly.

'How would they have petrol if they weren't from the government?' Eve asks.

Lukas shrugs. 'Who knows? The could have a cache of it some-where. But it's more likely it means the government has found a new supply.'

'You think it's the Chinese?' Virat asks.

Lukas looks at him. On the mainland the Chinese government has been annexing land for food production under the aegis of disaster relief, but until now there has been no word of them here on the island.

'Maybe,' he says. 'Let me talk to some of the others.'

Although their gate is well back from the road and hidden behind a stand of wattles Lukas planted when he first bought the property, this is not the first time strangers have turned up on their doorstep. The first year after the Melt, when things were at their most chaotic, people came drifting up the road every day or two. Most were small groups, usually men, or men with a woman or two, but some were families, the adults hungry and scared, the children pale and exhausted. Lukas made sure they never came up the drive, but was always careful to offer them a loaf of bread and clean water or something they could spare. Once or twice they refused to leave, and there were words exchanged, or even blows, but they always moved on eventually.

Since that first winter the numbers arriving at the gates have thinned, presumably because the scarcity of fuel means fewer people make the journey this far out. Even so, it is unusual for a month to go by without a wanderer or two turning up at the gate.

Sometimes there are raids and thefts as well. In their first winter somebody stole the cattle from the high field. It was done under cover of dark, and in silence, and though none of them know who it was, Lukas and some of the others suspect one of the farmers further south. After that they were without milk for three weeks, until they convinced Jemima Rawson to let them buy one of her cows in exchange for a promise to help her work her fields when the summer came. Since then they have been careful to ensure the animals are checked hourly at night, but there are still incidents: a year ago somebody stole a trailerload of feed, and three months after that seven chickens disappeared overnight. Worse, though, are the acts of vandalism, the fences knocked down or crops destroyed. Whether these are kids from the surrounding farms or something more sinister nobody knows, but each time it happens they are left feeling angry, violated, a little less safe.

Eve knows their neighbours share this sense of vulnerability. Since last summer there has been a market in the town every second

Saturday, a place for them to bargain and trade what little they have. Yet its real value lies in the talk afterwards, the informal gathering of locals in the old pub, and the forum it creates for ideas and sharing.

She knows many of them are wary of Lukas: he is too young, his manner too abrupt. But he has found a way to work with Jemima Rawson and her wife, and over the past few months he has discussed them pooling their resources more often. But all know their presence here is tenuous: last winter people chopped down the trees that lined the road up from the town, leaving the land broken, bare, and as the summer approaches the threat of fire is greater. They have all seen the images of what is happening elsewhere.

This is different, though, and not just because the men were armed. Until now they have been protected by the chaos in the cities. But together with the reports of the Chinese on the mainland, these men and their talk of a provisional government suggest the world outside the valley is changing, and not for the better.

That evening there is a meeting in the old hall in town. Gathered together, the people of the valley look rough and worn. Lukas has spoken to a number of them already, and they have all had similar visits. Before the Melt many were city dwellers; Lukas believes more than a few of them have not fully accepted the world has changed forever, meaning the reality of the new world frightens them, angers them, and no more so than tonight.

Eve slips in late and takes a seat against the back wall, anxious to avoid the stares of the others. People are talking and shouting, their faces agitated, afraid. Finally Lukas stands up and calls for quiet. Gradually the hubbub subsides.

'You all know why we're here. And I know everybody is worried,' Lukas says. 'But we need to have a plan in case they come back.'

'*When* they come back!' interjects one of the women.

Lukas nods. 'When they come back. Because they will. I think we can count on that.'

'Is it true they had guns?' asks somebody at the back. Eve turns. It is Damon Brenner, who runs the vineyards up on the old Hill Road.

Lukas hesitates just slightly. 'Two of them had rifles. But I think we should assume they all have weapons. And that they're prepared to use them.'

At the back of the hall the door opens again and Sami appears. He closes the door quietly and takes an empty seat in the back row.

'I thought the government was gone,' says one of the others.

Lukas looks at them. 'It is. Or effectively at least. But that doesn't mean there won't be people trying to fill that vacuum. We need to take them seriously.'

'Then what? We should just give them what they want?'

'No. But we need to present a united front, force them to negotiate with us as a group. They need to understand they can't just walk in here and take what they want.'

There is a murmur of unease. 'But what if they try to force us?'

Lukas stands, staring at them. 'Then we defend ourselves.'

There is silence for a moment, then everybody talks at once. Although she could not say why, Eve feels some kind of line has been crossed. In the back row Sami stands up, and with a quick look at Lukas, heads back to the door and disappears.

Once the meeting is over, Eve goes outside. Thinking Sami might still be waiting she looks around, but he is nowhere to be seen. Behind her people are beginning to drift out, but suddenly she wants to be alone, so she heads out onto the road and begins to walk.

It is half an hour on foot to the house, but the night is mild, so she decides to go the long way, meaning it is almost an hour before she wanders back up the drive towards the house. Lukas is sitting on the veranda smoking a cigarette.

He regards her thoughtfully as she climbs the stairs. He looks tired.

'Where have you been?' he asks.

Eve shrugs. 'Walking,' she says. She turns and looks up at the vast span of the Milky Way. Since the lights of the cities have faded the stars have come back, brighter than ever.

'I know it's frightening, but we shouldn't be surprised. Capitalism feeds on crisis. It was only a matter of time before it began to reshape itself.'

'Do you think they'll really hurt us if we don't give them what they want?'

Lukas doesn't answer at once. Instead he looks past her.

'I do. But we need to negotiate, make it hard for them.'

'What if they decide they can just take it?'

'Then we don't let them.'

Lukas takes a drag on his cigarette. 'You don't think it's a coincidence?' he asks.

Confused, she shakes her head. 'What?'

'Sami turning up at the same time as Drago and his thugs.'

She hesitates. 'How could it be?'

A wary look crosses his thin face. 'Do you know where he is now?'

Eve shakes her head.

'You need to be careful of him,' Lukas says.

Eve doesn't reply.

'What is it?' he asks.

She turns to him. 'You never told me why you stopped being friends.'

Lukas snorts softly. 'It's a long story.'

'Tell me.'

Lukas nods. 'After I finished school Sami lived with me for a while. I still had my parents' house, but I was on my own, and I had a room to spare, so I let him have it.' He pauses, thinking. 'Sami was using by then; I think he'd been using for a while, and he used to borrow money off me, never pay it back, but that didn't worry me. Anyway, one day I came home, and somebody had broken in, been through the place. They hadn't taken much, but most of what was missing was jewellery that had belonged to my mother. I knew I should call the cops, but before I did I called Sami. Usually he answered straight away, but that night the phone rang twice, and then diverted to voicemail. He didn't come home that night, or the next, but when he did, he acted surprised about the break-in, and when I asked him if he knew anything about it he got angry, told me he couldn't believe I'd think it was him.'

Lukas stops. Dropping the cigarette to the ground he grinds it out with his foot. 'I told him to get out and not come back. It wasn't the fact he'd taken the stuff that bothered me. It was the way he lied to me, the fact he thought I'd just believe him.'

Eve doesn't know what to say, and for a long time they sit in silence. Finally Lukas stands up. 'He is what he is, Eve. Just don't let him hurt you.'

Once Lukas has gone she sits in silence on the front step for a long time. Lukas's story has unsettled her. She knows Lukas well enough to know he is telling the truth. But would Sami have done such a thing? And if he did, does that mean he would do it again?

Finally she stands up and walks out through the garden towards the goatshed. As she gets closer she can smell their warm, dusty scent. Eve checks the padlock then slides open the small window in the side. In the darkness their sleeping forms are almost invisible, but Eve is pleased to see her favourite, Smilla, outlined in the light from the window. Closing the window, she turns just in time to see a figure detach itself from the blackness of the trees on the far side of the field and move quickly towards the house.

This time she knows it is Sami immediately: his thin figure and fast, forward-leaning walk are unmistakeable. He hurries to the fence that separates the field from the gardens around the house and, glancing around, swings a leg over it and darts inside. Eve knows she should find Lukas and tell him Sami is back, but something holds her back, and instead she just stands, staring after him at the dark shape of the house, the restless wind moving about her.

When Eve first arrived at the compound she could not have imagined how close she would come to feel to this small space of land. Still deranged with grief, she barely spoke as Lukas drove her up through the hills and helped her unload her things into the room that has become hers.

The others greeted her warily – later she would learn that several of them had resisted her being allowed to join the group, and that it had only happened after Lukas insisted – but for the first weeks their uncertainty about her manner and appearance were of little interest to her. She spoke seldom, preferring to work alone, or spend her days in the bush behind the property.

Then in her third week she was assigned to help Carla and Tomas clear a fire break along the eastern boundary. The week was warm, the work hard, and at first, Eve laboured in silence taking her breaks alone and speaking only when spoken to. On the second day, though, Carla followed her when she retreated to the shade to rest.

'You're strong,' she said sitting down beside her. 'This would have taken twice as long without you.'

Eve shot a furtive glance at the other woman. Until then she had assumed Carla was older than the others, her direct, practical manner making her seem more responsible; up close it was clear she was not much older than Eve herself.

'Thank you,' Eve said. She felt maladroit, lumpen, yet Carla's gaze was kind.

'Lukas said your mum died not long before you arrived.'

Eve's throat closed up. She nodded, unable to speak.

'That's hard,' Carla said. 'My mum died when I was in my last year of school. It gets better, but it doesn't stop hurting. I still miss her every day.'

Eve stared at her hands.

'If you ever need somebody to talk to, or just to be with, just tell me. I know you're friends with Lukas, but he's not the most emotionally available guy, if you know what I mean.'

Eve snorted, a snotty, tear-filled laugh breaking free. Carla pulled a handkerchief from her pocket. 'Here,' she said, 'take this.'

She never took Carla up on her offer, but after that, things were easier. And they needed to be, because that first year was harder than even Lukas had expected. After a long summer of blazing heat and fires, the winter never really came, months of sunshine and no rain leaving the ground parched and bone dry for the spring, so their first crops failed.

They were hungry then, fretful. Lukas said it wasn't just about food, that they were all traumatised by what had happened, by the sense the world had unravelled around them. 'We had forgotten how to imagine other worlds,' he said to Eve one evening, 'and then everything we know got swept away. It's not surprising people are confused and frightened: they're grieving.'

Yet as the summer stretched on they began to find their way. They brought in a small crop of wheat, and the sheep lambed. There were still crises, arguments – Virat broke his arm two days after Christmas; Malla and Otis still can't be left alone together – but gradually things improved, and they began to become a community, at least of sorts.

It is after midnight before she sleeps, yet she is on breakfast duty, so when the morning light wakes her she hauls herself out of bed and dresses. When she first arrived she found the proximity to the others' kitchen duties demand uncomfortable, and so avoided them wherever possible. Yet as the months passed she came to enjoy the sense of shared purpose and easy comradeship they inspire.

For a time she let herself believe this feeling meant she was really one of the group, but one night last winter she was reminded it was not that simple. She was outside the kitchen when she heard Malla and Octavia, speculating aloud about her mental capacity. 'On the spectrum, for sure,' Octavia said. 'Could it be something genetic?' Malla asked. 'She's so weird-looking.'

Eve had turned and run out into the yard. She was at the goat shed when she began to sob. But she couldn't avoid them forever, and that night when they had gathered for their meal, the two had chatted to her as easily as ever. Perhaps they had no idea she had overheard their conversation, but even so, it seemed strange to her they could say such things and then carry on as normal. It confuses her, this talent for duplicity, the ease with which sapients lie and dissemble leaving her feeling slow and stupid. Is it simply their nature? Or is it the price of their society? Their constant competition for status and power?

Either way, such moments only ever serve to leave her feeling agitated, trapped in her separateness.

In time her sense of hurt and betrayal has faded, but she still finds it difficult to trust Malla and Octavia, and so is pleased to discover she is rostered on with Carla and Sophie. At the meeting the night before Sophie had been visibly agitated, arguing both that they should try to accommodate whatever demands were made of them and that they couldn't allow themselves to be taken over. This morning she is calmer, but clearly still anxious.

'Virat said they were at the school yesterday as well,' she says at last.

'Who? The guys who were here yesterday?' asks Carla.

Sophie nods. 'They wanted the names of kids. Laura told them she wasn't allowed to give them names.'

'Are you sure?'

Carla nods. 'Laura told Virat after the meeting.'

'Why would they want the kids' names?' Eve asks.

The other two look at her for a long moment. 'I don't know,' Carla says. 'But I think we can assume it's not out of concern for their welfare.' She turns to Sophie. 'Did Virat tell Lukas?'

Sophie looks uneasy. 'I'm not sure.'

Carla stirs the porridge, her face grim. 'We'll tell him at breakfast.'

Eve doesn't reply.

After breakfast Eve heads up to the enclosure to check on the goats. They run towards her, bleating and nuzzling. Crouching down, she strokes them, delighting in their yellow eyes and gentle nature. After a minute or two they seem to decide she does not intend to feed them, and begin to drift away, until only Smilla remains. Eve kneels down, drawing the young goat's face close to hers, and Smilla butts her gently. Laughing, Eve glances up and sees Lukas approaching from the house. He stops a little way off and smiles.

'How are those goats?'

Eve smiles and stands up, her hand on Smilla's side

'They're good,' she says, blushing. 'You weren't at breakfast.'

Lukas shakes his head. 'I was up early. Tomas and I have been moving stores up into the hills.'

Eve lets Smilla nuzzle her hand. There is a hidden storage area under one of the sheds; the fact Lukas has decided not to use that surprises her. Does he think it is no longer safe? The idea of Drago and his men tearing the place up frightens her.

'To the caves?'

Lukas nods. Smilla moves slightly, and Eve rubs her head, caressing the ridge of her skull.

'What about the animals?'

Lukas's expression tells her that this is what he has come to discuss. 'We need to take some of them up there as well.'

'How long for?'

'I'm not sure. A few days, maybe longer.'

'How many?'

'Half of them. And most of the females.'

'What will happen to the others?'

Lukas pauses. 'Hopefully nothing. But we need to be prepared.'

Eve nods, and Lukas smiles. 'They'll be fine, Eve.'

She nods again, but as Lukas turns away he pauses and looks back. 'One thing? Let's keep this between us.'

*

Eve spends the morning selecting which of the animals will be taken up to the caves. The task is not easy: she knows there is no guarantee those that are left behind won't be taken when the men return, but eventually she assembles a group to relocate, Smilla among them. Lukas is in the house with Tomas when she returns; seeing her, he steps out and follows her back up to the barn.

'Good work,' he says.

It is hot and windy as they lead the animals through the bush and up towards the caves, and in the trees the leaves rustle and shift. But despite the sound of the leaves the forest itself is silent, devoid of life.

The caves are low, wide shelves set into the broken stone of the cliff. Perhaps they once offered shelter to the Aboriginal people who cared for this country, but now they are empty, their recesses cool and musty with the smell of earth. As Eve tethers the goats and the cow she stares at the sacks of grain and bags of vegetables and boxes of jars Lukas and Tomas have already concealed at the rear of the caves.

'We need to bring water up from the creek,' Eve says.

Lukas nods. 'I'll help,' he says, and together the two of them head down towards the creek, filling buckets and hauling them up towards the cave. By the time they get back Tomas has finished winding out a roll of wire and staking it, creating a small fenced area. Eve leads the goats and the chickens in, setting down the buckets and scattering some hay and grain.

'We need to make sure the goats can't get at the food,' Eve says.

Tomas nods. 'I'll make sure it's walled off.'

That night the table is quiet, those seated around it apprehensive. All know tomorrow is the day the men said they would return; all know it is an encounter that is unlikely to end well.

Yet despite the sombre mood, Sami seems buoyant, talking and laughing, answering questions from the others. In the past day or two he has looked better: his skin clearer, his eyes brighter. For a time he entertains the table with stories about Lukas as a teenager, rambling anecdotes about wild times at parties and other adventures. Watching him Eve struggles to reconcile this Sami with the one Lukas described. How could Sami have betrayed him in such a way?

Lukas by contrast is restless and distracted, barely looking up as he eats and then leaning back and staring at Sami as he talks. Finally, when Sami tries to engage Lukas, he snaps at him, cutting him off.

'Stop talking shit,' he says.

Sami's rounds on him. 'Fuck you, Lukas,' he says, getting to his feet, his sudden anger startling Eve. 'You think you're so good.'

'Remind me why you're here again?' Lukas asks.

Sami shakes his head. 'Because I thought you were my friend, that you might be able to help me.'

'And nothing else?'

Sami stares at Lukas with sudden loathing. 'Whatever.' He stands up, his rapid motion sending his chair toppling back onto the floor with a loud crack, then stalks out. The back door slams.

For several seconds the room is silent. Eve looks at Lukas, expecting him to say something. But he continues eating in silence, his hand lifting the food to his mouth robotically, his anger palpable. Gradually the others begin to speak again, but Eve does not. Instead she keeps her eyes down, afraid to meet the gaze of the others.

Later, she knocks on Sami's door.

When he emerges he looks jumpy, angry. Wary, Eve asks him if he is okay. He opens his hand in frustration.

'Fucking Lukas,' he says. 'He thinks he knows everything.'

'He shouldn't have spoken to you like that,' Eve says. 'I'm sorry.'

Sami looks at her. 'It's not up to you to apologise, it's Lukas who should be sorry. He's always been like this. Acting like he's better than everybody, treating me like I don't matter.' He hesitates, looking at her. 'I like it here,' he says. 'You've all been really good to me.'

Eve smiles, although she is confused by his sudden change in mood.

'I didn't see you this afternoon,' he says.

'I was busy.'

'With Lukas?'

Eve nods. Sami pauses, looking at her. 'I saw you up by the barn with the goats this morning. Are you worried about them and these guys?'

'Of course. But I think we can keep most of them safe.'

'What do you mean? How?'

Eve hesitates. 'I'm not supposed to say.'

'What do you mean?'

Eve shakes her head, but Sami looks hurt.

'It's all right. I understand.'

She stares at him, remembering Lukas's story. But then she reminds herself this is Sami.

'No,' she says. 'It's okay. Lukas has been hiding stores in the caves above the farm. We took some of the animals there today. That way they'll be okay if these men try to take any of our stock.'

Sami looks at her. His eyes are dark, liquid with concern.

'You have to promise me you'll be careful if they come back. These sort of people are dangerous. You should do what they want.'

Eve nods. 'Of course,' she says. 'We just want to stay safe.'

The men arrive at midday. This time there are four utes, and they don't park by the gate. Instead they head up the drive. Lukas is in one of the back fields, but as they begin to climb out he appears and, vaulting the fence, heads towards them. Drago walks forward with two others to meet him. Drago has a black pistol tucked into his pants, its grip protruding in front of his shirt; the other two carry rifles in their hands.

'Nice to see you again,' Drago says.

'I wish I could say the same,' Lukas says.

Drago smiles, the expression entirely without warmth. 'I'm sorry you feel that way. But that doesn't change the fact we need to work out what you've got up here.'

'And then take it?'

'You catch on quick.'

'And what if we say no?'

'I wouldn't advise that.' He points at the barn. 'Your livestock are up there?'

'What we have.'

'And what about stores? Grains, vegetables?'

'Mostly in the house.'

Drago turns to the other two. 'Go take a look.'

Virat steps forward to block their way but Lukas raises a hand.

'It's okay,' he says. 'Just make sure they don't damage anything.'

Eve steps aside as the two of them push their way through the front door. As they pass, the smaller of the two leans close to her, pushing his face into hers.

'Jesus,' he says. 'Get a load of this bitch. What a fucking freak.'

His companion laughs, and the first man darts towards her; not enough, but enough to make Eve start. He snorts.

'That's right. You should be scared.'

Still shaking, Eve follows them to the kitchen. Together with Carla she stands and watches as the pair fossick in the pantry, then begin loading jars and bags into crates and carrying them out to the cars.

'This seems pretty thin,' says Drago once they are done. 'I expected you'd have more.'

Something in the way he says it makes Eve fall still. Not the threat, but the sense there is something else here, something Lukas, who is smiling and shaking his head, hasn't understood.

'Sorry,' says Lukas. 'But that's it.'

'Really?' Drago asks. 'Are you sure about that?'

Lukas hesitates. 'Quite sure.'

Drago nods. 'That's a pity. Because we hear you have a whole other cache up in the forest.' He looks at the one behind him. 'In the caves, wasn't it?'

Eve freezes.

Lukas has gone pale. Drago smiles unpleasantly. 'What? You thought we were stupid?'

Lukas tenses. Drago steps forward. 'I warned you what would happen if you lied, didn't I?'

Lukas is about to speak when one of the others steps in from the side and clubs him in the side of the head with the butt of his shotgun. The sound is blunt and sickening. Lukas grunts and tumbles sideways. Drago gestures to the other two, and they lean down and hoist Lukas to his feet. He slumps between them, his head lolled forward, blood running down the side of his face.

'Just remember,' Drago says, 'this was your choice.' As he speaks he punches Lukas hard in the face, then the stomach, then again in the face.

And then, without thinking, Eve hurls herself at Drago, slamming into him and sending him sprawling. Spinning around she sees the other two have let go of Lukas and are reaching for their weapons.

With a snarl she grabs the nearest by the arm and hurls him sideways, sending him cartwheeling to the ground. Turning to the other she lunges at him as well; he stumbles back, his face pale. Dropping down beside Lukas, she cradles his head in her arms.

Behind her Drago is back on his feet, wiping blood from his face. 'What the fuck!' he shouts, groping for his gun.

Eve looks around. Although he is taller than her she is stronger than him. Drawing back her lips she growls, the sound low, bestial, and Drago hesitates. Perhaps in some deep place he recognises her for what she is: the more powerful creature.

'Take the food,' she hisses. 'But don't hurt him.'

Drago stares at her. 'What kind of freak are you?'

She snarls, a low sound that emerges from deep within her. For a long moment he does not move. Then he steps back.

'Forget it,' he says. 'Just get the food.'

Eve watches him back away, not taking her eyes off him. In her arms Lukas is breathing in a slow whistle and gurgle. But it is only when she sees Sami standing by the fence, waiting for the men, that she grasps what has happened, and her part in it.

Eve carries Lukas to the house and lays him on the bed. He is bleeding, fading in and out of consciousness.

'Go find Malla!' Tomas shouts at Otis.

'And have them do this to her as well when they get back?' demands Carla, her face wild. 'We can't stay here. We need to get away. Hide.'

'Lukas can't be moved,' Tomas says, pushing his hair aside to examine the wound on the side of his head.

'And you!' Carla says. 'What did you think you were doing? Now they'll kill all of us.'

'They would have killed Lukas,' Eve says.

'Better him than all of us,' says Carla. There is a silence.

Eve swings around. 'What?'

Carla looks wild, terrified, either of Eve or of what she has said. Or both.

'It was your friend that brought them here, wasn't it? Sami. He told them about us, about the stores.'

Eve growls.

Carla takes a step back and shifts uneasily. 'What the fuck *are* you?'

Eve turns back to Lukas. 'Get out,' she says quietly. 'And tell me if they come back.'

An hour passes before Drago and the others arrive back. Eve stands in the doorway looking out as they carry the sacks and animals towards the cars. Nervously she counts the goats, only to realise Smilla is missing. Then she sees a small shape slung limply over Drago's shoulder. She gasps, tears starting in her eyes, but does not move, her feet rooted to the spot. Once they are finished loading, Drago and two of the others walk back towards the house. As they set off Sami falls in a few steps behind them. Pushing the screen door open, Eve heads down to meet them. They stop, facing each other.

'We'll be back in a month,' Drago says.

Eve doesn't reply.

'Hopefully this won't be so difficult next time.'

When Eve remains silent he snorts. 'Be like that, then. But this is how it's going to be. You fuckers don't get to sit up here with food while we starve. It's time to share.' He glances at the others. 'Come on,' he says. 'Let's get out of here.'

As they turn away Sami hangs back, staring at Eve. He looks pale, thin, frightened. Eve lets out a noise of disgust, but as she turns back towards the house he steps forward.

'Eve,' he says. 'Wait.'

She looks back at him. 'You told them,' she says.

He flinches. 'Please, Eve. You have to understand, I didn't mean for this to happen.'

She turns to face him. 'Is that why you came here? To spy on us? Were you working for them all along?'

He purses his lips and for a second Eve thinks she sees tears in his eyes. But then she remembers Lukas telling her that Sami wasn't to be trusted, that he only cared about himself, and as she does the memory of Lukas's ruined face flashes before her eyes. She advances on Sami.

'It is, isn't it? You came here for them, not for us. Not for me.'

Sami backs away.

'Go away, Sami,' she says. But as she turns away Sami speaks.

'That night, in the cabin after the party. You told me something.'

She falls still. Sami takes a step towards her.

'You remember?' she says.

He nods. 'I'm sorry. I was a dickhead. I shouldn't have run off like that. It was just . . . just, I didn't know what to think. I always knew you were different. But that . . .'

She sniffs. 'I trusted you.'

'I know.'

She shakes her head. 'So, what? You're here to tell me how sorry you are? That you didn't mean to hurt me?'

Sami shakes his head. 'It's not like that.'

'Then what is it like?'

'I found something. Online. A story about an experiment in France.'

There is a moment's silence. Then he takes another step forward. 'You're not the only one.'

THE SILENT WORLD

At first she thinks it is some kind of tent, a bedraggled hide or rug stretched across poles; it is only as she draws closer that its shape resolves, revealing itself in all its mute ruination. One of Davis's mammoths, its carcass foundered on the forest floor, skin stretched between its bones. As if at some unseen signal crows rise, their cries disturbing the air, and settle on nearby trees. They have survived. They always survive.

The smell is overpowering but she presses her sleeve to her face and forces herself to move closer. The rib cage is huge, half as tall again as she is, the scraps of flesh and skin that hang on it flapping in the wind, viscera coiled and bloated in a pool within. Its head is intact, the trunk splayed in front of it, the thick, mahogany-coloured hair matted with leaves, the black skin visible beneath it.

She knows the Foundation released mammoths in Lithuania, but how did it end up here, more than a thousand kilometres from that site? And what happened to it? She has heard stories about humans hunting the new beasts, killing them, but there are no signs of violence apart from the depredations of the birds. Perhaps it grew sick. Or hungry. Or perhaps this is where its kind have begun to bury their dead. Her arm still pressed to her face, she turns, scans the forest around her. Save for the crows watching her from the trees it is empty and silent.

Not so long ago this woodland would have been alive, information flowing through it like the wind that ripples through the leaves, a system that trembled on the edge of sentience. Back then these trees would have been filled with slow awareness, whispering to each other in patterns of electricity and biochemicals, a deep web connecting them not just to each other, but to past and future, a wordless remembering. Now, though, it is dead, the smell of it lingering like the stink of the mammoth carcass. Is there a word for that loss? A word that might name this rupture in the world? A word that might capture the way all that has happened has sundered this place from its past and left it storyless and alone?

Taking a step back, she sniffs the breeze: mingled with the reek of the mammoth's carcass she smells smoke, from either the fires to the south or perhaps somewhere closer at hand. Yesterday she passed a campsite, a confused straggle of tents and structures made of packing containers and a handful of ruined trucks and cars, their wheels removed, windscreens stoved in. At first she considered stopping to ask for food, but the faces on the children were enough to tell her it was better to hurry on.

She has passed many such places on her journey. Although she has mostly avoided the cities and the towns, dissuaded by the roadblocks on their outskirts, the plumes of smoke rising above them, in the lands outside them life is changing, growing wilder. The roads are scattered with travellers and refugees, some in cars or on contraptions pulled by horses but most on foot, and here and there military and security patrol the roads. Yet these travellers are only part of the displaced. Elsewhere others live in old buildings, supporting themselves in ways she does not understand, dirty children roaming here and there, gangs of teenagers or men who seem to be hunting, even if they do not call it that, and two days ago she glimpsed people living in caves, a fire crackling in front of them, tattered clothes and tarpaulins spread between the trees to shield them.

History runs backwards. The beginning becomes the end.

She takes one last sniff and heads on. Although she has grown used to the smoke, its constant presence is a reminder of the speed with which things continue to change. This year the summer in these northern latitudes has lasted six months, the heat stretching on and on. With so many people on the move the trees are being felled, and fire is racing through what is left of the forests. The world is burning.

In the years since the Melt, the warming seems to have accelerated, although whether that is because the survivors have been torching the forests to make fields or because the feedbacks in the system are now too intense to hold back, nobody knows. Yet there is no longer any question that the planet is undergoing a transformation. Much of southern Europe is now deserted, as is south-west Australia, subequatorial Africa, India. To the north the ice is melting faster and faster. The deserts are spreading, growing. It is as if the entire planet is convulsing, slipping free of their models, their fantasies of control.

It has taken her nearly a year to make her way here. In the aftermath of Drago's visit she helped nurse Lukas and do what they could to rebuild, though with so many of their supplies and livestock gone it was difficult to know where to begin. The mood of the group was different as well: the divisions between the different personalities more pronounced. One night Carla and Callum argued; the next morning he was gone. Meanwhile Tomas and Lukas became harder, more secretive. Eve found their disagreements exhausting and difficult to manage, a reminder of her own separateness. And so she did her best to keep to herself, to hold their arguments at arm's length. Yet even as she did, she could not put Sami's words out of her mind, and so, one night a few weeks after Drago's visit she sat down with a screen and used Lukas's satellite connection to connect to the net.

The uplink was slow and unreliable, but eventually she found the article Sami had told her about. Armed with the name, she searched for more information, and finally sent a message to the journalist who wrote the article, explaining the situation and asking to know more. Weeks passed with no reply, until she decided it had never been true in the first place.

And then, one night three months after she began her search she logged on, waiting while the interface slowly loaded. It was a surprise it was there at all: for the past fortnight there had been almost no signal, an intimation of what might come next, of the darkness that was spreading. And then, as the inbox appeared, she saw a reply.

He asked for a photo, some proof she was who and what she said she was, so she sent him one, and he replied with a location. When she wrote back he did not answer, although she didn't know if this was because something had happened or simply because the network had gone down.

After a fortnight she knew his answer was not coming. But by then a plan had begun to form in her head. She would go to him.

She had money, cash left to her by Kate, and so with Lukas's help she found a boat heading north, across the Strait, a yacht skippered by a man who used to be a lawyer and now did runs to Melbourne. The day she left was hot and humid, high cloud and smoke discolouring the sky, and as they tacked out of the Derwent and into the ocean the sea's surface was smooth, almost oily, but as they caught the wind and the boat knifed forward she felt her heart quicken.

As the boat travelled northward she sat, watching the coast pass.

It was strange, seeing the island from this angle, the way the land folded up from the water, the scraps of towns in the inlets. The marks of human habitation were clearly visible in the boxy shapes of houses, the pale emptiness of the fields and paddocks, yet elsewhere the trees still grew dark and heavy, their solidity suggesting these other marks were just transitory.

When they rounded Cape Portland, the shape of Barren Island rising to the north, they changed course, tacking out, into the Strait. A tremor passed through her as the island shrank towards the horizon. Out here it was quiet, the only sound the wind, the smack of the waves, and as the day drew down and night fell she sat and watched the horizon, astonished by the size of the world.

That night she slept below decks, lulled to sleep by the sound of the water outside the hull lapping against her head, but deep in the night she was roused by a low, mournful sound, and for a time she lay in the dark of the cabin, listening, not sure what she was hearing, until all at once she realised it was whale song.

Wrapping a blanket around herself she clambered up the stairs onto the deck. The stars were visible in places, the moonlight moving on the surface of the ocean, but there was no sign of the whales, only the sound of their cries echoing through the water. She remembered Lukas telling her they had been almost drowned out by the noise of human ships and industry, yet as the ocean emptied they were singing again. For a long time she stood, listening, trying to imagine those vast bodies moving weightlessly through the oceanic night, slipping and pulling as they rose towards the moonlight and then dove again. What were they saying, what meaning passed between them in this song? Was it for pleasure or was it simply to remind each other that they were here, that they were not alone? Only later did she wonder whether they had been crying out in hunger.

Outside Port Phillip they waited for the tide to change, then sailed in. Most of the docks had been lost beneath the water during the Melt, but new piers were already being constructed, crowded, makeshift arrangements built from old metal and timber.

She spent a week looking for passage out. There were still planes, but they were sporadic, mostly used by military and private security, meaning most people who tried to travel did so on container ships, which was how she did it eventually, finding a berth on a German freighter heading east towards Panama and then on, to Hamburg.

The northern summer had begun by the time they reached Germany. Hamburg was a maze of flooded wharves and drowned equipment. They docked at a floating wharf, dismounted into the city. The air smelled of wood fire and sewage. Shouldering her bag, she slipped away without goodbyes and headed south, taking a highway towards France.

She has been walking for almost a month. Long enough to see how much of the old world is gone, something of the new one that is growing. At night she has slept in the forest, beside roads, in abandoned barns. Sometimes she has walked with other travellers, standing aside to let the military vehicles roar by. They say there is war brewing further south, and to the east in India and Pakistan, but here it is mostly quiet.

Before she arrived she wondered whether she would know this place, whether its light and trees might speak to some ancestral memory of these northern lands, but although she sees beauty here sometimes, it has not sparked anything in her. Perhaps it would be different if it were living, if she could not feel the loneliness of it. Sometimes in the night she hears cries, the howling of wolves, the eerie call of an owl, but mostly what she feels is absence, the emptiness of a place almost devoid of life.

By the end of the lane the road dips, then rises again. Will they still be here? Has she come all this way for nothing? As she begins to climb again she feels her step slow, her legs trembling beneath her. And then ahead of her she hears a voice, speaking in French, a woman's laugh. She comes to a halt, staring forward. Two figures are walking towards her. They are broad, powerful, their thick hair hanging loose over faces larger than those she knows. The woman sees her first, falling still, then the man. They are older than her, but not by much. Behind them a child, of three or maybe four. Eve opens her mouth but words do not emerge. She cannot speak. For a long moment nobody moves, then the woman steps forward and, grasping Eve's hand, pulls her close.

ACKNOWLEDGEMENTS

This novel has benefited from the input and assistance of a great many people. Although they may not have realised it at the time, Paul McAuley, Ben Ball, Delia Falconer, Melissa Ferguson, Garth Nix, Kim Stanley Robinson, Jonathan Strahan, Sean Williams and Geordie Williamson all offered ideas and perspectives that helped me find the book I was looking for; likewise Patrick Bradley, Craig Hargreaves, Jason Martin and Margaret Morgan provided advice and answered questions about security, technology and medicine. I am extremely grateful to all of them.

I am also indebted to Sophie Cunningham, Ashley Hay, Jane Rawson and Adam Roberts, all of whom read various drafts of the manuscript. Their insights helped make this a much better book than it might otherwise have been, and helped me keep faith at moments when I needed it most.

I also want to acknowledge my former agent, the late David Miller. David was my agent and my friend for almost two decades, and one of the kindest and funniest people I have ever known. His absence remains a source of continuing sadness.

Since David's death I have been represented by Jennifer Hewson, now of Lutyens & Rubinstein, and Matthew Turner of Rogers, Coleridge & White. I am grateful to both of them for their consistently excellent advice and support, but I owe a particular debt of gratitude to Matthew, whose energy and enthusiasm for this novel has been deeply inspiring.

I would also like to thank everybody at Penguin Random House Australia, but particularly my editors, Rachel Scully and Claire de Medici, for their rigorousness and attention to detail, and my publisher, Meredith Curnow, for her thoughtful and illuminating questions.

And finally I would like to thank my partner, Mardi McConnochie, and my daughters, Annabelle and Lila. Their love and support is a constant reminder of what matters in the world.